"What's the matter…haven't you seen a man stripped to the waist before?"

Alice bridled at the taunt in his voice, eyes snapping open once more. "What? Nay, don't be ridiculous. Of course I haven't!" she blurted out.

Bastien's eyes moved over her flushed face. "Of course, my apologies. I forgot."

Lord, but she was beautiful, standing before him, her delicate build framed by the rough-hewn oak of the door. The wide V-neck of her gown revealed an expanse of fragile skin below her neck, the dark fur edging the collar brushing against it. She had changed her gown, was now wearing one that fitted her exactly; his eye traced the rounded curve of her bosom, the fine seaming that followed the indentation of her waist. Something knitted within him, deep within the kernel of his heart, igniting a delicious energy, a need. Inwardly, he groaned.

Alice frowned. *Forgot?* What was he talking about?

"I forgot you were an innocent," Bastien answered her unspoken question.

* * *

Captured by the Warrior
Harlequin® Historical #322—December 2011

MERIEL FULLER
Captured by the Warrior

TORONTO NEW YORK LONDON
AMSTERDAM PARIS SYDNEY HAMBURG
STOCKHOLM ATHENS TOKYO MILAN MADRID
PRAGUE WARSAW BUDAPEST AUCKLAND

Recycling programs
for this product may
not exist in your area.

ISBN-13: 978-0-373-30631-2

CAPTURED BY THE WARRIOR

Copyright © 2010 by Meriel Fuller

First North American Publication 2011

www.Harlequin.com

Printed in U.S.A.

Chapter One

Shropshire, England 1453

'Sweet Jesu!' Beatrice Matravers moaned with her usual peevishness, raising a quaking white hand to her high, unlined forehead. 'This infernal bumping will be the death of me!' As if acknowledging her curse, the cart lurched violently, causing Beatrice to reel against the padded interior. There she stayed, supported by the side of the cart, her eyes shuttered, her mouth twisted into a forbidding expression of grim dissatisfaction. Her maid, Joan, lolled at her side, deep in a comfortable sleep.

'Take heart, Mother, try to rest.' Alice Matravers leaned forwards, smiling, patting her mother's knee by way of encouragement. The elaborate gold embroidery decorating Beatrice's gown rasped against her finger-tips. Alice sat back, raising one small hand to part the thick velvet curtains that covered the opening, trying to establish their location. Stifled by the warm, tense atmosphere of the cramped interior, she pushed her face

out beyond the curtain, relishing the fresh morning air
on her skin. Outside the day was clear, bright; the beech
trees, dressed in their gaudy autumn colours, towered
up and over the narrow track that ran through the forest,
their trunks smooth boles of dark grey wood.

A thin trail of annoyance threaded Alice's veins, the
result of this long journey coupled with her mother's
continuous whining since they had left Bredon earlier
that morning. She sighed. Her mother would have been
far happier if Sir Humphrey Portman had found Alice
more amenable, more fitting as a potential bride. There
was no question that he had found her distinctly lack-
ing in all the qualities needed to become the lady of a
manor; why, he had positively scowled when Alice had
marched confidently up to the top table, greeting him
with a broad smile. The day had lurched downhill from
then on.

'We should be home by the four o'clock bell.' Alice
sagged back against the feather cushions, blinking rapidly to adjust her eyes to the dim, shadowed interior
once more.

'That is some consolation, I suppose,' Beatrice
replied faintly. Her wide blue eyes, the image of her
daughter's, swept over Alice with a mixture of irritation
and puzzlement. 'Of course, we would still be there if
Sir Humphrey had found you more accommodating. I
had hoped…this time…after our little talk…' Beatrice's
words drifted off, disappointed.

'I am sorry, Mother,' Alice apologised. Guilt scraped
at her insides. Her parents only held her best interests at
heart: to see her happily married to a wealthy husband,
a brood of smiling children clutching at her skirts. She
wished for that as well, but with a man she could truly

love, someone who would give her the freedom and independence to which she was accustomed, not some elderly suitor twice her age who would curb her ways in an instant!

'Well, there's always Edmund.' Beatrice smiled wanly. 'He's keen to marry you, and he's due to come into his inheritance quite soon. Although it will be less than all your previous suitors possessed.' The blue shadows under her mother's eyes seemed deep, heavy, evidence of countless nights without sleep. Even now, with the war in France at an end, there had been no news of Alice's brother, who had left to fight for his country two years previously, and had still not returned.

'Edmund's a good man,' Alice agreed. 'It's just that…' How could she tell her mother that the prospect of marrying Edmund filled her mind with insipid pictures of unending dreariness? Comfortable, aye, but dull. She had known Edmund since childhood; she liked him, he was a good companion, but she did not love him. But her mother's ravaged face forced her to reconsider; it would make both her parents so happy if she married.

'…it's just that, I don't love Edmund,' she blurted out finally.

Beatrice fixed her with red-rimmed eyes. 'I've told you before, my girl, love does not, should not, come into it! We need coin, coin that your useless father fails to provide, and a rich marriage for you is the only way to acquire it.'

Alice bit her lip, frowning. In comparison to Sir Humphrey, Edmund appeared a far better prospect. And maybe, if they married, love would blossom between them. The weight of responsibility dragged at her shoulders. Abruptly, she stood, clinging on to the curtain for support. 'I'm going to ride for a bit; I need some fresh air.'

As Alice swung down from the lumbering cart, her soft leather slippers sinking into the spongy ground, she half-expected her mother to call her back, to entreat her not to ride in the elaborate, fashionable dress that she had worn especially for this visit. But Beatrice seemed subdued, forlorn even, caught up in her own thoughts, and Alice was happy to leave her to them.

Seeing her spring down lightly from the moving cart, one of the escort soldiers shouted a brief command for the entourage to stop. Alice smiled gratefully up at him, picking her way carefully through the muddy ruts to the back of the cart where the soldier led her dappled grey mare. She knew, without looking down, that the long sweeping hem of her gown dragged through the mud; as she stuck her toe into the stirrup, the claggy earth smeared the bottom three inches of the beautiful green silk.

'May I be of assistance, my lady?' The soldier leaned forwards as if preparing to dismount, the smooth metal plates of his armour gleaming in the filtered sunlight.

'Nay, no need,' Alice reassured him hastily, swinging herself up into the saddle to sit astride. The soldier turned his face away, hiding a smirk; the lady Alice was well known for her tomboyish ways, which never ceased to cause amusement among the many members of the royal entourage.

'Er...you may want to...' The soldier indicated the vast bundle of skirts bunched around her slight figure.

'Oh, yes, of course.' Alice grinned, wriggling in the

saddle so that she could pull out the back of her gown, and then the back of her cloak, to lie flat across of the rump of the horse. 'I'm not used to wearing these sort of clothes.' Turning around, she shifted her balance as the entourage set in motion once more, pleased that she had possessed the forethought to wear a cloak for the journey, something her more fashionable mother refused to do.

Yet despite the cloak's heavy folds, after the cloying heat of the cart she still shivered in the chill autumn air. Her mother had insisted upon her wearing an elaborate gown, sewn from an expensive silk velvet. A silver gilt thread formed the weft of the material, so the dress sparkled with every movement, but the lightweight material offered little protection against the outside elements. Accustomed to wearing more understated, practical clothes, Alice baulked against the ostentation of the garment. It represented everything she hated about living at court with King Henry and his French wife, Queen Margaret of Anjou: the vanity, the constant sniping and bickering of the Queen's ladies-in-waiting, of which her mother was one, and the long hours frittered away in pointless needlework. Thank the Lord for her father, a physician to the royal court, who also found time to tend to the poor outside the royal circle. Much to her mother's disgust, Alice would accompany him on these trips, dressed in her older brother's clothes so as not to draw attention to herself. Thomas! Her heart squeezed painfully at the thought of her brother, his bright, laughing face flitting through her mind. As children, they had been constant companions, running wild through the royal forests, riding bareback, climbing trees. Thomas had forged a love of the outdoors in her, how to relish the wind in her hair, the fine rain on her skin. How she missed him!

Her mother's head poked out from the cart, her jewelled U-shaped head-dress sparkling in the sunshine, the vivid material strangely at odds against the drab colours of the forest. The side pieces, attached to this padded roll, were each fashioned from a net of thin gold wire, covering her ears. Alice knew her mother's hair to be the same burnished blonde as her own, but the fashion of the moment dictated that every scrap of a woman's hair should be hidden. Alice stifled a giggle as she watched the head-dress snag on a loose thread of the curtain; this type of fashion was completely impractical for travelling.

'Alice,' Beatrice's fractious tone whined over to her, 'I need to rest for a bit. I feel sick.'

Alice's heart sunk a little. She had hoped not to delay the journey any longer than was necessary, and was surprised her mother wanted to stop—there might be news from Thomas at home.

'Could we stop here?' Alice lifted her wide blue eyes up to the soldier beside her. 'Maybe have something to eat? My mother needs to rest.'

Exasperation crossed the soldier's face, swiftly suppressed.

'I'm sorry,' Alice mumbled, catching his expression. 'I realise you and your men wish to return to Abberley as quickly as possible.'

'No matter, my lady.' The soldier's face cleared. 'But these are troubled times. I would not wish to tarry too long.' He ran his eye along the serried rank of beech trees that crowded in along the sunken track. 'There's a clearing up ahead,' he announced. 'I'll ride on and tell them to stop.'

Lady Matravers perched bolt upright on the woven wool rugs that Joan had spread out in the forest clearing. Now the servant was busily drawing out the many muslin-wrapped packages prepared for them by the staff in Sir Humphrey's kitchens. He might be a miserable old bore, thought Alice, but he certainly didn't stint on food. Her stomach growled at the sight of roasted chicken legs, rounds of creamy cheese and crusty bread.

At the sight of all the open packages, Beatrice shot her a loaded look, as if to say, 'Look what you're giving up'. Never had her mother's disapproval been more apparent, more tangible.

'Here, mistress, take some food, it will make you feel better.' On her knees in front of the wicker basket, Joan passed across to Beatrice a flat pewter plate laden with delicacies. 'And the same for you, my lady?' The servant turned her well-worn features towards Alice, who loitered on the edge of the clearing.

'Maybe later.' Her limbs felt pinched, stiff after the long hours of sitting in the cart. Riding her horse had eased the feeling slightly, but the experience had been curtailed too soon to have any real benefit. 'I think I'll take a little walk.'

The dangling pearls attached to her mother's headdress swung violently, as Beatrice's head bounced up, her eyes narrowing. 'Then take a soldier with you.'

'Oh, Mother, it's not something I want a guard to see.' Alice said, implying that her walk involved a matter of a more delicate nature.

'Ah, I see…then Joan.' Her mother floated one pale hand in the direction of the servant.

'Mother…' Alice smiled '…I'll be careful. I'll not go out of earshot. It's perfectly safe.'

As she stepped away from the clearing, and her mother's piercing regard, Alice drew in a deep lungful of the verdant forest air. Beech husks crackled beneath her slippers as her footsteps sank into the soft mass of decaying leaves and rotting vegetation. For the hundredth time that day, she cursed the inadequacy of her footwear; when she ventured out with her father, she always wore stout, laced boots.

Every now and again, the sunlight managed to pierce the thinning canopy above, sending a column of spiralling light down to the brown earth. Occasionally the sun's warm fingers touched her face, reminding her of the balmy days of summer, making her want to shut her eyes and turn her face up to the light. Above her head, birds fluttered and chirruped, darting in and out of the branches, hardly heeding her quiet steps. The strain across her shoulders and neck began to diminish, released by the exercise, the tension of the past few days beginning to ease. At her back, she could still hear the low guttural tones of the soldiers as they ate their midday meal at the side of the track; she determined not to venture too far.

Over to her right, she caught the faintest sound of water: the high, bubbling notes capturing her interest in an instant. She pushed off the open path, through the undergrowth, all the time checking back to make certain of her direction. Brambles caught at her cloak, low branches snagged at her simple head-dress, but Alice would not be deterred.

And there it was. Water gushed over a rocky outcrop, bundling and frothing down into a small pool, trickling away into a narrow stream. The noise of the water drowned out all other sounds in the forest, and she felt herself mesmerised by the melodic bubbling and churning of the water, enchanted by its supine fluidity.

A sweaty hand clamped over her mouth. 'Got you!' A rough voice jagged at her ear, as she was pulled unceremoniously backwards, away, away from the water, away from the track where the cart and her mother waited.

A searing panic vaulted through her limbs, her blood slackening with fright; she wrenched her shoulders first one way, then the other, trying to loosen the man's fearsome grip. An odious stench of masculine sweat overlaid with a clinging smell of stale grease assailed her nostrils as the man hauled her backwards, her heels bumping, dragging uselessly against the earth. Thick clammy fingers dug into the softness of her cheek, the palm clenched so tightly across her mouth and nose that she found it difficult to breathe. A huge arm circled the upper part of her body, clamping her arms firmly to her sides, preventing her from trying to raise them up to dislodge the hold.

Then the man's grip was suddenly released and she was sent spinning to the ground in a flurry of rich embroidered skirts. A chorus of ribald male laughter encircled her; her heart skittered with jerky fear. How many? she wondered. How many men stood above her, laughing at her? For a moment she lay there, face down in the wet leaves, the smell of rotting vegetation climbing in her nostrils, the damp seeping into the bodice of her gown, before the same fear galvanised her, forced her to lift her head. In a quick movement, she pushed herself up on her arms, twisting around, opening her mouth to scream and scream. The sound reverberated in her ears, a piercing, desperate noise—surely someone would come to her aid!

'Shut the silly bitch up, for God's sake!' The order was swift, threatening.

One of the younger men bent down, binding a length of dirty rag across her mouth, his fingers snagging in the back of her veil as he tied a crude knot. He sniggered as she shook her head this way and that, trying to prevent him from tying the gag. 'Looks like you've picked us a feisty morsel—' the young soldier finished the knot and murmured approvingly, touching the silken skin of her cheek '—and a pretty one too.'

Slowly, reluctantly, Alice compelled herself to focus on the men around her. Her heart plummeted. Five soldiers surrounded her, crowded in on her neat, seated figure, staring down at her with hungry, bloodshot eyes. Orange rust blighted their dented plate armour, mud and what looked like dried blood splattered their long cloaks; their surcoats were torn and dirty. White exhaustion clouded their faces, the shadowed hollows beneath their eyes only adding to their expressions of ruthless desperation. And on the front of their tunics, God forbid, the distinctive coat-of-arms of the Duke of York! Her eyes widened fractionally; these men were knights, not common soldiers, and as knights should be bound by the chivalric code, the first rule of which was to treat any woman with respect! A fierce, wild anger began to replace her initial fear; before anyone could stop her, she sprang to her feet, tearing at the gag across her mouth.

'You will pay for this!' Her eyes, flashing blue fire, swept derisively around the circle of men as she jabbed her finger at them. 'I am under the protection of King Henry the Sixth himself, not some serving wench to be dallied with in the forest!' Her voice was shrill.

The soldiers guffawed. One burly man stepped forwards, towering over her. 'And what King's protection lets a maid walk unaccompanied through the woods, tell me that, eh?' He shoved at her harshly, causing her to stagger back into the younger knight, who caught her easily under the arms. 'You're the youngest, John, I suggest you go first.'

Bastien de la Roche drained the last drops of liquid from his leather flagon, before placing it back into the satchel at the back of his horse. Squeezing his knees, he set his animal in motion once more, slowly following a narrow trackway that skirted the edge of a forest. To his left, the land swept away in a series of gentle hills and hollows; to his right, the forest was alive with the sound of birds, a slight breeze riffling through the tops of the branches. It felt good to be back in England again. Almost. His mind paused, stilled for a moment on the distant memory. Nay, he would not think of that now.

He had forgotten how soft the land could look; the extended fighting in France had kept him away for too long. And now it was lost, all lost. France, the country that successive English kings had fought long and hard to keep, had finally slipped from their grasp. England had conceded victory to the triumphant French and now the English soldiers tramped home, despondent, defeated and often with no homes towards which they could head.

Under the restrained, jogging gait of his destrier,

the stallion that had carried him all the way back from France, he unbuckled the chin strap of his helmet, lifting it from his head. Tucking the visored metal under one arm, he pushed back the hood of his chainmail hauberk. The chill breeze sifted deliciously through his hair, and he pushed his fingers through the strands, savouring the cool release against his scalp.

Idly, he wondered where his soldiers had stopped in this vast forest. His horse had cast a shoe and, while a village blacksmith had fitted a new one, he had sent his soldiers on to rest, and eat. His men were keen to reach home; another two or three hours of riding would see them back at his estates in Shropshire. He hadn't set eyes on his home for nearly two winters; now he relished the thought of good food in his stomach, fine linen sheets against his weary skin and a warm hearth, even if it did mean seeing his mother again. The time in France had been spent in a pointless circle of attack and retreat; some nights had been spent under canvas, with the rain beating hard and thick to soak the heavy material of their tents; other nights had seen him and his men ensconced in a hospitable castle.

A scream pierced the air. A woman's scream. Further on, up to the right, a mass of rooks flung into the sky in one swirling, orchestrated movement, shaken from their tree-top perches. Bastien grimaced, nudging his horse in the direction of the sound; instinctively he knew that his men were involved. They were hungry, tired and dirty after the long months of campaigning in France—no doubt they believed English society owed them a little fun.

The springy turf muffled the sound of his horse's hooves as he cut into the forest from the main path, sure of his direction. Now he could hear the men's voices, their ribald laughter echoing through the trees as they taunted some common wench. Dismounting swiftly, he secured his horse's reins to a nearby branch and continued to approach on foot, his hand poised over the hilt of his sword.

He could hear a woman's high tone, raised in trembling anger now after the high-pitched screaming, the clear, bell-like notes castigating his men with ferocious persistence. The main bulk of his tall frame hidden by the generous trunk of an oak tree, he slid his head around cautiously to gain a better view and almost laughed out loud. A maid, a noblewoman by the quality of her garments, stood to one side of the clearing, both hands wrapped around the hilt of a sword that was evidently too heavy for her. He recognised the sword as belonging to one of his men; she must have managed to grab it from one of them. The heavy blade dipped and swayed as her diminutive frame struggled to hold it horizontally, every now and again sweeping to the left, then the right with it, to ward his men off, to stop them from coming close. What utter fools his soldiers were! Sweet Jesu, there would be women enough on his estate to warm their beds—why couldn't they have waited a few more hours?

The maid's face glowed with a pearl-like lustre in the shadowed pale-golden light, her eyes wide and anxious as she stared at the semi-circle of soldiers. Her mead-coloured hair was caught back into a heavy bun at the nape of her neck, secured into a golden net. A silken veil fell in a series of stiff pleats from the simple heart-shaped headdress. Against the dusty, travel-stained garments of his soldiers, she stood out like a bright jewel, an exquisite flower amongst common brambles.

'I will take my leave now,' she was saying, her small, oval face set with determination as she gave the sword another couple of swipes for good measure, 'and you will not follow me.' Behind the tree, Bastien grinned; from the expression on her face, it was obvious she had no idea what to do next. If she turned, then the men would jump on her; if she backed away, unsure of her path, then the thick undergrowth would prevent fast movement.

Bastien advanced stealthily into the shadows behind her, his step light assured as a cat. The mouths of his men dropped open in surprise at the sight of him; John, the youngest, began to blush. He knew he had done wrong and that they would pay for it. The maid retreated tentatively, the sword point drooping as her narrow shoulders and slim back began to close the gap between herself and Bastien.

'And if any of you dare to follow me,' the maid continued in her high-pitched, imperious tone...

'...they will have me to deal with,' Bastien murmured behind her.

Her lithe body jumped and turned, quick as a hare, bringing the lethal sword point slashing round. He grabbed the wrist that held the sword, squeezing the fragile bones that gave her fingers the strength to hold the weapon. Green eyes, flecked with gold, glittered over her.

'Let go,' he said, patiently, 'I am not your enemy.'

The small bones in her wrist crushed under his strong fingers and the sword dropped into the undergrowth, a slither of sound as the blade landed in a heap of brambles.

Alice's mouth scraped with fear. Her eyes, darting sapphire, widened with a mixture of horror and rage as she gaped up at him, this man who towered over her, his broad chest covered by a white woollen surcoat bearing the personal seal of the Duke of York: the falcon and fetterlock. He stared down at her, down his proud, straight nose, his chiselled features accented by the verdant shadows. Within the hard, angular lines of his face, the shape of his mouth came as a shock. His lips were full, sensual, with the promise of an easy smile. Fixing her gaze on the ground, she cradled her wrist, trying to gather her scattered wits, to slow her racing heart.

Nay, this man was not her enemy, but it was a well-known fact that the Duke of York was not well liked by Queen Margaret, the King's wife, who would always do her utmost to keep him out of King Henry's circle of advisors. As the King's cousin, as well as the top-ranking military commander in England, the Duke of York was favoured by the masses to be the King's successor. And by wearing his seal, these men followed the orders of the Duke of York, as opposed to the King. Alice needed to tread carefully.

Chewing her lip, she wrenched her eyes upwards. 'Your men...your men...' she spluttered out, unable to elucidate the full awful truth of what his men had been about to do.

'My men should have known better,' the soldier began, shaking his rough blond head: an unexpected shaft of sunlight turned the strands momentarily to gold, surrounding him with an aura of light that magnified the sheer size of his body. The hood of his chainmail hauberk gathered in metallic folds over his shoulders, emphasising the corded strength of his neck.

Alice gulped.

'But they were only having a bit of fun,' the soldier added pleasantly, folding his huge arms across his chest. In this curious half-light, the intense leaf-green of his eyes deepened, drawing her in reluctantly with their magnificent colour.

'Having a bit of fun?' she snapped out, clenching her fists against the folds of her gown, disbelieving this man's audacious defence of his men. 'My God! Have you any idea? Why, they nearly…they very nearly…!'

'Calm yourself, mistress,' he murmured, his voice neutral as he contemplated his men over the top of her head. Dark brown lashes framed his magnificent eyes. 'Nothing would have happened here, believe me.'

'Oh, you think to know your men so well, do you!' Rashly, she poked a finger into his chest, her mind jolting as it registered the unyielding flesh.

Mild amusement mixed with astonishment crossed his sculptured features—the maid's boldness was quite astounding. 'I would run, my lady, run back to where you came from, before anything else happens,' he advised coolly.

But she seemed not to hear his words, incensed that he seemed incapable of comprehending the severity of the situation. She whirled away from him, furious, challenging his soldiers. 'Look at you, hanging your heads in shame—you know the truth, so why not tell him?'

'Enough, mistress,' Bastien said, more sternly now. 'I will hear their story, and punish them accordingly.'

Alice spun back to face him, her hands planted firmly on her hips. 'Which, in my opinion, should be nothing less than a horse-whipping.'

Bastien raised his eyebrows. 'You seem to have a great deal of opinion for…a maid.' A faint note of annoyance marked his reply; this woman was beginning to severely irritate him, with her argumentative tone and challenging manner. The relentless pace of the last two days travelling began to cloud his brain; he felt weary and in no mood to remonstrate. As far as he was concerned, women were only good for one thing, and even then he preferred them if they kept their mouths shut.

'You need to understand, you need to listen to me…' Her voice rang in his ears, scolding, reprimanding.

Self-restraint, laced tightly, unravelled. 'Nay,' he ground out dangerously, 'you need to listen to me.' His blond head dipped, one thick arm snared her waist, jamming her against the inflexible slab of his chest. His men cheered as he lowered his lips to hers, primitive, demanding, insistent.

He had meant to scare her, to stop that relentless tirade of speech that needled its way into his very soul, but the first touch of her soft sweet lips made him almost groan out loud with desire. Too long! He'd been too long without the pleasure of a woman. The gruelling days of battle, the dust, sweat and heat—all those memories faded, dwindled with the sweet smell of her skin, the luscious pliability of her slender frame hard up against his, the rounded swell of her bosom. Sweet Jesu! Desire rattled through his body, building steadily, inexorably.

Foolish! Foolish girl! Why hadn't she kept her mouth

shut? Alice squeezed her eyes together, holding her body rigid as his lips came down over hers. She had a fleeting impression of wide green eyes, tanned ruddy skin, before his lips touched. Shock ricocheted through her veins at the impact, breath snatching in her throat as her heart thumped uncontrollably against her ribs. His mouth roamed against hers, wild, plundering; she crumpled against him, knees suddenly weak. Her mind scrambled, his lips luring her, drawing her towards the edge of a plunging abyss, a whispering place of tantalising promise, of…

'Alice! Where are you? Alice…?' A peevish, wheedling voice drifted over from the other side of the forest, calling.

Bastien tore himself away, breath ragged.

Alice reeled backwards, shaking, dazed. Senses shredded, she managed to lift one trembling finger towards Bastien, eyes hot with indignant accusation. 'How dare you!' she screeched at him, her mouth carrying the hot bruise of his kiss, her cheeks flushed with shame. 'You insufferable pig! You tell me you'll reprimand your men, and then you take advantage yourself! How dare you!'

'Steady yourself, my lady.' Bastien regarded her tensely. In truth, he was having trouble calming himself. He tipped his head on one side, listening. 'Someone's searching for you; go now.'

The deep cerulean pools of her eyes lobbed him one last stinging look, before she turned, stumbling away through the undergrowth towards her mother's voice, veil sitting askew on her head.

'Dear Lord, I thought she'd never stop!' muttered one of his soldiers. 'What a shame on such a beauty.'

Bastien followed the maid's slender back retreating through the trees, her sparkling skirts flowing over the mossy ground. As soon as she was out of his sight, he told himself, he would forget her completely; women had no part to play in his life, especially bossy, unbearable girls who scarce came up to his shoulder. Women were of no importance, in his opinion. Not after what had happened with Katherine.

Chapter Two

Alice swept her eyes around the great hall at Abberley. Aye, it was all still there: the sumptuous intricacy of the huge tapestries hanging from floor to ceiling, concealing the uneven stone walls; the high dais at the far end where the King and Queen and their attending nobility sat above the murmured hubbub of people gathered together to eat. Pausing in the doorway, Alice attempted to draw some comfort from the familiar surroundings, but her perception seemed tarnished, different, somehow. She knew why—a pair of emerald-green eyes and a shock of tousled blond hair loomed with unnerving regularity across her vision, unsettling her normal confidence. Aye, and that kiss. That treacherous kiss.

Light filled the space, spilling out from a combination of rush torches slung into iron brackets along the walls, and a roaring fire. Soldiers and servants alike crammed along the wooden trestles in the main body of the hall, knives jamming into the large serving platters of steaming roast meat. There was Queen Margaret, her small neat head held erect and proud as she listened to a nobleman at her side, her eyes wide and intelligent as she nodded in agreement once or twice. The height of the table obscured the round smooth bump of her pregnancy. Alice liked the young Queen, drawn by Margaret's ambition and vitality; it was said that she had enough energy for both herself and her husband. Of King Henry, there was no sign. He had recently become unwell, and was confined to his chambers to recover.

'Alice!' A fresh-faced young man moved across her line of vision. Edmund! A sense of relief flooded through her, his jovial expression for a moment shutting out her unpleasant memories of the journey. 'Alice, did you not see me waving? I saved you a place beside me over there!' His open, candid features searched her face.

She laid a careful hand on his arm, allowing him to lead her around the edges of the hall to an empty table, mindful that her mother was up on the top table, and would be watching. Maybe if Beatrice saw her with Edmund, it would shake off her mother's current mood. When Alice had finally returned to the cart in the forest, Beatrice had been furious, berating her for keeping the entourage waiting. Alice, humbled by her encounter, had crept to a corner of the cart without a word. Now, as she met Edmund's warm brown eyes, she hoped his easy companionship would drive away the bad memories.

'Tell me, what was he like?' Edmund asked softly at her side. At one-and-twenty winters he was the same age as her, his rounded features holding the pink bloom of youth.

Alice jumped, needles of fear firing through her, fingers curling around a floury bread roll on her platter. How did he know? she thought frantically, her scrambled brain trying to make sense of the question. An image of a strong, sinewy hand manacled around her own wrist intruded into her consciousness. A hard mouth upon her own.

Edmund nudged her with his elbow. 'Sir Humphrey... Surely you haven't forgotten about him already?'

'Oh...yes!' she gasped with relief, shaky laughter covering her confusion. 'Oh, Edmund, he was well enough, but unfortunately for my dear mother, I wasn't up to the mark, as usual.'

'Well, thank the Lord for that,' her companion breathed out. His plump fingers, whiter than her own, searched for Alice's hand under the table, squeezing it gently. His shoulder nudged hers, close, insistent. 'You know I've spoken to your parents...'

Alice's heart flipped. Could she do this? Could she marry Edmund? Her eye searched along the row of nobles at the top table, found her mother's anguished features, watching them. 'I know, Edmund.' She patted his arm, biting her lip.

'You know I come into my inheritance soon; your parents would be well looked after.' His brown eyes, riveted on hers, wavered momentarily, shifting to a point beyond her right shoulder.

'Thomas...' she breathed desperately, her toes curling in her shoes, as if providing a physical resistance. If Thomas came back, then he would provide for them, he would care for them in their old age. The responsibility on her to marry would lift, and she would have the freedom to do as she wished. But even as she had the thought, the small flame of hope in her belly flickered and died.

'Marry me, Alice,' Edmund urged, his voice low,

persuasive. 'I will look after you…and your parents.' His white fingers curled possessively around her sleeve, his smooth chestnut hair flopping over his forehead.

Alice took a mouthful of bread, chewing slowly. She had known Edmund since late childhood, when his father had become a knight for the King and moved his family to live at Abberley under royal protection. She and Edmund had immediately liked each other: they shared the same interests, of music, art and culture. True, she also enjoyed being outside, riding or walking, as opposed to Edmund, who preferred to stay inside, but that seemed to be the only difference in them. He was kind, considerate and gentle, and, unlike many of the potential husbands her mother had introduced her to, the same age as she.

Beside her, Edmund watched her closely. If only the girl would agree! He had to physically prevent himself from drumming his fingers on the tablecloth, frustration mounting in his gullet. His uncle's generous offer would not be around for ever; somehow, he had to persuade her. He knew her mother was willing—he had seen the flare of greed in her eyes on her return this evening when he mentioned the amount of money he would receive—now all that remained was to gain the agreement of this stubborn maid!

'Am I such a bad prospect?' he asked, holding one hand to his chest—a theatrical gesture of false sorrow. A huge sapphire ring glittered on his little finger.

Alice laughed. 'Nay, you're not.' She took a deep gulp of wine, setting the goblet back on the table with studied determination, pulling her spine straight at the same time, making a decision. 'I will marry you, Edmund.'

* * *

A heaviness weighed down Alice's eyelids as she attempted to open them the following morning. Her sleep had been restless, worn through with the uneasy threads of half-snatched dreams, dreams fringed with the anxious memories of the day before. She had tossed and turned in the stuffy curtained interior of the four-poster bed, thumping the goose-down-filled pillow with an impatient regularity. Everything had become irritating: the crackle of straw in the mattress beneath her, the bunched lumpy feathers beneath her loosened hair, the shouts of the soldiers piercing her consciousness at some ungodly hour...

Soldiers...? Alice bounced upright, the rippling cascade of her hair spilling on to the bedcovers, sparkling in tangled glory. Flinging back the furs, the linen sheet, she sprang from the bed, fighting her way through the heavy curtains. Her full-length nightgown billowed out over her bare toes as she flew over the wide elm boards to the window casement, pressing her nose up against the thick, uneven panes of hand-blown glass. Nothing. Her sleep-numbed fingers fiddled with the iron latch, pushing the window open so she could lean out. The chill morning air stung her heated face and neck. Eyes watering, she dashed the wetness away and looked down. Soldiers filled the inner bailey, their red surcoats vivid in the luminous pre-dawn light, their armour glinting dully. Grooms ran hither and thither, fetching fearsome-looking weapons, adjusting buckles on saddles and stirrups and attaching saddle bags with practised efficiency. Cold fear slid through her veins: these men were preparing for battle.

Throwing a simple gown over her voluminous

nightgown, Alice yanked her unruly hair into a braid, binding the curling end quickly with a leather lace. Pulling open the door, she raced down the corridor to her parents' chamber. With her mother's elevated status as one of the Queen's ladies-in-waiting came all the associated privileges of such a position: warm, well-appointed rooms, as well as clothing and food.

'Father!' Alice burst into her parents' room without knocking. Fabien Matravers, busy at a table by the window, lifted his weary eyes to acknowledge his daughter with a smile. He raised a finger to his lips, nodding in the direction of the bed, where her mother slumbered. Clamping her lips together to prevent her next question, Alice closed the door quickly and tiptoed over. The table held a collection of medical equipment: bandages and salves, sewing needles fashioned from animal bone, and fine thread made from sinew. These items were disappearing one by one as her father packed up a sturdy leather satchel.

'What's happening?' Alice whispered, her periwinkle blue eyes wide, curious.

''Tis what Queen Margaret feared, 'tis what we all feared.' Fabien's face clouded. 'The Duke of York has challenged the King's leadership, now that we have lost France. He has mounted an army, and awaits the King's men on a high plateau not far from here.'

Alice nibbled at a fingernail. 'Will King Henry fight?'

Fabien's mouth turned down at the corners. 'Nay, not he, lass. You know he's…he's not well at the moment. But the Queen is fully aware of the situation; she intends to send two or three of the King's more loyal dukes.' He tucked the last roll of bandage into a corner of the satchel and sighed. 'I only hope that this will be enough. The Duke of York's men are notorious for being savage fighters.'

Alice's heart lit with excitement. 'Let me come too, Father. Please.'

But Fabien was already shaking his head, his hands stilling momentarily as he looked at his daughter. In the light beginning to filter in at the window, the grey streaks in his hair seemed more prominent, the lines on his face more pronounced. 'Nay, Alice,' he said finally. 'The battlefield is no place for a young lass. Especially one that is betrothed.'

Alice gasped, colour flushing into her cheeks. 'You know!'

Fabien nodded. 'Edmund came to me last night, to tell me.' He smiled, his mouth creasing up at the corners. 'And I gave him my blessing. As I give you mine now.' He leaned down, planted a soft kiss on his daughter's forehead, smoothed her wayward blonde hair with one hand. 'Your mother is relieved,' he added.

Alice frowned, fiddling with the curling end of her loose braid. A curious reluctance sheared through her, a reluctance to share in her father's obvious joy at the news of her marriage. 'I suppose it was inevitable.' Uncertainty weighed her voice.

Fabien caught her glum look. 'Is it not what you wish?'

Alice's head snapped upwards. The last thing she wanted was to load any further worry on to her parents. 'Nay, of course not, Father. It's happening so fast, that's all.'

Fabien's head whipped around at another shout from below. He touched his daughter's cheek. 'I have to go,

Alice. We will talk again about this…I wouldn't want you to enter into anything you're unsure about. And marriage is a huge undertaking.'

She nodded, distracted by the sounds outside the window. 'Please let me come, Father.' Already she had a sense that times such as these, helping her father, supporting him, would dwindle and eventually die out, even with a liberal husband such as Edmund. 'I've been with you before,' she reminded him. 'I—'

Fabien stopped her sentence with a hand on her arm. 'Aye, you've come with me to the village or to some minor skirmish between two landowners.' His blue eyes, set in his tanned, weathered face, regarded her gently. 'Your skills are excellent, daughter, but I would not lose another child on the battlefield.'

Alice stepped quickly around the table, coming to her father's side. 'Don't speak like that, Father! We don't know that he's dead!'

'We've had no news for two years, Alice. What am I supposed to think?' His quiet burr hitched with emotion as he recalled his son, Thomas. He smothered a deep sigh, unwilling to show the depth of his true feelings to his daughter.

'I miss him too, Father, but until we hear definitely, I cannot believe that he's dead.' Alice's voice held the edge of conviction. 'Look, you need me with you; I'll wear some of Thomas's clothes. Nobody will have any idea.'

Fabien laughed, patting Alice's hand. A sense of elation crowded into her chest; she knew she had won.

To the south of Ludlow, the lands belonging to the Duke of York stretched away in a series of low, folded hills, green and fertile. Balanced on the edge of slopes, or flat in the valley bottoms, the fields were small, bounded by hawthorn-sharp hedging and narrow, stony lanes. High on one of the ridges, where the west wind blew the horses' tails into fans, dark strands against the clear blue sky, two riders sat, almost motionless, surveying the land spread out beneath them.

'Ah, it's great to have you back in England!' One of the horsemen, Richard, the Duke of York and cousin to the King of England, slapped Bastien companionably on his back.

'I thought I'd come home for a rest!' Raising his visor, Bastien grinned at his friend, the metal of his helmet cold against his cheek. He hadn't even returned to his own manor, having been waylaid by the Duke as they had passed through Ludlow.

Richard gave a swift snort, his square-shaped face set into a scowl. ''Tis unlikely we'll have much rest with that feeble-minded cousin of mine in charge of the country. He's let the land go to the dogs, the barons are feuding under his very nose, and what does he do? Nothing!' His dark hair, untouched by grey despite being Bastien's senior by ten years, stuck out in tufted spikes from under his helmet. 'I need to see the King, Bastien, to talk to him, but his Queen protects him like a child. She won't let me near. The only way is to openly challenge the House of Lancaster in battle.'

Bastien shrugged his shoulders. 'So be it, my lord. My men are willing and ready, although they are tired from the long march home.' As he was, he thought wearily. Yet he sensed the frustration, the annoyance emanating from the Duke, and understood his motives.

Richard ran a critical eye over Bastien. 'Still not wearing full armour, I see.'

Bastien openly shunned the body-plate armour worn by most knights, preferring to wear just chainmail over a padded gambeson with a steel helmet. By contrast, Richard wore a full set of plate armour that had been made especially for him: breast and back plates, articulated steel gauntlets covering his whole arm, and leg pieces attached to the front of his shins by leather straps.

Bastien adjusted himself in the saddle, the leather creaking with the movement. 'Plate armour is too heavy, it weighs me down too much.' The tint of a far-off memory laced his voice, the familiar whisper of guilt licking along his veins. After all these years, he just couldn't forget.

'So you said in France, young man,' Richard chided him. 'I've told you before, you take too many risks.'

'And you move too slowly, laden down with all that steel,' Bastien teased. 'Admit that I'm quicker and faster than you in a fight.'

Richard smiled. His friend's prowess on the battlefield was legendary. 'Just make sure you don't get yourself killed by your own foolhardiness.'

'I'll try not to,' Bastien replied, dropping his visor down. But in truth he didn't really care.

Alice helped her father erect the tent beneath a line of beech trees; their distorted, knotty roots afforded some shelter from the north, and the ground, though rough and sloped, was reasonable once she had kicked the stones out of the way. The stained white canvas flapped and strained in the breeze, the guy ropes pulling insistently against the heavy stone that held them taut. Securing the door flap back with a leather tie, Alice stood for a moment, surveying the land below her. Over to her right, moving across the flat river valley that was the declared battle site, the Lancastrian army marched purposefully, their red tunics glowing in the rising sun, flanked on either side by knights on horseback. Outriders held banners aloft, triangular pennants flapping the colours of King Henry.

Fear bunched in her mouth. Through the shifting mist drifting from the river, she could see the Yorkists, mostly knights on horses, spread out in an imposing line along the opposite slope—hundreds of them. She closed her eyes, and ducked back into the tent to where Fabien laid out the tools of his trade.

'God in Heaven, Father, there's so many!' Panic threaded through her voice.

Fabien surveyed his daughter critically; she had made an excellent job of disguising her sex, but his heart clenched with the risk he took by bringing her.

A large, leather hat completely covered her bright hair, the brim pulled low to shade her delicate features. Her brother's cote-hardie was long on her, but did not look out of place, and the intricate pleating that fell from the shoulders, front and back, did much to hide her feminine curves. A thick leather belt secured this over-tunic loosely on her hips, and the hem fell so low, that only a glimpse of her fustian braies could be seen. Somehow, she'd managed to walk in Thomas's big leather boots; they reached her knees, already dirty with mud.

'Do you want to go home?' he asked at last.

'Nay!' she shook her head vehemently. 'I shall stay… and help you!'

'That's my girl!' Fabien smiled back at her, hearing the courage in her voice.

For the next few hours, against the echoing back-drop of the battle raging in the valley below, against the shouts and the clashing of armour, they worked, patching up the soldiers and knights that were brought up the gentle slope. For that was all they intended: to stabilise any injury and to stop the bleeding, enough so that each man could be taken back to the safety of the castle. Alongside Fabien, Alice worked slowly and patiently, murmuring a question or a comment to her father now and again. Immersed in her work, she barely lifted her head when Fabien told her he was needed to attend to some soldiers on the battlefield.

'Stay here until I come back,' he entreated softly, slipping out through the canvas. Alice nodded vaguely in response, her tongue between her teeth as she con-centrated on stitching up a long gash in a soldier's arm.

The sun had risen to its highest point by the time Alice could take a rest. With nobody in the tent, she whisked off her hat, rubbing her face with one hand, trying to erase the stiff, exhausted feeling from her skin. A rawness pulled at her eyes; clapping the hat back on, she reached for the leather water bottle behind her and took a long, refreshing gulp. Replacing the cork stopper, she realised the sound from the battlefield had become noticeably subdued. No longer could she hear the roar of men as they rode into attack, or the clash of steel against steel. Yet it had been a fair while since her father had left the tent—did he still tend the injured?

Alice stuck her head out through the canvas flaps. She had to go to her father, to find him, but the thought of tip-toeing through a field loomed before her as a daunting prospect. She gritted her teeth—think of Thomas. He would go to their father, he would find him. But Thomas was not here; it was her responsibility.

The spongy earth pulled at her boots as she advanced stealthily. In front of her, a high earth bank topped with a hedge obscured her view of the battlefield. Hoping it would also hide her from the enemy, she pulled herself up the loose earth of the bank, digging her fingers into the gnarled beech roots as a makeshift lever and hoisted her slight figure up to peer through the bare branches.

Bodies lay everywhere. A slight sound of horror emerged from her lips as she squeezed her eyes shut, unwilling to look at the carnage strewn before her. Her fingers curled around the branch, the twiggy whorls cutting into her flesh. How could she? How could she walk through these dead and dying men? And what if her father was one of them? The thought galvanised her—she had to find him! Through the net of branches, she could see a group of soldiers, King Henry's soldiers, thank the Lord, making their way up the hill, battle-worn, bleeding, but thankfully alive. Springing down backwards, Alice entered the field through a gateway further down the bank, and began to pick her way warily across.

'What's happening?' She ran up to the soldiers, the air of defeat surrounding them like a cloak.

The tallest one eyed her warily, obviously puzzled by

the young boy's presence in such a place. 'They won, we lost. Simple as that.' He spat on to the ground.

'Then why—?'

'Why aren't we prisoners? They let the common soldiers go; it's only the noblemen they want, and they've got them,' the soldier growled out between his blackened teeth.

'Let's keep going,' growled another, and made as if to push past her.

'Wait a moment, please.' Alice's voice rose a little higher, and the tall man looked at her sharply. She lowered her head quickly, realising that her voice had been too high for a young lad. 'Have you seen my father, the physician? Do you know him? He came this way to help tend some men.'

The soldiers looked at each other. 'I'm sorry, lad, but he was taken, along with the rest of them. Look, over there.'

Alice screwed her eyes up against the freshening wind, following the soldier's pointing finger to search the horizon. And then she saw it. A long snake of walking knights, trudging wearily away between the white tunics of the Yorkist horsemen. She hoped with all her heart that these soldiers were wrong, that her father wasn't among them. But, for her own peace of mind, and for Thomas, she knew she had to find out for herself.

Chapter Three

The loose chain of prisoners straggled up the hill, shoulders slumped, feet shuffling over the crumbling earth of the track. Yorkist soldiers flanked the line of men on either side, hemming them in with the strong, shining flanks of their destriers. At this shambling speed, the journey back to Ludlow and the Duke of York's castle would take at least a day and a half, allowing for a night's rest in between.

As they mounted the hill, the green lushness of the river valley receding, the countryside opened out, spread, studded here and there with a massive oak, or a small grove of beech trees. With the sun warming the back of his neck, Bastien pushed his soles against his metal stirrups, raising himself in the saddle to stretch and flex the muscles in his legs. He baulked at this ambling speed, more familiar with the rapid movement of professional soldiers, but he resisted the temptation to break into a full gallop to break the monotony of the journey.

'I'm not sure about that one, my lord.' Alfric, one of Bastien's younger knights, rode alongside him at the back of the line of prisoners. He nodded towards an older man, not dressed for battle, who strode with the others. 'Maybe we should let him go? He's no knight.'

'Nay,' Bastien agreed, 'but he's certainly a nobleman.' He pushed his visor upwards, relishing the fresh air on his skin, his high cheekbones still flushed from the exertion of the battle. 'Look at his clothes.' Although the man's garments were of a simple cut, his cote-hardie was fashioned from a fine silk-woollen material, shot through with gold thread and his boots were of good leather. 'And there's another very important reason why we cannot let him go.'

Alfric's eyes widened

'He's a physician,' Bastien replied, grinning at the fervent curiosity in the young man's face, 'and obviously well known among these noblemen; most of them call him by his first name. He can help tend to the injuries…on both sides.'

'They endured more losses,' Alfric interjected. 'A good victory, methinks.'

'Undoubtedly,' Bastien murmured, but a hollowness clawed at his heart. There was no joy in following the hunched, defeated knights as they bobbed forlornly in front of him, no elation in this victory. He was tired, that was all, tired of the endless fighting, the bloodshed, and he had had no time to rest before this latest fight against the House of Lancaster.

His head jerked around suddenly to the row of trees over to his right, catching a tiny movement out of the corner of his eye. The trees were a couple of fields away; he scanned the dark trunks, the hedgeline, unsure that he'd seen anything—a flash...of blue, maybe? Something untoward, anyway, something not quite right. His green eyes narrowed, emerald chips as he pulled gently on the reins, slowing his horse.

'What is it?' Alfric hissed.

'I think someone is following us,' Bastien replied quietly. 'Alfric, you stay here, maintain the rear guard. I'll have a snoop around these woods.' Knees gripping at the saddle sides, he yanked his helmet off, dumping the heavy, shining metal into Alfric's lap. 'Hold on to this, I have no need of it.' Clods of earth flew up as Bastien kicked the horse into a gallop, thundering towards the tree line, reining in sharply at the serried oak trunks. The wood was overgrown, impenetrable; he would have to search on foot. Jumping down lightly, he secured the horse to a branch, noting the position of the sun to gain his bearings.

After the clamour and mayhem of the battle, he relished the quiet hush of the forest, the damp smell of the vegetation crushed beneath his boots. Despite his muscles easing, every sense remained open, alert to the tiniest noise, the smallest movement. He was certain now that he'd seen a glimmer of blue in his peripheral vision; if someone was tracking them, then he would find them. Bastien plunged through the thick undergrowth, brambles tearing at his surcoat, snagging in his hair. For a moment, he stood still, listening, hearing only the marching feet and shouts of the army he'd just left.

The breeze lifted the branches, a sighing sound. And then he heard it. A cough, hurriedly smothered. Bastien smiled to himself, locating the position instantly, beginning to pad forwards on silent feet. If the years of war had taught him anything at all, it was how to approach the enemy without being heard or seen.

As she watched the large knight break away from the back of the prisoners, Alice's heart plummeted with fear, annoyed with herself that some noise, some moment of inattention, had led to her being spotted. Up to now, she had been congratulating herself on how well she was managing to keep up without being seen.

Her natural athleticism, so heavily condemned by her mother and the other ladies at court, served her well, enabling her to sprint across the fields, to jump and climb. Many happy days in her youth had been spent with her brother, scrambling through the forests and valleys, much to her mother's disgust. Now that she was older, and had to behave in a manner befitting a lady at court, she relished any opportunity to be in the open air, to race about.

Except now...now it had all become a bit more serious. Her palms scraped against nubbled bark and her knees wobbled as she peeked around to see where the knight had gone. There was something vaguely familiar about him, but he was too far away for her to determine exactly what it was. Now would be the time to turn and run, to speed all the way home and raise the alarm. But nay, she told herself sternly, that was the way of the weak and she had travelled too far to abandon her father when she was so close. Lord knows what they would do with him!

Edging carefully around the trunk once more, Alice saw that the knight had left his horse in the open field at the forest boundary, the bridle looped casually over some low-hanging branches. The glow of an idea kindled in her mind. Certain that the knight had entered the very depths of the forest, Alice inched forwards. If fortune smiled on her, the Yorkist numbskull would become hopelessly lost, or caught in an animal trap, enabling her to escape.

She endeavoured to keep her breathing deep and even, not easy as fear whipped around her veins, making her jittery, nervous. Blinking, she tried to focus her vision, scanning her immediate environment to ensure she didn't catch against anything that would make a noise, or tread on any dead twigs. Before her, not far now, the destrier pawed the ground, shaking its head, the bit jangling menacingly between its huge yellow teeth. The animal was enormous, powerful, a warhorse in every muscle, every sinew of its well-built frame—very different from the docile mares she was used to. Alice swallowed, the saliva in her mouth all but dried up. She paused, unsure, until the distant shouts of the army reminded her that her father marched along with them—wasn't that reason enough to overcome her fears? Thomas would do this, Thomas would rescue him! Her brother's voice echoed in her mind, urging her on, giving her the conviction she needed, that she was able to do this. She had to climb on that horse, and ride like hell after him!

A few feet from the horse, still hidden in the shadow of the trees, she halted again, listening carefully. Nothing. The silence loomed in her ears, an eerie quiet. She wanted the knight to thrash about, to make a noise, so that she could be certain of how far away he was. If anything, it was too calm, too hushed. Sweat sprung to her palms as she contemplated the enormity of her actions. No matter that Thomas had taught her a hundred times how to vault on to the back of a horse—this time, it was different.

In a flash, her poised figure erupted into a sprint, leaves crunching under her feet as she covered the small distance between herself and the animal. Before the horse had time to look around, to even deduce what was occurring, she placed two palms flat on the horse's shining rump and jumped. A shout from behind burst into her brain, and she snatched for the bridle, breath punching into her lungs as the leather strap broke free from the branches. Clamping her knees to the horse's sides, she dug her heels viciously into its flanks, unable to reach the stirrups. Her head and neck wrenched back wildly as the horse, unnerved by her unfamiliar weight, her clumsy handling, leapt away at speed.

Alice prided herself on being a fast runner; indeed, in previous years her lean, agile frame had been known to beat half the boys in the castle. But Bastien, despite his broad, muscular build, was a lot faster. The crackle of leaves underfoot had drawn his attention, followed by the glimpse of blue clothing as the boy shot towards *his* horse! For that was all he chased: a weedy stripling of a lad, not some grizzled, bloodthirsty assassin, as he'd been expecting, determined to drive an arrow into the Duke of York. He almost spat on the ground with disgust! But when the lad took a flying leap on to the back of the horse, anger rose in his gullet, spurring him into action. Thought he to steal his horse, did he? The impudent lad! He crashed through the undergrowth, low branches breaking against his arms, his body, as he ran out over the open ground.

His long, powerful strides covered the distance easily. If his horse had been at full gallop, then he would never have caught them. But luckily, his highly strung, temperamental animal decided to act up, bucking and side-stepping under the unknown rider. The boy was obviously having trouble trying to stay on the destrier's back, kicking in vain with his heels, while clinging to the reins and mane with small, pale hands. In one fearsome, full-length leap, Bastien was upon him, gripping at the youth's arms to drag him bodily from the horse. Man and boy fell in a graceless, clumsy heap, a tangle of legs and arms thumping heavily on to the ground, into the shining windswept grass. The lad struggled violently, trying to punch out with his fists, his puny legs kicking out in chaotic, laughable randomness. In a trice, Bastien twisted the lad so he lay face down in the dew-wet pasture, his arms locked up painfully behind his back, and sat astride the boy to prevent all movement.

Nose and mouth choked full of dank, slimy grass, the cold press of earth against her cheek, Alice realised she was beaten. Hot tears sprung beneath her eyelids, tears of frustration, of desperation. She bit her lips against the painful agony of her arms, as, with one fist, the man wrenched them up between her shoulder blades. Sheer arrogance had led her into this situation—an errant, idiotic belief that she could outwit, and outrun, any man. What a fool she had been! The oaf astride her, the man whose brawny thighs pressed hard against her buttocks, her hips, was nearly twice the size of her and clearly, unfortunately, not stupid.

'Who are you?' he was shouting at her now. 'What do you want with us?' With her mouth jammed into the ground, she was unable to answer, merely shaking her head in futile desperation. Deftly, he flipped her on to her back, a movement so swift that she barely registered the slight release of his weight before it descended heavily on her once more. Dismay blotted her senses as she recognised him… Nay, not him! That rude arrogant knucklehead she had encountered in the forest, the man who had kissed her! God forbid that he should recognise her; admittedly, he had let her go once, but now the House of Lancaster and York were fighting, she doubted such luck would come her way again. His massive chest and shoulders towered over her, forming a dark, intimidating shape against the periwinkle blue of the sky.

'Who are you?' he asked again, gauntleted fingers digging painfully into the small bones of her shoulders, lifting her upper body off the ground and thumping it down once more, hard. The rock-hard muscles of his thighs flexed against the outer softness of her hips with the movement, and she flushed painfully at the intimate contact. Never before had she come into such close proximity to a man! A prickling of unwanted sensation peppered along her veins, a sense of…what was it? Excitement? Her eyes squeezed shut in shame as the touch of his mouth broke into her memory.

'My name is Duncan of Abbeslaw,' she responded at last, deliberately keeping her voice low, gruff. 'I was out hunting, when you attacked me—'

'When you stole my horse,' Bastien broke in, correcting her, his voice grim. One big palm still held her pinned to the ground by one shoulder. Amazingly, her large hat had stayed on throughout the whole encounter, the double knot in the leather lace tied under her chin firmly in place.

'Aye, I'm sorry about that, my lord,' her words stumbled out, breathily. 'I was thrown from my own horse, and when I saw your horse standing—'

'Stop it!' He cut her short harshly, his tone abrasive, blunt. 'You've been following us for miles—did you really think we wouldn't notice?' He ran a derogatory eye over the bright blue of her cote-hardie, as if to indicate the stupidity of her choice in clothing. 'Who are you spying for? Who's paying you?' Her blood froze as she heard the slither of a knife, and suddenly he was up against her, the ice-cold blade at her throat, his left forearm pressed painfully along her chest. His breath was warm against her cheek. 'Tell me,' he demanded, his voice stern, forceful.

Panic danced in her brain, rattling her senses—did he really intend to kill her? The prick of the knife against her windpipe certainly indicated his intentions. Tears slid from beneath her lashes; now, she was truly frightened. 'It's not what you think,' she stuttered out. 'Take my hat off… you'll see who I am.'

Frowning, still keeping his blade at the boy's throat, Bastien wrenched at the large hat, the leather strings straining, cutting into the soft white skin of the boy's throat. Frustrated at the tight lacing, he used his knife to slice roughly through the leather strips, pulling the head covering away. As the strings released under the swift movement of his blade, Alice fainted dead away, truly believing he would cut her throat.

He stared at her in astonishment. A maid! Sweet Jesu! How had he never guessed at the lad's true sex? It all made sense: the lad's pathetic attempts to fight back with puny arms and legs, and the lack of a weapon, and aye, he knew it now, the supple contours of the body beneath him. He had merely intended to frighten the boy into speaking, but now, gazing at the pale white oval of the girl's unconscious face, he felt oddly guilty.

He recognised her with a jolt. The same maid who had confronted his soldiers in the forest a few days back. The same maid he had kissed, to stop her endless scolding. Her name? Her name was Alice; he remembered the plaintive call through the trees. On that occasion, her shiny, honey-coloured hair had been bundled back into an expensive golden net and veil, but now it was coiled, pinned rigidly to her scalp, emphasising the fine, sculptured bone structure of her face, the high cheekbones, the wide, rosebud mouth. Baggy clothes disguised her slender shape, clothes more befitting to a yeoman farmer. The last time he had seen her, she had been dressed as a member of the nobility, her garments rich and fine. She had been bossy, argumentative but now, her face as white as milk, she was utterly vulnerable. What game did she play? Leaning over her, his hands cupped her shoulders, he shook her brusquely.

Her eyes opened.

The fierce blue of her eyes punched him hard in the solar plexus. Deep azure blue, like the sea on a calm, hot summer's day. His gloved hands dropped from her shoulders, fell to his sides. Sweet Jesu! Framed by thick, spidery lashes, those burning, fathomless pools threatened to drag him under, sucking at the very core of his body, visceral, greedy. She squirmed beneath him, trying to release his weight upon her, slender curves against his own hardened muscles, and his body responded, flooded with unexpected desire. What was the matter with him, damn it!

He sprung to his feet, his only thought to create some distance between their two bodies. He had been too long without the pleasure of a woman, that was the problem. Under normal circumstances there was no way such a maid would be attractive to him, little thing that she was, but with a mouth to command a whole army if he remembered correctly.

Her pupils dilated, widened, as she surfaced back to consciousness, struggling to focus on his face. He saw the fear in them, the fleeting panic as she recognised him, remembering once more the situation she was in, and some odd little whisper hinted that it might be kind to tell her not to fear him, that she was safe with him. But nay, he wouldn't do that; kindness was not part of his nature.

'I thought you were going to kill me,' Alice breathed out in a whisper, her mind lurching back into searing consciousness. She lifted one hand tentatively to the back of her head; the long pins securing her hair dug painfully into her scalp, her head pillowed by the arching grass.

'There's still time,' Bastien growled out. 'What, in Heaven's name, do you think you are doing? Shouldn't you be tucked up in a woman's solar somewhere, working on a delicate piece of embroidery?'

Head swimming, Alice forced herself to sit up. A clamminess coated her palms. 'I told you,' she stared mutinously at the ground. 'I was out riding, and my horse threw me.'

Fern-green eyes raked down over her, over her faded, overlarge clothes, critical, assessing. 'The last time I saw you, you informed my men that you were under the protection of the King himself, a lady of the royal court, no less.' The wind ruffled his gilded hair, loose strands sifting like fine gold thread.

'I am,' she replied simply. 'I am Lady Alice Matravers, under the protection of the King.' Now she realised he was not about to kill her, some of her old confidence returned. 'And you would do well to remember that.'

'Oh, I would, would I?' he drawled. Had women changed this much since he'd been away? He'd never met any lady quite as outspoken as this one. 'Well, Lady Alice Matravers,' he rolled her name out with sarcastic emphasis, 'mayhap you could deign to tell me why you are out riding dressed as a boy?'

'Dressed like this I can ride out on my own; I prefer it that way…it's safer.'

He angled his head to one side, his eyebrows raised in exaggerated disbelief. 'Not quite safe enough today, methinks.'

Nay, not safe at all, Alice thought, her exhausted brain skittering in all directions, searching for a way out of this mess, all the time thinking of her father, marching in line, moving further and further away. Mustering all her energy, she scrambled inelegantly to her feet, painfully aware of the difference in height between them, the top of her head teetering on a level with his shoulder.

The deep laurel of his eyes glimmered in the sunlight, edgy, unpredictable. His face held the sculptured contours of stone, and was just as unyielding. She was uncertain how to deal with men like this, men associated with weapons, with battle and the harsher realities of life. His very masculinity unbalanced her, made her doubt her own courage, her own determination. Every pore of him oozed power, and a dangerous arrogance that made her angry and fearful at the same time.

'And now I'll take my leave of you,' she stuttered out formally, her words tinged with faint hope. If only he would let her walk away, then she could double back and follow her father, with more care this time.

'I think not.' He grinned back at her congenially, arms folded high across his chest. In one swift glance he absorbed the peculiar details of her attire: the oversized cote-hardie engulfing her small frame, its countless pleats falling from the shoulder-line failing to disguise the narrowness of her shoulders. Her fustian leggings fell in loose gathers about her knees; both they and her leather boots were obviously too big for her. A leather bag sat on her right hip, the strap crossing diagonally across her chest. The woman was a puzzle; she was up to something, but with the battalion heading over the hill, he had no time at the moment to find out what it was.

'I'm nothing to you,' she whispered, her large turquoise eyes observing him warily. 'Just let me go.'

'You're coming with me.' He reached out and grabbed her delicate hand, crushing the soft fingers within his leather glove.

'I will not!' she protested vehemently, as he angled down to scoop up her fallen hat, wedging it tightly back over her head. The split side of his mail coat fell open beneath his white surcoat, revealing one long muscled leg encased in close-fitting linen braies. His strong thigh muscle strained against the thin gauziness of the material.

'Keep that on, otherwise I cannot vouch for the consequences,' he warned, ignoring her objections. 'My soldiers are hungry men, in more ways than one, and there's no telling what they would do at the sight of an available woman, albeit a scrawny one.'

Her temper ignited, hot, fuming; she twisted her

fingers in his grasp, throwing her body weight back to try to escape. The ligaments in her shoulder wrenched painfully, but his fingers held firm. 'How dare you, you big oaf!' she railed at him. 'You can't frighten me!' She dug her heels into the ground as he started to pull her across to the place where his horse nibbled the grass. 'I'm not coming with you, I'm not…oof!'

Her head spun crazily as, without warning, Bastien ducked, tucking his shoulder into her soft midriff, to sling her easily over one shoulder. Flailing wildly, her hands scrabbled for a hold against his broad back, fingers sliding over his surcoat to lodge, finally, in his leather sword belt.

'You can't…!' she squeaked, outraged, as he tossed her up to lie face down over the neck of his horse.

'Save your breath, my lady…I don't have time for this now.' He cut across her protestation, his tone bored, laconic. A heavy hand squeezing down in the middle of her back prevented her from slipping forwards as he mounted up behind her. Alice squirmed violently, wriggling under his grasp, blood rushing to her head, as she reached out to clutch on to the leather strap that held the saddle in place.

'You'll pay for this,' she screeched up at him, her throat constricted, raw. 'You've no right to treat me like this!' Her head bounced against the sleek flank of the horse as Bastien kicked the animal into a trot.

She was rewarded with a short, emotionless bark of laughter. 'I'll treat you exactly as I like, my lady. And there's not a thing you can do about it.' He spurred his animal on into a full gallop, with no intention of making the ride back up to the line of prisoners any easier on his own captive. Alice held on grimly, her fingers knotted into the girth strap, her whole body jolting uncomfortably, awkwardly. Yet there was no risk of her falling; in his fist, Bastien held on firmly to the back of her tunic, the fine blue wool bunched into his leather gauntlet.

The marching prisoners had reached the brow of the hill, approaching a knot of pine trees, their dense green forming a strong silhouette against the cerulean sky. The sun was high now, and beat down hotly on the soldiers' heads, captor and captive alike. Alfric, bringing up the rear of the party, looked around for Bastien in concern; his master had been absent for a long time; he wondered whether to double back and look for him. He smiled in greeting as he spotted Bastien, and his horse straining up the hill to catch them.

'So your hunch was correct…' Alfric eyed the boy slung across the front of Bastien's saddle '…but it seems your catch was small.' Bastien grinned in response, a faint sheen of sweat shining on his face as he ground his fingers more firmly into the boy's back to stop Alice wriggling herself free.

'There's more than meets the eye with this one,' he explained, 'and I aim to find out precisely what it is.'

At his words, Alice moaned inwardly. Why, oh, why did it have to be him? Why not some bumbling, ignorant soldier who she could outwit in a moment? Her whole body ached from being continually pounded against his horse's flank, the muscles in her back and neck stretched almost to screaming point. The warmth of his big body pressed into her back as he leaned down low over her, his mouth close to her ear. 'Now, do you promise to be a good girl and walk nicely with the rest of the prisoners?' His hot breath caressed her lobe, silky, seductive. Her heart jolted, despite his mocking, taunting tone and she bit her lip, trying to ignore its rapid beating. Anything, she thought, she would promise anything to be away from him and his annoying presence! 'Aye!' she forced out, her throat dry, scratching.

'Do you promise?' he repeated lightly.

Sweet Jesu! He was infuriating! The blood sung in her ears at his patronising tone. 'I promise,' she muttered, lamely.

Relief whooshed from her lungs as he pulled gently on the bridle, not bothering to dismount as he dragged her off haphazardly. Disorientated, her head whirled dangerously, the blood rushing back to her limbs; she swayed. His hand gripped her shoulder, steadying her for a moment. 'If you value your well-being,' he reminded her once more, 'then keep that hat pulled low.' She had scarce time to nod, to indicate that she heeded his words, before he gave her a rough shove towards the line of shuffling prisoners.

The low curve of the sun brushed the hill tops, turning their smooth slopes into purpling lush-green velvet, when the order came from the front of the line to halt for the night. After tramping all day across the hills, the Yorkists had finally led the prisoners down into a wide, wooded valley, through which ran a small river. It was an ideal place to stop; a place where the horses and men could drink and wash, and sleep in the soft, cushiony grass of the flat meadows beside the water.

Alice's eyes felt hollow, burnt out with weariness. More than anything she wanted to fold her knees and drop at the next step, but the urge not to show any form of weakness, any clue that might single her out from the rest of the men, was far stronger. She was in no doubt that her captor was a man of low morals and low principle: he would most likely take great delight in seeing her humiliated in front of his men. That one thought forced her to keep her back ramrod straight and her shoulders square, and to push her feet one in front of the other, over and over again. No longer did she secretly sweep the crowd for a glimpse of her father; now all her energies were devoted to saving her own strength. Her feet ached the most, ached from the strain of trying to keep on her oversized boots that slipped and wallowed with every step; no doubt her heels were peppered with blisters. She was hot, hungry and thirsty, but she would not give up.

From his vantage point at the back of the line, Bastien studied the maid. When he had first met her, a spoiled rich girl dressed in all her finery and lost in the forest, he had dismissed her from his mind instantly. But now? Now she presented him with something of a puzzle; a puzzle dressed in boy's clothes and striding along with the rest of the men as if it were a routine activity for her. Why, they had covered nearly twenty miles today—the majority of women would be mewling wrecks by now. His own mother, Cecile, would barely totter more than a few steps before lifting one limp, white hand to be assisted into a litter, to be carried everywhere, like a child. His lips curled at the unwanted memory. Since his older brother's death, she had become even worse, hardly able to walk at all without assistance. Yet if he were around, which was seldom, she would whip her head around with such force it would stun everyone, and fix him with a baleful eye, pinning her younger son down with such bitter accusation, such acrid blame that it knotted his stomach for days. Cecile had chosen to punish him for what had happened, but surely the guilt that he carried around, day after day, was punishment enough?

Chapter Four

Huddled in the voluminous folds of the cote-hardie, Alice closed her eyes momentarily, head resting in the cradle of her arms balanced on her upraised knees. Up to now scant attention had been paid to her and she hoped by this position to remain as inconspicuous as possible. Every muscle in her body ached; her stomach growled with hunger. The woollen fabric of the cote-hardie tickled her nose, the tangy smell reminding her of her brother. Mother of Mary, she wished he were here now; he would know what to do. She prayed fervently that he had somehow survived the war in France, that he was alive somewhere and would come back to them eventually.

She shuffled uncomfortably, the moisture from the damp ground beginning to seep through her braies. A knotty root from the wide oak behind her pushed uncomfortably into her right hip. Lifting her head, she scanned the seated prisoners, searching, scouring the gathering for her father. A tall, lean figure snagged her eye; her heart plummeted as she recognised the knight in charge: Lord Bastien. He moved among the Yorkist soldiers, gave terse orders to various men, his every move practised, efficient. His lips twisted with irritation as he saw one soldier fumble with lighting a fire; in one swift movement he had dropped to his haunches to strike his own flint with a blade. His large hands cradled the spark in the puff of dried grass, nurturing the flame until it danced and crackled through the kindling. An animal energy seemed to course through his body, a dynamism that fired all his movements with an effortless grace. A lick of desire coursed through her; she ducked her head, remembering his big body pinning her own to the ground, straddling her. A memory she wished fervently to forget.

The smell of meat cooking made her lift her head once more, her mouth watering. Every sinew in her body ached with the pain of walking, ached with the need for some sustenance. Surely they would be fed? The Yorkist soldiers gathered around the main cooking fire, the thin line of smoke rising up to mingle with the darkening haze of the evening. Sitting cross-legged, their helmets glinting in the grass beside them, they swigged from leather flagons, and carved off hunks of roasted meat with their knives to chew heartily, lips slick and shiny with grease.

Starving, Alice also chewed at the inside of her lip, aware of a low muttering to her right from the other prisoners. A soldier barked across at them to be quiet. Was this how it was going to be? Were the prisoners to receive no food at all? Anger flowed up in her, replacing the gnawing hunger. She had little knowledge of such things, but she was certain that all nobles, be they prisoners or not, were treated with deference and courtesy. Surely it was part of the knight's code?

Suddenly one of the prisoners clambered to his feet, beginning to pick his way towards the Yorkist soldiers. He seemed older than the rest, and was dressed in fine clothes, not chainmail...her father! Alice's breath stopped in her throat. She knew what he was doing, but she feared for his safety with these low-born thugs. Approaching the fire, her father spoke in low tones, deferential, and nodded towards the roasting meat. A hum of appreciation rippled through the watching prisoners. One burly soldier put down his leather flagon with studied deliberation, wiped his greasy hands down the front of his woollen braies, and eased himself into a standing position. He stared at Alice's father with a blank, insulting sneer. Then he raised his fist and punched him, hard, straight in the face. Her father reeled backwards, clutching his cheek. The soldier moved forwards, making as if to hit him again. But he didn't get the chance.

Alice cannoned into the back of the soldier with a force that surprised even herself. Her blood fired, coursing hard and fast through her veins, replacing the dragging exhaustion that had plagued her earlier. She wasn't about to sit around and let her father be kicked down like a mangy dog!

'Leave him alone,' she yelled huskily as the soldier staggered sideways. 'You have no right to treat prisoners this way!' The man recovered his balance, coming towards her, a snarl on his face.

'I'll show you how we treat prisoners!' he growled out, his voice thick and guttural. He had no intention of being made a fool of in front of his fellows, who smirked and sniggered by the fire.

Alice kicked out at his shins, as he smacked her across the face. The soldier's surly face, his mean, narrow eyes, blurred before her. Her head spun wildly as the impact sent her reeling, pain buzzing in her jaw, her cheek. For a moment, the world went black, then resurfaced in a cloud of dazzling stars. She fought to keep herself on her feet. Was she awake, or asleep? Alice shook her head, trying to recover her senses, lifting her arms above her head as she saw the thick fist begin to descend once more.

'Enough!' The sharp order sliced through the night air. Alice sensed, rather than saw, Bastien's big body come between the soldier and herself. 'Go and sit down…now,' he commanded Alice and her father. His voice held the thread of steel. Limbs turning to water, knees barely holding her upright, Alice followed her father back to a spot underneath an oak tree, and sat down before she collapsed. Her hands shook with fear, body trembling with the shock of being hit. Her jaw throbbed.

'Thank you,' her father said. 'Thank you for taking the risk for me.'

She hardly dared speak, deliberately keeping her head lowered, cradling her swelling cheek beneath the shadowy brim of her hat. When her voice finally came, it was thin and tentative. 'Father, it's me.'

Her father's body tensed with the jolt of recognition; she heard the sharp intake of breath. 'Alice?' he said faintly. She nodded her head, imperceptibly.

'Good God!' he murmured, but it was impossible for him to say anything further, too dangerous. Now the Yorkists had finished their meal, they had begun to patrol the area, circling the prisoners like carrion around dead meat. Yet, unseen by the others, her father's hand reached out across the grass to seize her fingers, to squeeze some reassurance into her frozen veins. She drew comfort from his touch, knowing that somehow, and in some way, they would extract themselves from this mess.

Stretched out on his back, his head propped comfortably by a wide trunk of oak, Bastien's thoughts prowled unceasingly through the scenes of the day, scattered images continually shot through by a pair of limpid blue eyes. He sighed, turning on to his left side, then adjusting a few moments later to lie on his back. In retrospect, life in France now seemed gloriously uncomplicated. At least there, on the other side of the Channel, women had behaved like women. He had never known a maid to behave in such a way before, with such bravery, or foolishness. How different she was from Katherine. Katherine. His fingers sought the leather lace tucked into his tunic, the cold metal of the betrothal ring. Pain lanced through him, the pain of loss, of bereavement. He would never know such beauty, such love again.

Opening his eyes, shoving the shrouded memories from his brain, he explored the darkness above, trying to gain some meaning from the maid's behaviour. Why had she leapt to save the older man, when he had warned her to keep a low profile? Either she was profoundly dimwitted, which he doubted, owing to the dexterity of her speech, or there was some other reason. His fingers dug into the soft, damp ground beneath as he recalled the sheer horror he had experienced when the soldier had hit her.

Bastien had been high on the hillside when it happened, his eyes sweeping the area for any sign of attack, his body restless, uneasy. Yet the girl screeching by the fire had drawn him immediately into a powerful sprint; he saw her jump on the soldier from behind, dragging down at his arms…and had tasted fear, like iron filings in his mouth. What a fool the girl was!

Around him, sprawled haphazardly amidst cloaks and blankets, the men slumbered, some snoring gently, others muttering in their sleep. After the stiff breeze earlier, the air had calmed to stillness. Sounds seemed more rounded, amplified, by the utter quiet. The flow of the river plashing against the rocks was interspersed occasionally by the screech of a lone owl, or a furtive rustling of an animal in the undergrowth behind him. Bastien tracked the stars in the sky, searching for and naming the familiar constellations in an attempt to force his mind to drift off. But it was hopeless. Why had the maid leapt to the defence of the older man like a stone from a catapult? Slowly he turned his head to the left, in the direction he knew the girl to be, then propped himself up on one arm, his eye roaming over the sleeping bodies, hunting. Yet it wasn't her smaller profile that gave away her position, it was the clear, bell-like tones of her voice, carried to him in a whisper on the night air. Hell's teeth!

Bastien vaulted upwards, his approach stealthy and efficient. His target, the two figures in the moon-shadow of the wide oak, lay as if sleeping, but Bastien knew better. At the sight of him, the old man's eyes flashed with alarm; he murmured a low, swift warning. Crouching, Bastien clamped his hand to the maid's mouth as she twisted her head back to see who it was. Under his touch, her body jerked with fright, her soft lips moving tentatively against the inner creases of his palm. An unexpected warmth flooded his body, sensual, erotic; his heart thudded. He dismissed it, bending down to whisper in the girl's ear, 'We need to talk.' A light flowery perfume rose from the skin of her neck, rose into his nostrils, assailing him. He dragged his head upwards, away, away from the temptation of that wonderful scent. At Bastien's words, the old man seized his forearm, shaking his head, his eyes full of concern.

'She'll be safe with me, on my knight's oath,' Bastien reassured him as he hauled Alice up, one hand under her upper arm.

Don't believe him! Don't! Alice wanted to scream and shout at her father, as Bastien led her away in to the forest. Don't let me go with this thug! She hung back, deliberately slowing her steps as Bastien jerked her along, his fingers tight on her wrist. Oh God! she thought, her imagination looming with foreboding images of her fate. This was it! This was how she must pay for her stupidity, her utter, utter foolishness! Digging her heels in with even more force, Alice twisted her wrist this way and that, trying to loosen the muscular hold.

'Oh, for pity's sake, stop resisting me, will you?' Bastien stopped abruptly, impatient with her dragging steps. 'We need to be out of earshot.' So they can't hear my screams, she thought wildly, tears beginning to run down her face. His grip lessened slightly as he spoke and, seizing the opportunity, she wrested her hand with a sharp tug, freeing herself momentarily. Spinning on her toes in the loose leaves of the woodland floor, she made as if to run, but Bastien caught her in an instant, one huge forearm looping around her waist.

'Hell's teeth! I have no time for this!' he growled out, hauling her backwards, her toes flailing in the air. 'Stop behaving like a ninny! I've told you, I'm not going to hurt you!' Slammed up against his body, she caught the musky scent of his skin, a seductive mixture of woodsmoke and leather. Swinging around, he carried her before him with a powerful stride before dumping her down in a small clearing much further down the river.

'The noise of the water will drown our voices,' he explained, perusing her wan, exhausted face. In the moonlight, he could see the tears tracking down the exquisite lustre of her skin, over the purpling mark caused by the soldier. Exasperated, he shoved one hand through his hair, the movement ruffling the golden tendrils. He wore his hair shorter than most men, cut to the nape of his neck to expose the tough, lean line of his jaw. 'What in Heaven's name is the matter with you? I only want to talk to you.'

'I don't believe you!' she sobbed out breathlessly. 'Look at the way you're treating me! You're a thug… like the rest of your soldiers.' Her lissom frame vibrated with fear. Did she really believe he would attack her? His hands moved to her upper arms, to steady her, calm her. 'Nay…you misunderstand,' he murmured mildly.

But Alice refused to hear him, her mind whirling with stark images of what she thought was about to happen. She made a last, desperate bid for freedom. 'For your information…I am betrothed, you know… and he…he…my betrothed…' she struggled to find the words, for in her heart she struggled with the concept that Edmund would be her husband '…wouldn't be very happy with what you're about to do.'

'And what am I about to do?' Bastien tried to look stern, but in reality, he was finding it extremely difficult not to laugh. Under the white sheen of moonlight, the contours of his face seemed carved, sculptured from granite.

'You're…you're…' Alice hiccoughed '…going to…' She stopped. A frown creased her brow. Something wasn't quite right. Surely he would be throwing her to the ground right now, trying to tear her clothes off? The very thought made her blush furiously, and she studied her feet, praying that he couldn't see her face in the moonlit shadows.

'Methinks you flatter yourself, my lady,' he replied, his tone faintly insulting. 'You're far too short for most men's tastes. And dressed in all that garb you resemble little more than a suet dumpling. Hardly seductive.'

Dumpling? His words sent a storm of angry humiliation through her. 'How dare you speak to me so! You're outrageous!' she reacted instinctively.

'Would you rather I raped you?' he asked slowly, shockingly, his face looming close to her own. Her mouth closed with a snap as she caught the feral glitter in his eyes. She shook her head at his words, drawing away from him slightly. 'I thought not,' he continued, 'so let's hear no more on the subject.' He tilted his head in the direction of the camp. 'Tell me, why did you leap to that older man's defence back there?'

Alice touched one finger to the side of her mouth, throbbing and sore from the impact of the soldier's fist. 'Your soldier hit him, because he asked for some food.'

'Even after I warned you not to draw attention to

yourself?' The bruise on her mouth appeared as a dark splotch, mottled in this light, lines of blood creasing her lip. Guilt laced his gut. He should have stayed with the group; the Duke of York's men were renowned for their cruelty. He should have been on his guard. 'It was a foolish thing to do,' he murmured. 'What were you thinking?'

I wasn't thinking, she mused silently. I saw my father, my own kith and kin in trouble and I had to help him. Alice raised her chin, pulling her spine straight. 'I was not going to sit by and watch that man being beaten to a pulp.'

'I wouldn't have let that happen.'

'What?' she replied, appalled, her voice rising a couple of notches as she stared up into his tanned face, her eyes wide with bright intelligence. 'You mean you saw what was going on and you did nothing to stop it? How could you be so callous?' Her expression held nothing but accusation, blame. Anger flared over him, unearthing memories he didn't want: his mother's bitter voice, her cold stare.

He leaned down so his face was on a level with hers, his own expression blank, hostile. 'The Lancastrians are our prisoners,' he reminded her, rigidly. 'This is how prisoners are always treated.' And worse, he thought silently.

His face was inches from her own, but she held her ground, incensed by what he had told her. Her earlier fear of attack had disappeared; he obviously had no feelings towards her as a woman—indeed, he seemed to have no feelings at all, for anybody. Her fingers curled, compressing into her palms, clenching her resolve. She knew he was annoyed, sensed the ripple of irritation seizing his body, saw it in the diamond sparkle of his eyes. Yet something pushed her on; a sense of righteous indignation, of some higher moral code, she knew not what.

'You should be ashamed of yourself. Those men are human beings, just like you and me, and should be treated with respect and courtesy.' She exhaled, her breath expelling from her lungs with force: she hadn't realised how tightly she had been holding it.

Her words needled him. Everything about this situation was so wrong; he couldn't remember a time when he had heard a woman speak thus, or behave in such a foolishly courageous way. She had put aside her own safety in order to help another human being, and had suffered the consequences. Cupping her shoulders, he gave her a rough shake; the fragility of her shoulder bones under his touch surprised him, and he dropped his hands immediately. 'You meddle in matters that don't concern you.' Although his voice remained low, she caught the warning.

'What would you have me do, my lord? Sit back and watch that old man punished, all for want of a morsel of food? If I am there, watching, then it concerns me.' Unable to bear the merciless sparkle of his regard any more, she lowered her head to stare at the ground.

'And that's where you should have stayed. Watching.' Faced with the rounded crown of her hat, Bastien struggled to comprehend her motives. He stared down at her, frustrated, wondering at the secrets that danced in her head. 'You're in a tricky enough predicament as it is. Why make it worse?'

She couldn't tell him. If the House of York knew the identity of her father, then they would know how important he was to them. He was close to King Henry, as was she, and that would put a price on his head, for sure. She had to throw Bastien off the scent, distract him, somehow.

Alice jerked her head up. 'And it was you who put me in this predicament, my lord! You could have let me go in the forest. You could let me go now.'

Aye, he could have. But there was something about this maid that made him want to keep her by his side, something about her enigmatic, puzzling nature that made him hesitant to release her. He told himself it wasn't because of those wide cornflower blue eyes, or the sweet curve of her cheek as she turned her head from him, because he wasn't affected by such things. Certainly, he took his pleasures as readily as the next man, but on an impersonal level only—no involvement, no responsibility. It suited him that way.

'And if I let you go now, you would carry on following us, until you're spotted once more,' he replied. 'And it might not be me who finds you next time.'

'Are you telling me I should be *grateful* that it was you who picked me up?' She toed the ground, releasing the dank, powerful smell of mossy earth.

He grinned, briefly, the lopsided twist to his mouth lending him a boyish expression. 'Other men might not have treated you as well, once they knew your true identity.'

'You think you have treated me well? Why, the way you've hauled me about—!'

'Is nothing, compared to what other men might do,' he warned her.

'Come, let us go back, and sleep. And remember, don't try anything stupid again. I'll be watching you.'

He led the way back through the scrambling, moonlit undergrowth, safe in the knowledge that she would follow him, that the older man in the group of captives meant something to her. He knew that she withheld information from him, and that was why she had to stay; but the vaguest niggle in his conscience told him that wasn't the only reason he was reluctant to let her go.

Chapter Five

In the hazy heat of an early autumn afternoon, the imposing structure of Ludlow Castle seemed to drift on a raft of white mist: a magical, ethereal place. Yet there was nothing insubstantial about the towering, fortress-like walls, the square-cut crenellations. The fortified stronghold of Richard Plantagenet, Duke of York, rose impressively from a rounded green hill, overlooking the River Teme. The sheer, soaring walls, built from purplish stone, glowed with pink hues in the sunlight. The Duke's flag flapped listlessly in the occasional breeze, the black needlework of the falcon and the fetterlock stark against the white canvas background. No one could doubt the power of the Duke of York, even without this impressive fortification; tales of his notoriety were tittle-tattled with glee within the court of Henry, although not within the King's or his feisty wife's hearing.

Tramping steadily after her father, Alice tried to damp down the fear that clambered in her throat. Ever since they had been roused by a soldier's sword-point at dawn, and forced to march northwards without a bite to eat, the opportunities to escape had been few and far between. Indeed, if she admitted it, they had been nonexistent. The soldiers had kept them in close formation, stopping only once for a glug of water from a leather bottle passed around the prisoners, before driving them on to Ludlow. Despite being late in the year, the day had been unseasonably warm, and now, as she forced her feet to step the last few yards towards the castle gatehouse, beads of sweat begain to trickle down her face from the constricting band of her hat.

Her mind descended into a fug of listlessness; a combination of the perspiration and dirt coating her skin, the cloying heat, made her sway, lose her balance momentarily. Upright, she told herself grimly, remain upright. She had only herself to blame for the mess she was in. At this very moment Alice longed for the quiet serenity of the women's solar at the royal court: the peaceful stitching, the gentle, lilting conversations, the wonderful smell of the beeswax candles. How laughable that she craved something that she so often kicked against! Licking her parched dry lips, she fought to control the nausea rising in her gullet, fearing what lay before her. Despite her waywardness, she realised with horror how sheltered her life had been, cloistered in the pretty, protected ways of the royal court; now a shrouding vulnerability swept over her, leaving her raw, exposed.

Following the line on horseback, Bastien watched Alice sway, and deliberately turned his head away. He curled his ungloved hands around the reins, feeling the leather bite into his palms, annoyed that, throughout the journey, she had continually pulled his gaze. He told himself it stemmed from a polite, formal deference he would extend to any woman, rather than from any genuine concern. In truth, it was a long time since he had experienced any dealings with women, apart from the occasional dalliance with a camp whore, and around Alice, his manners felt rusty, unused. Still, he had fought too many battles, and seen too many good men die, to be concerned about the finer details of how to treat women properly. He simply didn't care any more. All he knew was that he had warned her enough times to keep quiet; now it was up to her. He wasn't about to leap to her defence again. Yet as he tracked her stumbling, listing gait, he realised she was exhausted. Why, she was half the size of some of his soldiers, yet had kept pace with them nigh on a full day! He supposed it was an adequate punishment for her recklessness in pursuing them in the first place.

As he and Alfric beside him chivvied the prisoners through the shadowed recess of the gatehouse and into the brightness of the inner bailey, a short, stocky man barrelled forward to greet him.

'Richard!' Bastien grinned at the Duke of York, jumping down from the saddle and handing the reins to a waiting groom. 'I wasn't certain that you'd be here.'

Richard clapped him on the back. 'Naturally I would be here to congratulate you on your victory! I'm only sorry I couldn't be there myself. Looks like you had an excellent morning on my behalf.' He nodded approvingly at the prisoners jostling together on the cobbles. 'What a fine bunch. And all ransomable for a pretty sum, I'll be bound.'

'I haven't collected the names yet.' Bastien was aware

of a curious detachment. Normally he was excited as Richard about their success in battle; they had fought together often, ever since the day the Duke had spotted the innate talent in the keen battle-hungry lad, and trained him up to be one of the finest commanding soldiers in England.

'Well, let's collect them now,' Richard said briskly, striding towards the group. 'As soon as we have names, we can send ransom notes to their families, and extract some money from them.'

Not that he needed it, mused Bastien. The Duke was one of the richest men in England—richer than the King himself, some said. But his grudge against the King grew wider and deeper every day and his loyal supporters were anxious about the mounting crisis towards which the county was heading under King Henry's weak leadership.

'Scribe!' Richard clicked his fingers, and instantly, a pale-faced, harried-looking man scurried to his side, carrying a quill and a book of parchment. Beside him walked a small boy, carefully carrying an earthenware pot of ink as if it were precious gold.

'Holy Mary,' Richard barked, braking his stride sharply before Alice's diminutive figure. She stood drooping at the end of the lined-up prisoners. 'They're sending them young these days, are they not?' He threw the comment back at Bastien, then turned to address the boy. 'How old are you?'

'I'm one-and-twenty, my lord,' the lad mumbled back.

'Hm! Older than you look, then.' The Duke appeared puzzled. 'You seem mighty short for a lad that age. What's your name?'

No answer. The lad stared resolutely ahead, eyes seemingly fixed on a distant horizon. Bastien frowned, a small crease appearing between his fine green eyes. Why did she not give a false name, and be done with it?

'I said...' the Duke leaned into the boy's face '...what...is...your...name?'

For a moment, the lad stood there, resolute, before his whole body seemed to fold in on itself, looping around in a soft spiral, before crashing down on to the cobbles. It happened so suddenly that no one had time to act, to leap or grab, and now all eyes were riveted on the lad that lay on the ground. Nay, not a lad. A maid!

Alice's hat had dislodged itself in her fall, and now lay some feet away from her crumpled body. Her golden hair, intricately braided, shone brightly in the sunshine, the severe style exposing the gentle line of her jaw, the smooth curve of her cheek. The older man, the one she seemed so familiar with, had dropped to her side, his fingers on her neck, finding her rapid pulse, assuring for himself that all was well.

He turned exhausted eyes up to the Duke. 'This has gone on long enough,' he muttered. 'My lord, may I present my daughter, the Lady Alice Matravers.'

'Good God, man, what were you thinking?' The Duke, his weatherbeaten faced creased with astonishment, glared down at Bastien, sprawled languidly in an oak chair by the fire in the great hall.

Bastien stretched his long legs out in front of him, his thigh muscles straining a little after the battle followed by two days' riding. Against the dusty leather of his boots, the stone floor gleamed a shiny grey; despite his reputation as a warlord, Richard always insisted on the highest of standards when at home. Bastien stared into the flames, continually damping down the guilt that flared within him, every time he thought of that woman.

'Well?' The Duke, his stocky build dwarfed by the massive stone fireplace behind him, hankered for an answer.

Bastine shrugged his shoulders, mouth twisting wryly. In contrast to the Duke's tetchy movements, he seemed calm, unmoved. 'I suppose I thought to teach her a lesson,' he replied finally. The image of the girl's limp body, her head lolling back over the crook of her father's arm as he carried her up the stairs, ran through his mind. He shifted against the hard wooden back of the chair. Lord, but these seats were uncomfortable!

'What! By dragging her through the mud and the mire? By subjecting her to the rough, untethered ways of our soldiers? I haven't dared ask about the state of her face… Did you do that?'

'Nay! Never!' Bastien's head shot up. 'She meddled in a situation that she shouldn't have. Richard, she was the one spying on us, following us. Should I have just let her go?'

Richard rested his hand on the carved stone ledge above the fire, the flames picking up the gold trellis-work embroidery on his cote-hardie, making it sparkle. Around them, on various trestle tables and benches, the soldiers relaxed, engaged in dice games, or light banter with the servants of the castle. Already the mead was flowing, in celebration of their victory, and every now and again a burst of raucous laughter would rent the air.

'Nay,' said Richard. 'You did right to bring her along.

But maybe not in that manner, forcing her to walk all that way with no food.'

Bastien stood up, raking his hair with his fingers, as he stood head and shoulders higher than the Duke. 'Sweet Jesu! Richard, you're making it sound as if I took the girl out of her bed, dressed her in those ridiculous boy's clothes and forced her to come with us. She was the one who put herself in that position. And I say she got everything she deserved. A woman should know her own boundaries, and by overstepping them, should know what to expect.'

'You're too harsh, Bastien.' The look in the Duke's eyes hinted at something else.

'I stepped in when it was absolutely necessary. It could have been a lot worse.' Suddenly the fire warming his right flank seemed too hot; he stepped away, creating distance between himself and the Duke.

'Even so, I think you have let your past colour your judgement.' The Duke's tone was softer now. 'Not all women are like your mother.'

'That woman has nothing to do with this,' Bastien snapped. 'It's a completely separate matter.'

'If you say so,' replied Richard, in a tone that clearly implied that he didn't agree. 'Anyway, despite your best efforts, it's a good thing you managed not to kill the Lady Alice.'

'Give me one good reason why.' Bastien let out a long, deep breath.

'Because she is about to become extremely useful to us.'

Fabien ran another approving glance around the room to which he had carried his daughter a few hours

earlier. A fire had been hurriedly lit in the brick fireplace, fresh linens already adorning the four-poster bed.
Through two large rectangular windows, the evening
sun streamed, throwing shafts of light through the
warped glass and across the polished wooden floor.
'Why not eat up here, daughter, in the comfort and
privacy of this chamber?'

'What? And leave you to face the enemy on your
own?' Alice bounced up in the bed, propping herself
up against the pillows. A rosy blush had returned to her
cheeks; her eyes had lost their dull glitter, regaining
their customary periwinkle sparkle. One of the maid-
servants had painstakingly released all the tightly bound
plaits while she had lain, exhausted, in the bed, and now
her hair flowed over her shoulders like liquid honey.

Fabien smiled at his daughter's misplaced protective
instinct. 'I'm sure I'll manage to survive with them.'

'After the way they treated us on the march? Father,
who knows what will happen?

'You mustn't judge the whole of the Yorkist army on
the actions of one wayward soldier, Alice. The Duke of
York is a fair man.'

Alice reached out to touch her father's hand. 'You're
too kind, Father. I know it's what Mother says all the
time, but you are too forgiving.'

'It's what makes me a physician and not a soldier.'
Fabien smiled down at her. 'If you're determined to
come down, then I'll go and find a servant to help you.'

As the heavy elm door closed with a sharp click of the
ironwork latch, Alice flipped back the fine linen sheets
that lay across her, and swung her feet to the floor. All
her garments had been removed, save for the linen shirt
that she had worn under her tunic. She relished the cool

air against her bare feet and legs, standing up tentatively. Her head felt clear, full of energy, the previous swimming sensation having completely disappeared. She hoped her father would return soon with something to wear; it was one thing to be near naked in one's home, but in that of the enemy?

Alice moved over to the window, looking out. The view was breathtaking, stretching out for miles over the lush grassland that bordered the river: a rich patchwork of greens and yellows, some fields stacked with stooks of straw, some grazed by a herd of cattle. And in the distance, the blurred bluish outlines of the hills, and beyond, Alice's home.

Behind her, the door opened. Alice turned, expecting a fresh-faced maid with an armful of clothes. At the sight of Bastien, his large frame filling the doorway, her heart plummeted, then leapt once more in exhilaration. Her lips parted, as if to speak, but although her scrambled brain could find the words, she couldn't seem to put them in any order. The top of his head grazed the top of the doorway, the shine of his golden hair leaping out against the silvered oak of the lintel.

'Oh!' she stuttered, a hand to her mouth, unsure what to say next, aghast that her legs seemed to have started trembling again.

Bastien had changed his clothes, all the trappings of war replaced by softer garments. His tunic bore no embellishment, but was cut from a fine silk velvet, the pleats falling from the shoulder emphasising the impressive breadth of his chest. A leather lace fastened the tunic at the front; somehow Alice couldn't imagine him fiddling with all the tiny buttons so favoured by the nobles at court.

She drew a deep shaky breath, trying to gather her senses into some sort of order. His wet hair was raked back against his scalp, exposing the lean angles of his jaw. And even though they stood a few feet apart, she could smell the sweet, water-infused scent of his hair, almost taste the dampness of his skin. A coiling heat wound slowly in the pit of her belly—what on earth was the matter with her? And now he was staring at her, staring at her as if he had never seen her before in his life.

'Is this what you normally do, invade ladies' chambers without knocking?' she asked. Her clear lilt instantly condemned him.

His fingers dug into the pile of clothes in his hands, before he tossed them into the middle of the bed, a tumbled rainbow of silk and velvet. 'I'm sorry,' he said gruffly, 'I thought you were still in bed.' In truth, the guilt surging within him had won; he had wanted to see how the maid fared for himself and had collected the bundle of clothes from the maidservant on the way up.

Her eyes widened. 'What, you mean so befuddled with the world that I wouldn't notice whether you were in the room or not?'

He brushed away a cold drip of water that crept behind his ear. 'Something like that,' he muttered. Sweet Jesu! He wished fervently that she *was* still in bed. The last time he had seen her she had been bundled up from head to toe in boy's clothes, but now? Now she stood before him in a gauzy shirt that barely reached her knees! Fashioned from a cotton lawn so fine, he could see every detail of her slender body, highlighted by the streaming sunlight that came through the windows at her back. He groaned inwardly as his body responded to her shimmering beauty, her shining hair falling like spun gold over her shoulders. He longed to plunge his hands into it, to test its softness against his skin, to draw her sweet fragrance deep into his lungs... Stop! He wrenched his eyes away from her, pinpointed a knot of wood in one of the floorboards, forcing himself to trace the whorls and patterns of the grain, to slow his breathing. Hell's teeth! Hadn't he been with whores enough to stop his body responding to some stupid female?

Drawing at the very depths of his self-control, he forced his eyes back, compelling himself to focus on her face, her face only. He tried to ignore the jewelled depths of her periwinkle-blue eyes. Her skin, pale, pellucid, still bore the marks of the soldier's attack, the large purplish bruise beginning to fade to a mottled yellow. Alice raised her fingers, touching the mark self-consciously.

Bastien strode over to the bed, began ruffling through the pile of clothes, a raft of irritation searing through his body. He was a soldier, for God's sake, not some lady's maid. He pulled a garment out, threw it in her direction with such force that she almost staggered back under the weight of the fabric. 'Get dressed,' he ordered, thickly. 'The Duke wants to see you downstairs.'

'Then maybe I should start with a gown,' Alice said calmly, approaching the bed with soft steps. She laid down the cloak that Bastien, in his agitation, had thrown across to her, and picked up the dress that lay in a crumpled heap in the middle of the furs. As she reached down, the white linen of her shirt pulled back, revealing delicate forearms, her white skin laced with a tracery of blue veins. The rich mead colour of her hair rippled forwards tantalisingly as her head bent down with the movement.

His fingers itched, then, as if with a will of their own, they stretched out, brushed fleetingly against the silken strands, luxuriating in their softness. A faint smell of lavender lifted into the air, disturbed by his questing fingers. At his touch, she jerked her head up, backed away, astonished at the change in him.

'Your hair...' he whispered. His eyes burned down at her, desire evident in the emerald orbs. A log fell in the grate, the sound snapping across the stillness in the room.

Alice smiled broadly, trying to lighten the strange atmosphere. 'I know...it's a bit out of control.' She pulled down on the strands, trying to smooth the curling mass. 'My mother says she can't do a thing with it.'

'It's beautiful,' he said, then turned abruptly on his heel, left the room and closed the door with a sharp click.

Chapter Six

The diminutive maidservant drove another long pin against Alice's scalp, trying to secure the large heart-shaped headdress to Alice's hair.

'Ouch!' yelped Alice, raising one hand as if to ward off the onslaught of another attack by a pin. 'I really think it will stay on now,' she continued, a note of pleading in her voice.

'All done, my lady,' the maidservant announced, stepping back to run a critical eye over her work, frowning. 'Will you not let me pluck out those few hairs that are showing on your forehead? It would improve the look of the headdress.'

'Absolutely not!' Alice spun on the low stool to face the maid, touching her hand to the loose tendrils of hair that framed her face. 'I know all the other ladies at court do it, but it's not for me.'

'Ah, well, I've done my best then, my lady,' the maidservant responded doubtfully. She chose not to ask about shaving the lady's eyebrows off; her question would most likely be met with complete outrage. Yet it was what all the noblewomen chose to do; it was the fashionable look. This lady's eyebrows might be finely arched and coloured a rich sable, but most ladies preferred to shave them off, and redraw high arches using a fine charcoal pencil. The maidservant picked up an oval looking-glass, its frame and handle made of smooth animal horn, and offered it to Alice, who gently pushed it away.

'Nay, I know what I look like,' she explained her rejection. Bastien's compliment of her hair still sung in her head; her surprise at his utterance flowed in her blood, making her wonder at his words. He was wrong, of course. Her mother continually berated her for not following the court fashion, and she knew the women giggled and pointed at her hoydenish ways. But no matter, she knew there was more to life than just sitting around looking beautiful. Every time she went anywhere with her father, she honed her skill as a physician, sucking up knowledge like a sponge. Only this time she seemed to have received more than she bargained for.

The restrictive head-dress and heavy veil pressed down on her head, pulling cruelly at her hair, emphasising her feeling of imprisonment. Her gown, too, was of an elaborately embroidered silk, the loops and whorls of golden thread adding to the weight of the skirts. She felt unbalanced, as if she could hardly stand up, let alone walk. Her own mother would clap her hands together with joy if she could see her now, wearing the height of fashion; what irony that she was wearing these clothes behind enemy lines. She frowned. Both her mother, and

Edmund, would be frantic with worry now, probably sending out a search party at this moment.

Edmund. The man she had agreed to marry. Her mind rummaged through the chaos of the past few days, through the shock of capture, the exhausting march, searching for the details of Edmund's face, his gentle brown eyes. But every time she caught the faintest trail of him, the weak image was nudged away by an insistent, demanding pair of green eyes. Damn the man, that he had the power to corrupt her thoughts!

'Are you ready, my lady?' the maidservant enquired.

'As ready as I'll ever be,' Alice smiled tautly at the girl. 'You'd better lead the way.'

The maidservant nodded. 'I was told to make sure you arrived safely at the great hall, my lady.'

'Oh, really? To make sure I don't slip away?' Alice replied, studying the rising colour in the girl's cheek. 'Fear not. There's not much chance of me fleeing dressed in these clothes.'

The maidservant hoisted a blazing torch out of its iron holder, and pulled the door open, holding the flame aloft to lead the way down the steep spiral stairs. Alice's fingers trailed along the damp stone wall as she descended, countering her feeling of unsteadiness. The torch threw strange, flickering shadows up and down the stairwell, making the stone glisten under its shuddering light. Despite knowing her father to be in the great hall, Alice could not shed the feeling that she descended slowly to her doom.

After what seemed like an eternity, the maid halted before a wide, Gothic-arched doorway. Placing the torch carefully in an empty iron bracket at the side of the oak door, the maid turned the handle and pushed the door open slightly. 'The great hall, my lady,' she announced in a sonorous whisper. 'I'll leave you now.'

Heart thudding with—what…anticipation, a fear of the unknown?—Alice teetered on the threshold, allowing the sounds of merrymaking from the hall to wash over her: the click of dice, the roars of laughter and the light, bouncing tones of music. Her customary self-confidence drained away; she was about to enter a roomful of strangers—nay, not just strangers, but her enemies too, men who wished to harm her King. She edged backwards into the corridor. The maid had disappeared, no doubt assuming Alice would enter the great hall with no argument. But no, that was not how it was going to be!

Heart rate quickening, Alice turned, walking down the corridor with light rapid steps, skirts swinging forcefully. Now she would escape; she would seize this moment when no one was watching her. Her father obviously thought that by being pleasant to these barbarians, they would let him go; Alice was not so sure. Hopefully, dressed as she was, she would be mistaken for one of the ladies in the Duke of York's court, allowed to come and go as she pleased. Her pulse beat wildly in her throat and at her wrists. She had almost gained the small door at the far end of the corridor, its rectangular outlines looming out of the dimness towards her. Her salvation.

Her white fingers reached out to turn the handle, made contact with the forged iron ring. Oiled on a regular basis, it slid easily around, and she pulled… Suddenly a muscled arm shot forwards over her shoulder and smartly slammed the door shut again.

'And where do you think you're going?' His hot breath touched her ear; the skin on the side of her neck tingled. Alice eyed the massive palm in the centre of the door, and knew, without looking, to whom it belonged. Tears of frustration wetted her eyes…she had been so close!

She twisted angrily, trapped between Bastien's huge frame and the thick door behind her. In the half-light, she caught the gilded gleam of his eyes, smelled the heady scent of his masculine aroma.

'I was trying to leave,' she admitted, turning her palms heavenwards. 'I thought I had a chance.' Her voice sounded small in the cavernous confines of the passage.

'Did you think that we might have forgotten about you?' He tilted his head to one side in question, the high-rolled neck of his gypon creasing with the gesture. 'Do you honestly think we are that dim-witted?'

'I don't credit you with much intelligence,' she replied, sourly, annoyed that her escape attempt had been foiled. 'You Yorkists are known as men of war, who would kill first and ask questions afterwards.'

'Is that your own opinion, or one that you have gleaned from the tittle-tattle of others?' His well-defined lips twisted into a mocking smile.

She placed her hands on her hips, indignant. 'I don't listen to gossip! Nay, I've seen how you treat your prisoners; I saw the wounds you've inflicted on our soldiers on the battlefield…it's enough.'

'So you have formed your judgement on the basis of one battle, and on the hasty actions of one soldier?'

'I've helped my father many times; I've seen more than just one battle.'

'Hah!' he laughed, a short, caustic noise. 'You speak like a veteran soldier.' He leaned in closer to her, the taut angles of his face just inches from her own. 'Yet all you are is a maid completely out of her depth. Stop trying to second guess everything; in this situation you cannot win.'

Alice sagged back against the door, defeated. 'It was worth a try,' she muttered, her blue eyes flashing up at him, acutely aware of the closeness of his chiselled features. She swallowed; her throat was as dry as a husk.

'Has life at court become a little bit tedious?' he chided her. 'Is that why you persist in putting yourself in danger?'

'Nay!' she protested. Why did he have to be so close? 'I do it because I want to learn! My father teaches me, so I can heal people too!' He made her sound like she was a child, a bored wanton out for a bit of fun. He couldn't be further from the truth.

He glared down at her, blond strands of hair falling down across his forehead. This woman was impossible, frustrating; he couldn't label her, neither lady, nor peasant. She was so unlike any woman he had ever met before. How different she appeared even now! In the upstairs chamber, clad only in that diaphanous shirt, she had been free, flowing, her hair loose and tumbled. His throat constricted at the memory. Now her beautiful hair was hidden beneath an elaborate padded head-dress, her svelte curves emphasised by the fitted seams of the gown. The wide, curving neck of the dress displayed an expanse of white throat and neck, a frantic pulse beating rapidly at its base. A pang of longing for her faded linen shirt scorched through him. She was close, too close!

'Come on,' he muttered abruptly, turning on his heel. 'The Duke is anxious to speak to you.'

She trailed after him miserably, her feet dragging.

'You seem to have slowed down a bit since we marched to Ludlow,' he muttered drily, halting up ahead in the passage to wait for her.

'It's the gown,' she explained, frustrated. 'It's like walking in thick mud.'

He smiled at her analogy, catching at her hand, intending to speed her up, to help her, he wasn't sure which. 'You would never have escaped wearing that,' he chuckled, almost to himself. His lean, sinewy fingers tightened around her palm; a spark leapt up her arm, encircling her heart, burning.

Crowds of people thronged about the great hall, full of the Duke's soldiers and their prisoners. Alongside them sat the usual retainers of the castle: the servants, the estate workers and some of the villagers, too poor or too ill to provide for themselves. The air was thick, muggy from the fire smoke and the combined breath and sweat of the crowd. Raising the long sweeping hem of her gown to negotiate the wooden steps to the high dais on which the nobility sat, Alice was glad of Bastien's supporting hand on her elbow.

The Duke of York sat in the middle of a long length of oak table, talking animatedly to her father. Why, to look at them it could have been that they were the best of friends chatting and laughing with each other. But Alice noticed the lines of strain around her father's mouth, the redness around his eyes, and knew that he was not finding the conversation easy.

'Sit here,' Bastien ordered curtly, indicating an empty high-backed chair next to her father. His elbow nudged hers as he flung himself into a chair next to her. Alice slipped into her chair gracefully, her skirts settling around her in graceful folds.

The Duke, who, with her father had watched her approach, smiled at her. 'Well, my lady, are you well rested?' He ran appreciative eyes over her attire. 'I see the servants have found some appropriate garments. Doesn't she look well in them?' The Duke glanced at her father for agreement.

'She looks much better,' her father agreed, taking her small hand in his: a sign of silent support. With that gesture, Alice's heart lightened. They would come through this together. But when she looked into her father's eyes, she realised something was wrong; his whole demeanour seemed humbled, chastened. She caught the merest shake of his head, and realised she couldn't ask him all the questions that tumbled in her brain.

'Help yourself to something to eat,' the Duke advised her, 'and then we will talk.' He resumed his conversation with her father, and Alice was left staring at her empty pewter plate, her stomach churning with nerves, with fear. If only she could read her father's mind!

'What's going on, Bastien?' In her panic, she appealed quietly to him, sitting on her right. Suddenly the man who had taken her prisoner, who had dragged her through the mud and mire of the countryside and treated her hardly better than a common peasant appeared before her as her ally, her haven. To rely on such a man was the last thing she wanted to do, but, adrift in this uncertain situation, it seemed her only course of action.

Bastien had already loaded his plate: slices of roast chicken, crusty bread rolls and a pile of cooked vegetables formed a colourful mound before him. He shrugged his shoulders at her low question. 'You know as much as I do, maid. Where the Duke is concerned, his plans are often not revealed until the very last moment.' He grinned, the smile lighting his face, lines crinkling out from the sides of his eyes. 'Always keeps his enemies guessing…and keeps them on their toes.'

Her wide blue eyes swept over his face. 'But we mean nothing to him,' she hissed. 'He can't keep us here for ever. What would be the reason?'

Bastien stabbed his knife into a chunk of chicken, slicing a small piece off. A glorious scent arose from the woman next to him; a heady combination of rosewater, of lavender—she smelled like a summer's day. Shifting uneasily in his seat, he chewed slowly, methodically, willing himself to remain unaware, to still his heightened senses. Don't become involved, the logical side of his mind shouted at him, this maid's business is none of your concern. Why was she any different from the other women he had met over the years? She was not important.

'Listen, my lady, it's nothing to do with me,' he growled at her. 'All I want is a decent meal and some good wine, without you prattling away beside me!'

'Very well!' Alice stared in silent fury at the shining wood, the sparkling pewter-ware before her. She was sick of being treated like this, of being pushed around, of being told to wait, told to speed up. Despite her mother's best efforts to the contrary, she had been brought up to know her own mind.

Alice slapped her hand down on the table and stood up abruptly, turning towards the Duke. Red spots of colour bloomed across her cheeks. Bastien watched her jerky movements with mild amusement—just what did the girl intend to do now?

'My lord, I demand to know what you intend to do with us!' Alice cut across a conversation that the Duke held with a nobleman on the other side of him.

Her father tugged at her arm. 'Alice, sit down, do!'

'Nay, Father, I will not!' She didn't look at him, fearing her courage would fail before Fabien's gentle look.

'I beg your pardon?' The Duke's head swivelled round, his eyes narrowing on her. 'Do you address me?'

'Aye, my lord, I do,' she replied boldly, although a violent trembling shook her knees. At her back, Bastien watched as she touched her fingertips to the table top, as if to keep her balance. Despite her bold move to address the Duke, she was terrified. A grudging admiration grew in his veins: she had courage, this maid, he had to admit. He chewed slowly on a piece of bread.

'I could have you clapped in irons for the way you have just spoken,' the Duke replied tartly. His voice, soft, sibilant, held a dangerous thread. 'Or maybe sent to a nunnery to end your days. If you had been my daughter, I would have curbed your headstrong ways long before now—' he threw an accusing look at her father '—for they will bring you nothing but trouble.'

'Are you saying that it's better to be meek and mild and just accept one's fate?' The words burst from her mouth before she had time to think.

'Hold your tongue!' the Duke snapped. A muscle jumped in his square-cut jaw. 'This time, young woman, you will accept your fate, for I do have a plan that you will follow to the very last detail, otherwise...'

'Otherwise...?' Her voice emerged, small now, chastised.

'Otherwise your father will die.'

Her muscles slackened, crumpled beneath her, and she fell back into the seat, her eyes darting from her father's concerned face to the Duke's arrogant profile.

'Wh-wh-what?' she stammered. Sickness roiled in her stomach.

'Listen to me well, my girl. This country is in trouble. No one has seen hide or hair of King Henry for months. The barons are taking the law into their own hands, feuding, pillaging, kidnapping; it's all happening right under the King's nose and he doesn't seem to care.' The Duke sighed, leaning back in his chair to take a long sip from his pewter goblet. The rubies set into the thick stem flashed with a red brilliance.

'Nay, it's not true. Tell him, Father! Why, we saw the King not above a sennight ago!' Even to her own ears, her words were slick with falsehood. Her mind scrabbled to remember the last time she had seen King Henry.

The Duke set his pewter goblet down with studied patience, turning his light-grey eyes towards her. 'Do not feed me lies, young lady. Your father has told me of your close relationship with the Queen; I would use that to my advantage. You will return to court and find out what has happened to the King, find out what kind of mental state he is in.'

Beneath her fingers, Alice pleated, then unpleated the thick silk of her skirts. A cold stone of fear lodged in her stomach. She had heard Queen Margaret's talk at court, of how she hated the Duke of York, the king's cousin, convinced that all he wanted was to snatch the throne and be King of England himself.

'You're asking me to spy for you,' Alice whispered.

'Precisely.'

'And you'll keep my father a prisoner here until I come back with news.'

'Why, you do understand quickly,' Richard replied, a mocking smile on his face. His skin appeared stretched, taut, with the dark shadow of a beard about his jaw. 'And if you don't come back, why, then you will never see your father again.'

Tears welled in her eyes, and she hung her head, trying to hide her weakness, but her mind spun into action. How would they know that she brought the truth? She could return here with a bundle of lies to suit the Duke's ear and secure her father's release. What could be simpler?

'And to make sure you bring back the truth—' the Duke's speech jerked once more in her brain '—I'll send an escort with you. Someone I can trust.' He placed great emphasis on the last word, indicating that he didn't trust her in the slightest. 'Someone to make certain that you don't tittle-tattle.'

Alice lifted her pewter goblet, raising it to her lips. Some idiot of a soldier didn't worry her; she'd be able to outwit him in an instant, and he would be none the wiser. The thought of escaping this place, of rounding up support for her father, imbued her with sudden confidence. She took a deep gulp, feeling the honeyed liquid slide down her throat.

'Who's the lucky man?' As Alice set her goblet down, her eyes swept the room for a suitable candidate. Over there, lounging by the fire, a short man, with thickset brow and kind face—aye, that was the sort of person who could come with her. 'I'm sorry, what did you say?' Suffused with her own plans, her burgeoning hope, she had failed to catch the Duke's words.

'Lord Bastien will go with you, naturally.'

Alice's confidence drained from her limbs. Her father took her small, cold hands in his. 'It will be all right, Alice, you'll see.'

'Nay.' She jumped up, almost tipping her chair back with the violence of the movement, fixing her father with her imperious blue orbs. 'Nay, Father, it will not be all right!'

The gardens at Ludlow has been set out some years ago, in a formal pattern of rectangles and half-circles. Alice's skirts whisked over the low box hedges as she walked angrily down one of the main paths. The edge of her sleeve caught a rose head in its final unstable moments as a flower, and the pink petals tumbled down, emitting a sweet heady perfume as they fell in her wake, showering the uneven stone path.

Footsteps descended purposefully on the steps behind her, following her.

She spun round, believing it to be her father, searching the blue-fringed twilight for his familiar silhouette.

'Oh, it's you!' she blurted out, dismayed as she recognising Bastien's bright hair emerging from the shadows.

'I came to fetch you back,' he explained, a weariness in his voice.

'Oh, aye, I forgot. It wouldn't do to let me out of your sight now, would it?' she replied woodenly. 'Don't you realise this is all your fault?' An owl hooted, eerie and chilling through the oak woods that surrounded the garden. The rushing sound of the river broke through the trees, continuous, insistent.

'No doubt you have wrought some intricately ill-informed explanation.' Bastien cupped her elbow gently and began to lead her back to the castle, his manner deferential, formal. He had to maintain this emotional distance from her; it was easier that way.

She ignored his sarcastic comment. 'If you had let me go in the forest, then none of this would have happened. My father would not be a prisoner, I wouldn't have to spy upon my friends...' She wrenched her elbow away from him. 'Tell the Duke you can't do this, that you're busy!'

'I only wish I was!' Bastien stopped for a moment. His breath puffed out, short bursts of mist in the chill night air. 'Believe me, escorting a wilful young lady back to the King's court isn't my idea of a good time. But the Duke knows full well that I was intending to spend the winter on my estate sorting my affairs out.'

'See, you are busy. Someone else needs to go in your stead.'

'What, so you can give some poor unfortunate soldier the slip?' he chortled, the iron mask of his reserve melting away. 'I've only known you a handful of days, Alice, but even in that short time, I can read your mind.'

I can read your mind. The intimate words, husky and low, punched into her brain. Her hands flew up, covering her cheeks, as if trying to place a barrier between his large, imposing presence and herself. She didn't want this, didn't want him here, next to her, insinuating himself wholeheartedly into her life. The thought of him accompanying her back to Abberley filled her with horror. And then there was Edmund...

'And how am I supposed to explain your presence?' she asked desperately, her hands falling away from her face. 'Everyone will be most surprised that I have lost a father and gained a Yorkist thug in exchange. Edmund would certainly have something to say about that.'

'Edmund...?' He let the question drift over the evening air.

'None of your business!' Alice clamped her lips together, wishing she had never mentioned the name.

'Ah, the young beau,' he deduced quickly, alert to the tiny tilt of her head, the softening of her voice. 'The man you intend to marry.'

'The man I will marry,' she corrected him. 'Which will make it all the more difficult to explain you!' She jabbed a finger into the middle of his chest; underneath the soft pad, his skin refused to yield: a powerful cage of muscle and rib, bound together by his innate strength. Alice dropped her fingers hastily.

'I am the man who saved you from the evil clutches of the Duke of York and brought you home. It would be the least you could do to provide me with bed and board for a few days after such a daring rescue...'

'Nay, nay...' Alice backed away '...please tell me you jest.' The very thought of him staying at Abberley, of having to be nice to him!

'No jest, my lady, but the Duke's plan in every detail.'

'It won't work, you're completely mad, he's completely mad!'

'It's a good thing I'm thick-skinned,' he muttered. The wide span of his hands curved around her shoulders, the warmth from his skin flowing through the thin silk covering of her gown. 'Listen, it's not for ever, just until I have the information that the Duke needs. Then you need never see me again and can spend all your time with your pretty beau.'

The words rankled. 'He's not like that,' she responded irritably, feeling the box hedge push its prickly leaves through the material of her skirts and into the back of her calves. She felt uncomfortable hearing Edmund described as her 'beau', for up to this moment he had been a friend, and nothing more. Why, it was only a couple of days ago that she had agreed to marry him! Bastien's choice of words made Edmund sound like some sort of court fop. Unease sluiced through her veins, a trickle of doubt. 'You don't know what you're talking about; you don't even know him.'

'Aye, but I know you,' he shot back, 'and I know your demanding, wilful behaviour. No man in his right mind would put up with that, so your Edmund, well… all I can say is "good luck" to him.' Bastien shrugged his shoulders.

'That's it! I'm not staying here to listen to this a moment longer!' Alice pushed past his large frame, almost tipping herself into the flower-bed in the process. A shaft of pure rose scent burst into the air, strong and heady. 'Edmund is not like that at all!' she threw back over her shoulder before mounting the stone steps. Ahead of her, the arched doorway stood open, throwing out a shaft of warm light, like a beacon. 'At least he knows how to treat a lady!'

In two short strides he was upon her, one hand gripping her upper arm, preventing forward movement. His distinctive smell of musky leather, spliced with a tint of mead, curled around her. 'I would treat you like a lady…' his voice lowered, a tantalising baritone '…if you behaved like one.'

Chapter Seven

The morning sun sent brilliant shafts of light streaming through the arched upper windows of the great hall, the rays refracting slightly through the brittle, hand-blown glass. Few people moved about; the hour was still early. One servant scrubbed down the well-worn planks of the trestle tables, the bristle brush swishing rhythmically across the wood, the water in the bucket sloshing noisily as the servant kicked it along the floor to keep level with his cleaning. Another servant swept the large flagstones clear of debris from the evening before, heaping together a mound of wine-soaked straw before lifting it into a barrow. The new fire burned merrily in the grate, the damp sticks crackling and spitting.

At the top table, Bastien sat alone. Finishing his breakfast, he pushed the platter away. The high collar of his shirt dug into his neck and he reached up to pull at it, to try to stretch the stiff linen. Inadvertently, his fingers brushed over the leather lace that he wore beneath, next to his skin. The familiar circle of gold that dangled against his chest drew his fingers, almost against their will. Katherine! The name punched into his brain, clamouring, begging for attention. A raft of memory scythed through him, making him pull his fingers away abruptly, as if bitten. Why did he still wear it, if it caused him so much pain? He had hoped by this time the memories would have dulled, dwindled into the misty obscurity of the past, and the betrothal ring would remind him of the true love that had once been his. The fighting in France had helped; a mind totally focused on the intricacies of battle allowed little room to brood over what had happened. Yet even now, when he touched the ring, the memories leapt vividly into his brain as if they had happened only yesterday.

He needed to focus, to turn his attention to the task in hand. Where was the silly girl anyway? He'd sent the maid up hours ago to tumble her from her bed; he was damned if he was going to do it himself! Every bone in his body baulked against the Duke's plan. He'd wrangled far into the night with Richard about the sense in taking the girl at all—surely it made better sense to keep her prisoner here, for Bastien to go as a messenger? But the Duke had been stubborn, adamant. 'The Queen guards the King like a secret; no one has seen him for months. She is more likely to trust someone she knows. Think sensibly. The girl is a gift, our key to enter the House of Lancaster.'

His toes curled at the prospect of travelling at a snail's pace; with the girl carried in a litter it would take an extra day, at least. No doubt she was fussing and flapping with her clothes right now, in anticipation of seeing her family and friends once more. Tipping his pewter goblet to his lips, he drained the last dregs of mead, frowning. Somehow the thought of her preening before a looking glass didn't quite fit with the maid as he had seen her yesterday: covered in mud, exhausted and dressed in boy's clothes. He smiled to himself. She'd certainly have a lot of explaining to do when she arrived back home!

On the threshold of the great hall, Alice hesitated, courage draining from her limbs. What was it about this man that made her lose all sense of herself, become befuddled and gauche in his company? The sight of his big body sprawled comfortably into a high-backed oak chair made her want to run, run until she was sure he would never find her. As he tipped his head back to drink, the corded muscles of his tanned throat flexed, a picture of strength. Anxiety danced along her nerves, making her feel wobbly and uncertain. Her heart filled with foreboding—how could she leave her father with these barbarians? How could she travel with this man… all alone?

Bastien's gaze slewed upwards, catching her slight movement in the doorway. The sturdy oak of the door framed her figure, dwarfing her even, making her appear small and vulnerable.

'At last!' he muttered, a thread of exasperation in his voice. 'What in Heaven's name have you been doing? We need to leave!'

'I was saying goodbye to my father,' she replied tersely. 'I'm ready now, so let's go. I for one would like to get this whole charade over and done with as quickly as possible.'

'You need to eat something.' It was an order, not a request. He came down the steps and strode towards her, covering the distance between them with a graceful, loping stride. Like an animal, she thought suddenly, supple and strong.

'Since when have you become so concerned with my well-being?' Alice taunted, tilting her head to one side. As she moved over the threshold, a shaft of sunlight fell across her face, emphasising the flawless quality of her skin. It appeared almost translucent, the colour and lustre of a pearl: creamy-white with a delicate rose flush beneath the cheeks. Even the fading bruise on her jaw-line could not diminish her natural beauty. For a moment, his eyes drank in the beautiful sight, all speech stopped. The pads of his fingers tingled, wanting to touch; he curled his fingers in, forming rigid fists at his side.

'Since you became useful to us,' he replied bluntly. 'I can't have you fainting away in the middle of the journey.'

'I've never fainted in my life!' she snapped back. The hanging pearls adorning the net that held her hair in place shook violently with the movement of her head. From a central parting, her thick blonde hair had been looped into a smooth coil at the nape of her neck, secured with pins before the net was positioned. Yet the coil seemed quite loose, almost haphazardly pinned up. Idly, Bastien wondered if she had done her hair herself, eschewing the services of a maid.

'Apart from the moment when you thought I would cut your throat. And when the Duke asked your name, in the courtyard.'

Her mouth turned down at the corners, grudging agreement. 'Apart from then.'

His green eyes sparkled with victory. 'Well,' he continued mildly, 'I can't force you to eat. Let's just hope you don't slow us down.'

Alice stepped back, turning to lead the way to the inner bailey, disliking the feeling of him hulking over her. All along the corridor, he followed her, unspeaking, and the hairs on the back of her neck prickled with the awareness that he was there, behind her, the rounded leather toes of his boots whispering against the flowing hem of her step lagged.

Outside, the cool autumnal air seemed saturated with the rain that had passed over in the night, a cloying wetness that seeped into her bones. Alice hunched into her short blue cloak, now cleaned of the dirt gathered from the march to Ludlow. Most noblewoman never wore cloaks, as they travelled in litters and rarely spent any time outside in bad weather. A seamstress at Abberley had made the garment for her, after Alice became tired of becoming soaked and cold on the many expeditions with her father. Now it sat rather strangely over the more formal gown supplied by the Duke of York's castle.

A groom stood at the head of Bastien's stallion, holding the animal steady as it pawed impatiently at the cobbles. Beside him, two packhorses waited patiently between the traces of a brightly covered litter.

Alice stopped in her tracks, surprised, turning her face up to Bastien. 'I have no need of a litter,' she exclaimed lightly. 'I will ride!'

'Ride?' Bastien observed her bright face closely. A honeyed wing of hair was beginning to loop down below her ear. Was she jesting with him? No woman of quality travelled on horseback, especially if the journey was destined to be long. True, noblewomen would hunt on horses, but were never in the saddle for a long time.

'Aye, you know, on a horse,' she replied, a teasing note in her voice. Her delicate, rose-tinted lips curved into a smile. 'Like this. You remember, I've done this before.'

Before he could stop her, she bolted for his own horse, his *warhorse,* placed two hands on the saddle and vaulted into position, scissoring her legs mid-air so that one leg came down either side of the horse, perfectly in position. Bastien had a fleeting sensation of rippling skirts, a flash of white stocking covering a fine-boned ankle.

The groom's mouth dropped open, and his hands released the reins in surprise.

For a moment, Bastien was totally stunned, the sight of Alice's thin leather slippers resting comfortably against his horse, jarring with every sense of normality. Her tricks in the forest, when she had been disguised as the lad, returned to him with a horrible clarity. Dressed as a woman, he had forgotten her previous strength and agility, and now, it caught him completely by surprise.

In the forest, his horse had tried to buck her off. And it was happening again. The destrier shook its head violently, jangling the bit between his teeth, as Alice pulled on the reins, intending to ride around in a circle of victory, to prove to Bastien that she could ride, she was as good as any man. To her dismay, the horse had other ideas, pawing the ground fretfully, before rearing up on his hind legs, wanting to throw off her slight weight. Surprised by the surge of upward movement, she started to slide backwards in the saddle, slowly at first, then faster, backwards…

'Release the reins, I have you.' The order was rapped, sharp and hard, into her left ear.

Two firm hands clasped around her waist, the ultimate humiliation.

Bastien's eyes flicked to the groom, a silent instruction: *hold the horse steady,* as he swung Alice back from the horse. As soon as her slippered feet touched the ground, she rounded on him.

'You didn't give me a chance! He needed time to become familiar with me!' Alice stared up at Bastien, lifting one small white hand to loop a loosened strand of hair back behind her ear.

'He threw you off the last time, and he'll throw you off again, given half a chance,' Bastien replied quietly. 'He's not the sort of horse to try your stunts on; he's only used to me and my command.' Bastien contemplated her neat head, resisting the urge to push in another gold hairpin that seemed to be nudging its way out. 'The groom can fetch you a more suitable horse, and then we can start.'

Alice shrugged her shoulders, deflated. 'I *can* ride.' She had embarrassed herself in front of him, wanting to prove herself, and it had all gone wrong. She lifted one hand self-consciously to her hair, jabbing a pin back into her bun where it had dislodged itself. Looking down at the top of her neat head, Bastien could see it was not the only hairpin to have come adrift.

'Aye, you can,' he agreed, 'but maybe not that one.' His eyes crinkled upwards at the corners, the hint of a smile. 'We'll find you another, *more suitable* horse, and then we'll be on our way.'

The narrow path, weaving around and about the great trunks of oak and beech, forced the horses to walk in single file, with Bastien leading the way. The track was little used, and remained dry under the dense canopy of trees which made the going easier. Alice hoped that Bastien was sure of his direction; she certainly did not want to become lost...with him. His dark presence made her jumpy, skittering her normal self-control, reducing her to a mass of contradictions.

Down to Alice's left, the valley sides dropped steeply, leading to the banks of a fast-flowing river, the boiling water jumping and splashing over great slabs of rock, creating plumes of froth that spat up into the air. Deciduous trees clambered along the water's edge, gnarled boughs of oak dipping into the rushing water, interrupting the flow.

And up ahead, Bastien's straight, rigid back. She had stared at it for hours; her eyeballs felt dry, itchy. He had dispensed with his woollen cloak, rolling it up and securing it with leather straps at the back of his horse. His surcoat was fashioned from a plain green velvet, and shorter than normal to make riding easier. A wide leather belt secured the tunic just below the waist before it flared out to end at his knees. His head was bare, and when the weak autumn sunlight poked through the trees, it lit upon his short, ruffled hair, burnished with streaks of copper.

Since the groom had brought a docile grey mare out for Alice to ride, and helped her to mount up, Bastien had not said another word to her, had not even turned his head to see that she was following. He simply expected her to keep up. She wondered if he would notice if she started to drop back; the temptation was to look for a suitable gap in the trees to make a bolt for freedom. But the horse she had been given was slow, and would never be able to outrun Bastien's powerful stallion. He would catch her in moments.

Alice hoped they would stop soon. A dryness invaded her mouth; she needed a drink. Above the forest canopy, the sun had already begun to descend from its zenith; it was past noon. To her relief, as the trees began to thin out and the path dropped closer to the river, Bastien twisted in the saddle towards her.

'We'll stop down there.' He pointed down at a flat, grassy area beside the water, where the grass grew long and lush, before leading his horse into the middle of the area. His saddle creaked as he leaned forwards, scissoring one leg over to dismount. He let the reins drop, allowing his horse to crop at the grass in freedom. Quickly, Alice slithered off her own horse, not wanting him to help, or to witness her untidy dismount. She landed in a flurry of skirts, wincing slightly as her aching muscles protested. Despite telling Bastien she could ride, she honestly couldn't remember the last time she had ridden so intensively over such a long time. The ligaments in her legs seemed to have tightened in all the wrong places; and now, as she walked to the spot where Bastien had spread a rug across the grass, they screamed out at the unfamiliar activity.

'Come, sit and eat,' Bastien commanded her, his moss-green eyes sparkling over her. 'I'm famished, and so must you be, having eaten no breakfast.'

He began to unwrap the muslin packages: floury rounds of bread, hunks of fresh cheese, cold roast chicken. Alice's stomach grumbled.

'The Duke's servants never stint on good food.' Bastien stretched out his body on one side of the rug, propping his head up with his left hand, and bit into a chicken leg. Alice threw back the hood of her cloak, kneeling down on the rug. Her knees sank into the damp ground through the woollen fabric. Eagerly she reached for a bread roll, lifting it to her lips, before she noticed Bastien smiling at her.

She froze in amazement. The wide grin lit up his face, showing white, even teeth, making his eyes crinkle up with sheer merriment. It made him look much younger, more boyish somehow. It unnerved her.

Alice's fingers released the bread roll, letting it fall with a soft 'plop' on to the rug. 'What is it? What's the matter?' She coloured under his intense, teasing scrutiny.

'Er, well, it's your hair,' he replied, still grinning, trying to suppress an outright guffaw. 'It seems to have come adrift.'

'What?' Alice automatically lifted one hand to the back of her head, astonished to find that the net seemed to have slipped, and now was hanging down, secured by a single hairpin, while the rest of her hair had fallen down in soft coils. 'Oh, I see,' she replied calmly. 'It must have been the riding; it's all come apart. I suppose I'll have to put it up again.' She eyed the food longingly in front of her, torn between knowing she should tidy her hair and a ravening hunger.

'Eat first,' Bastien made the decision for her. 'Don't mind me.'

'I don't,' she chipped back at him, picking up the roll, her small teeth biting delicately.

A silence descended between them, but it was not strained. The air was filled with the sound of birdsong, chirruping through the branches, and the perpetual, relaxing sound of the river beside them. The sunlight finally managed to burn through the hazy cloud cover of the morning and filled the early afternoon air with heat. Having eaten his fill, Bastien turned his body slightly, closing his eyes, relishing the warmth washing over his limbs, as he tucked his arms behind his head, extending his legs, his thigh muscles flexing with the movement. Any other woman would be having seven fits about the state Alice was in, but she seemed unusually relaxed about the whole affair. The pinched, resentful face of his mother loomed into his mind's eye. He had never, even as a small child, ever seen her in a state of disarray. Her presentation had always been perfect, every pleat pressed within an inch of its life, all stray hairs plucked, all velvet free from lint and dust. Even on that dreadful night when he had returned home from the Duke of York's castle, carrying the news of his older brother's death, she had made him wait for hours, before coming to see him in full dress, an elaborate head-dress completely hiding her hair. In fact, he had never even seen his mother's hair, as high fashion dictated that not a scrap should be seen; he didn't even know what colour it was.

Next to him, Alice continued to nibble contentedly, trying to ignore the large man stretched out opposite her, until she realised he seemed to have fallen asleep. Then, through dipped lashes, she studied him covertly. What a size he was! She knew he towered over her in height, that she had to tip her head to look at him, but it was the sheer muscled breadth of him that took her by surprise. The hem of his tunic had fallen back, revealing long legs encased in buff-coloured wool chausses. These were covered from the knee down by his calf-length boots, the leather of which, although polished, was scarred and scuffed with use. Everything about him was hard, masculine—the cut of his tunic, the plain fabric of his shirt—so different from the other men at court, who competed to outdo each other with their complicated, elaborate costumes.

Darting a quick glance to Bastien's face to assure herself he still slept, Alice endeavoured to sort her hair out. Sleep seemed to erase the severe edges of Bastien's face; his proud, straight nose flared out around the nostrils—even his high cheekbones appeared softer, somehow. But his mouth still sent reverberations of shock through her, every time she looked at it, its softness unexpected in the harsh, craggy face of a soldier; wide, sensuous, with a full bottom lip, made all the more alluring by the set of his square, chiselled chin. For a moment, Alice just stared, drinking in the carved beauty of this man's face, able to do so because he slept.

A bird squawked nearby, startling her, breaking her out of her reverie. Ashamed at her blatant perusal, she tilted her head downwards, lifting her fingers up to dislodge the pins, the net, to start again, tearing with agitation at the tangled strands. Her breath emerged rapidly, her heart thudding strongly in her chest—what was the matter with her? Was she ill?

Hearing the rustle of sounds to his left, Bastien open his eyes a fraction of an inch. He had not been asleep, merely content to listen to the bubble of water, the wind sifting through the trees. Through the mesh of his dipped lashes, Bastien watched Alice as she pulled her fingers through the tumbling ripples of her hair, watched the curling ends pool in her lap. She reminded him of a mermaid, told about in the old myths of the sea, sitting on her rock, combing her locks. In the sunlight, her dark-gold hair burned with a brilliant fire, falling around her like a curtain of gold. Whereas before he had slumbered in a state of warm relaxation, now all the nerve endings in his body snapped to attention.

As she raised her arm, the material of the tightly fitted sleeve strained at her elbow, emphasising the slenderness of her limbs. She seemed to be having trouble coiling the unruly bundle into some semblance of order; every time she stabbed a long pin into the back of her head, another thick tendril came loose once more.

'Let me.' His voice, husky, poured over her with the sensuality of liquid cream.

Alice jumped. 'I thought you were asleep!' she squeaked. His eyes flared over her: an emerald flame. 'Nay, I can do it,' she protested limply as he sprang to his feet and came around to the back of her. She felt him kneel, felt his close, heated presence burn along the length of her spine.

'It will take too long if you do it,' he said, simply. His cool fingers brushed against her neck as he took the heavy weight of her hair into his hands.

His breath caught. He couldn't remember the last time he had touched something so lovely, so silken against his fingers. His many days of battle had been filled with roughness, with steel, cracked leather, mud and stone. This was something different, something silky and soft, so pure. Each strand of hair had a life of its own, sparkling with a slightly different hue from its neighbour, lending the whole mass of wondrous silk a dynamic intensity that he longed to bury his face into.

An excitement leapt through his body, filling him with fierce, longing need. Gritting his teeth, he tried to suppress it, tried to suppress the urge to bend his head, to drop his lips to the smooth, tempting curve of her neck.

Alice sat rigidly, her fingers balled into fists on her lap. Surely this wasn't proper? But she had long ago lost all sense of what was proper behaviour and her mother wasn't around to tell her. But it didn't feel proper; nay, it felt dangerous, as if someone was pushing her inexorably towards the edge of a blazing fire. She wanted to flee, to run away. Every time the rough pads of Bastien's fingers grazed her neck, a splinter of exhilaration drove through her, kindling a churning, fluttering sensation in her stomach, increasing her sense of unease.

One of his fingers glanced against the downy lobe of her ear. Her stomach flipped. 'I'll finish it,' she spoke hurriedly, wanting him away from her. This was not right! This man was her enemy—what in Heaven's name was she thinking? As she gritted her teeth against the heated feelings coursing through her blood, her hand whipped upwards and back, snaring his muscled wrist, trying to pull it away. The blood, pumping through the artery in his wrist, pulsed against her fingers.

'I've nearly finished.' He continued to pull the silken strands through his fingers, reluctant to relinquish the wonderful feel of her hair. Her slim fingers around his wrist felt cool, smooth.

'Enough!' she uttered, with sheer desperation, jerking her head forwards, pulling her hand back at the same time. Tears jumped to her eyes as the hair tore against her scalp, but she wrenched herself to her feet, stumbling backwards. 'I said I'll finish it!'

On his knees, Bastien stared up at her, his body a churning mass of heightened need. Alice's eyes glowed down at him, her azure orbs holding a heady mix of anger, frustration and, yes, desire. Her chest rose and fell rapidly, her neat bosom strained against the fitted fabric of her dress. By Christ, his need was such that he wanted to strip her right now, and take her swiftly, there on the rug. He saw it in her eyes; her need matched his.

'You feel it too,' he said, bluntly.

'I don't know what you're talking about,' she replied haltingly, studying the toes of her leather boots with unnecessary attention.

He leapt up then, the unfulfilled desire making his body restless, itching for action, and strode over to her so that she quailed at his threatening approach. He leaned down, whispered, close to her ear, 'I think you do.'

Chapter Eight

Bastien drove his heels fiercely into his horse's smooth, glossy flanks, urging the animal up the steep, wooded slope to gain the wider path that ran along the brow of the hill. Irritation seared through him; he was annoyed, annoyed that such a maid could arouse him so. He should never have offered to do her hair. How could he have known such a simple action would reap such consequences? Especially for him, a man who prided himself on keeping his emotions squashed down to nothing. Foolishly, he had believed he could indulge in the sheer pleasure of feeling the silken strands slip through his fingers and remain unaffected. How wrong he had been. Her hair had acted like a lure, reeling him closer, stealing in under the steel casing clamped around his heart, digging in, teasing out emotions he had long since forgotten. Emotions that he had no wish to remember.

Behind him, Alice followed at a more sedate pace, the head of her gentle mare nodding rhythmically as it plodded up the track. Her hands trembled on the reins; her body felt weak, sapped of energy. The wetness of her furious tears clung to her long, dark lashes, blurring her vision and she lifted one finger to blot them away. How ludicrous the whole thing was! The man had offered to tidy her hair. Yet she still felt the imprint of his fingers at the nape of her neck, and her body still clung to the embers of desire that he had kindled with that touch. What would have happened if she hadn't leapt to her feet, if she had let him continue? The memory of the look in his eyes as she had whirled about told her the answer. Sighing, gritting her teeth, she contemplated his fast-receding back. She forced herself to think about Edmund, Edmund, the man she had promised to marry. They both knew it would be a marriage in name only, but at least it would be *safe*.

Gaining the brow of the hill in record speed, Bastien pulled on the reins, wheeling the animal around to assess the maid's progress. Christ, she was miles away! He could just about make out her slim figure through the trees. And he could also see how she sagged in the saddle, her whole demeanour wilting with exhaustion. Serve the girl right, he thought savagely. She had chosen to ride, hadn't she? Wanting to prove that she could ride as well as any man? He wanted to punish her, wanted to give her a hard time for sparking such unwanted feelings inside him. If he made things tough for her, then maybe it would be easier to keep her at arm's length. To make her hate him would be a far safer option.

'You need to hurry up,' he ground out, as, finally, she drew level with him. A small, neat ankle, encased in white stocking, forced him to draw a swift breath. Alice flicked the hem of her skirt down over her foot, hiding it completely. 'I can't make this animal go any faster.' She regarded him through wide, periwinkle-blue eyes, her animated face glowing like a precious jewel beneath the shady canopy of the forest.

The neutral tone in her voice irritated him. He had seen her hands loose on the reins as she approached; he hadn't seen her urge the animal on once.

'Try,' he murmured tersely, 'or we'll not make Abberley by nightfall.'

'I'm not one of your soldiers who you can boss around all day,' she sniped back at him.

'I am well aware of that fact.' He glared pointedly at her rounded bosom. 'But at this rate, it would have been faster if you had travelled in a litter.'

'I don't believe you! We couldn't have journeyed this way if I was in a litter, and by using this path we've shaved hours off the journey time.'

He grimaced. She was right. Since when had women become so informed about the geography of their country? 'Well, come on, then,' he said at last, exasperated. Surely a whole army of men was easier to control than this one woman?

The wider path at the brow of the hill led them out of the forest and on to open moorland, vast tracts of high, rough grass where a few sheep grazed. The track become wider, with fewer hazards to negotiate, allowing both riders to break into a gallop. Above their heads, buzzards wheeled and circled in the rising warm air, filling the vast, open space with their haunting cries. This time, Alice kept up with him; he was surprised to see that she was merely a few feet behind him all the way. She was a good horsewoman, he thought grudgingly.

Now and again, they would slow to a walk, allowing the horses a short rest, before resuming the relentless pace once more. Bastien could go on like this for ever, days even; he had endured enough practice in this kind of travel in France, but the maid? He shrugged his shoulders inwardly, a small part of him wanting to see her reduced, suffering, just a little.

Dusk began to fall; the western horizon a mass of glowing pinks and purples, silhouetting the few lone trees on the moor with stark beauty. Most of the trees were bent over at an angle, like old men stooped, after being continually buffeted by wind through their growth. Bastien and Alice slowed once more to a walk. Silently Alice wondered how long this was going to go on. Her whole body was overheated and uncomfortable, coated in perspiration from matching Bastien's tireless pace; she now regretted turning down the offer of a litter. Ensconced in the curtained interior, she wouldn't have had to *look* at him all day.

'What's that, up ahead?' Alice broke the silence between them.

Bastien narrowed his eyes, focusing on a small group of shambling peasants up ahead. He could see two people, and it appeared that one of them was helping the other to walk along the trackway. 'No one of importance,' he muttered, keeping his eyes forwards, trained on the horizon. 'Come on.' He kicked the animal into a gallop, aiming to pass the group at top speed. 'Make way!' he roared at them. 'Move aside!'

The white, pinched faces of the peasants looked completely terrified as Bastien thundered towards them, the bit jangling wildly between his horse's large, yellowing teeth. The elderly man held up one hand, pleading, as Bastien approached. 'Stop, my lord, we need help.' Bastien ignored the man, his horse's hooves throwing up great clods of sticky white mud as he charged by. But almost in that moment of passing that pathetic huddle of humankind, he knew that he would have to stop— because *she* would stop. Hauling on the reins, he twisted his head round in time to see Alice slipping from her horse, an encouraging smile on her face.

'Alice!' he bellowed at her, leaping from his animal and striding back. 'We have no time for this!'

Alice's face appeared as an iridescent pearl through the twilight. His fingers twitched, wanting to touch, to test the fine exquisiteness of her skin. 'This will take no time at all,' she assured him coolly, her arms crossed high, defensively, over her bosom as she faced him. 'This woman has hurt her leg, I could see her struggling to walk from the bottom of the hill; I might be able to help.'

'It's none of our business.' His voice had softened, despite his annoyance at having been delayed. In the dimness of the evening light, the shadows beneath his high cheekbones appeared more pronounced, more sculptured, as if carved from polished wood.

'It's my business, Bastien. It's what I do.' Alice took a deep breath, pushing the flat of her hand against her horse's heated flank, as if to steady herself. He stared into her sweet, earnest face for a moment, noted the stubborn set of her mouth with a sense of resignation. He could force her to come now, drag her up before him, and link her horse to his own. But what would it achieve, except to turn her further against him? 'Then be quick about it,' he relented.

Alice nodded at him, the hint of a smile playing about her lips, before motioning for the woman to sit on the high grassy verge. She raised the woman's skirts to reveal bare legs, pale and lumpy in the half-light. The right leg was gashed, the edges of the wide wound puckered and swollen. The old man craned his neck to try to see, lines of concern etching his elderly face.

'The wound's infected,' Alice announced calmly. 'I'll clean it, put a poultice on it.'

'Put a poultice on it?' Bastien frowned at her, his body impatient. 'How long is this going to take?'

'Bastien, I can't just ignore this. It could infect her blood; she could die. I just can't ride on without helping.'

'But she's a peasant.' His voice cut across her, callous, unremitting.

Alice's head rolled back, her eyes glittering with shocked anger. 'How can you say such a thing? She's a human being, just like you and me.' She jumped up to fetch her leather drinking bottle tied to the back of her horse, unlacing it with short, jerky movements.

Bastien shrugged his shoulders, unconcerned. The maid was clearly insane. In his world, nobles dealt with nobles, and peasants? Well, they were nothing. He turned back to his horse, leaning down to adjust the strap that held the saddle in place, tightening it. One small fist jabbed him in the shoulder. Alice was beside him. Her blue eyes burned with fury, her lips pursed and rigid. Instinctively, he braced himself for another onslaught.

'What is it?' He straightened up, curious.

Alice tipped her head back, exposing the long, creamy length of her neck, the silken dip of her throat. He hulked over her, this barbarian of a man, too close, but she refused to step back, to be intimidated by his size.

'Do you really value human life so lightly?' Her mouth curled downwards in disapproval.

'I'm a soldier, Alice, what do you expect?' he replied bluntly.

'I expected more understanding from a nobleman, more compassion.'

'Compassion doesn't come into it when you're in the thick of battle.' He wrenched the girth strap tightly.

'Maybe it should.'

'And maybe—' he rounded on her, eyes flinty with annoyance '—you should stop lecturing me about my moral values and hurry up with treating that woman.' He pushed his face close to hers, wanting her to back down, to run away, but she didn't move one jot.

'It would be quicker if you helped me.' His skin smelt musky, a tantalising mix of horse and woodsmoke. Her heart rate skittered, then jolted into a faster pace. She ducked away then, unable to maintain that close contact, frightened of what his presence did to her body, without waiting for his answer. Dropping to her knees in the mud, she began to clean the wound.

Bastien watched her with annoyance. Since when had a woman taken him to task on how he lived his life? He had been fêted as a hero on both sides of the Channel for his prowess in battle; Alice made him feel he had crawled out from beneath the nearest stone. Was there any truth in her accusation? That human life, any human life, held no value for him? Since his older brother's death, he had fought harder, longer than any man in France, earning the reputation of the most feared opponent in Europe. The endless fighting had driven away the memories; he had been glad of that. Now, home again, to his utter disgust, the memories had come flooding back, those of his older brother and…Katherine. He wanted to be fighting again, out in the cut and thrust, the mayhem of the battlefield, not nursemaiding some girl in the hope that he would see King Henry. And yet, what was the alternative? Home, to his estates north of Ludlow, and what joys awaited him there? Only his mother, and he had no burning wish to see her.

Bastien hunkered down next to Alice, who was busily cleaning the woman's wound with most of the contents of her water bottle. Her face was set with an earnest concentration, her touch deft and assured. Although the wound must have pained her, the woman made scarcely a sound.

'What can I do?'

Alice glanced at him, startled. 'Fetch my bag, please.'

Feeling chastened by her earlier, heated words, Bastien did as he was told.

'Take out the linen bandages, and beneath you'll find an earthenware pot of ointment,' Alice continued. 'Then smear the ointment over the middle of one of the bandages—don't stint.'

Bastien opened the leather satchel fastened to the mare's side. The orderliness of the contents within astonished him—the neat row of rolled-up bandages, the labelled pots, and small leather pouches—all seemed at odds with Alice's disregard for her own appearance. Only one pot was made from earthenware; he removed the wide cork stopper, digging his fingers into the cold, waxy substance. A foul smell rose to his nostrils; he wrinkled his nose in disgust as he spread it across the bandage.

'Thank—you.' Alice barely looked up at him as she took the length of bandage between her fingers. Her skin creased a little between her eyebrows as she concentrated on applying the length of cloth around the woman's calf.

'There.' Alice tied a simple knot to secure the bandage, before sitting back on her heels to survey her handiwork. The woman was smiling, thanking Alice over and over again.

'We have nothing to give you, to thank you with,' the old man said forlornly.

Alice smiled up into the gnarled, worried face. 'I don't want anything; it's enough that I could help,' she explained gently. The woman stood up, putting her full weight on her injured leg, and started to walk, gingerly at first, then with more confidence.

Kneeling in the earth, an incredible fatigue washed over Alice, a cold fog sweeping through her brain, muddling her thoughts. From the intense concentration a few moments ago, now she couldn't even think straight, merely content to sit back in the mud and watch the old couple walk off, heading in an easterly direction, waving and smiling. She wanted to close her eyes and slump forwards, pillow her head in the soft, lush grass of the verge and sleep.

A hand grasped her upper arm, dragged her up. 'Come on, Alice.' Bastien's strong voice punched into her. 'Let's keep going.' Weariness made her sway on her feet before him, a slender reed buffeted by the wind. Smudges of blue formed dark semi-circles beneath her eyes, evidence of her exhaustion.

'How much further is it?' Alice rubbed at one eye, trying to erase the grittiness clouding her vision. She wilted under Bastien's grip, fast about her upper arm. He realised that instead of helping her up, he was in fact supporting her. His intention had been to ride through the night; the sky was clear, and already the waxing moon had begun to cast its ethereal light across the land. But the girl was exhausted, he could see that now.

'We need to find somewhere to rest for the night,' he found himself saying.

'I thought you said we were in a hurry,' she murmured, tilting her head to focus on his face.

'I still need my sleep,' he answered.

Alice peered at him suspiciously. His eyes were bright, alert, sparkling out of a face alive with energy. He didn't appear to be in any need of sleep.

'You mustn't stop on my account,' she protested limply. 'I can carry on...once I'm back on my horse.' She tried to inject more rigidity into her stance, pulling her spine straight.

If she had been one of his soldiers, marching across France, Bastien would have bawled her out, there and then, forcing her to keep going, to push through the tiredness. But she was not one of his soldiers, merely a woman who, despite what she believed, simply did not have the physical reserves to keep going.

'Let's find some shelter.' Bastien led her over to where the horses cropped the grass, placed his hands on her waist and lifted her easily on to the saddle. Out of habit, she swung her right leg over so she could sit astride, grabbing the reins. Mounting up, Bastien squinted through the twilight into the distance. To find shelter would mean dipping back down into the valley, contrary to their direction, but Alice's slumped figure in the saddle forced his decision in the matter.

Following a trail down into the valley's limpid darkness, it wasn't long before the outlines of a building loomed out of the shadows. A haybarn, double height, with no homestead or other domestic buildings attached to it, probably used to store the cut grass from the upper meadows—dried grass used as additional feed for the animals in the winter.

Alice's head bounced back awkwardly from her chest as her mare came to a halt in front of the barn, and she forced her eyes to open wide, to discern her surroundings through the drifting layers of sleep around her. As Bastien clicked open the iron latch of the wide barn door, and shoved at the swollen, damp timbers with the muscled bulk of his shoulder, she managed to slither from the horse, to secure the reins around the spiky branches of a low-growing hawthorn.

The smell of dried grass, heady and pungent, assailed her nostrils as she walked into the barn. The bound stooks had been carefully stacked upright; Bastien cut the string around the waist of one stook, releasing the hay to spread it over the earthern floor. He spread another, then another, building up a mound of inviting softness.

'Our bed for the night, my lady.' His bow was low, formal.

She flushed, aware of the challenge in his tone. Fear throbbed in her veins, thrilling her. Her scalp tingled; the memory of his deft fingers tidying her hair knocked into her. '*My* bed for the night,' she corrected him, primly. 'You can sleep over there.' She pointed to the furthest corner of the barn.

'You'll freeze; there's not much warmth in here.'

'I'll take my chances,' she replied, sinking down into the delicious heap of hay, feeling her muscles relax into the sweet softness. 'I don't sleep with men like you.'

Undoing another stook of hay, Bastien snorted with laughter. 'What kind of men do you sleep with, then?' he paused, his face crinkled up in a teasing smile.

Lying on the straw, Alice smiled back. He had caught her, fair and square. Once again, she hadn't thought before blurting the words out, not realising how they must sound. 'You know what I mean,' she hastened to correct his laughing assumption. His teasing reminded her of her brother, in the early days when they were children, before he had become a knight. Her heart gripped with loss.

'Don't worry, Alice. You're as untouched as the day you were born.' Bastien sat down on the hay mattress he had made for himself.

'Wh-what…?' Alice shot to a sitting position, horrified by his words. 'You…you can't say that to me!'

'I just did. Now calm down, and get some sleep,' he advised her.

'How can you be so…so crude?'

In the darkness, his eyes glittered, feral. 'I'm sorry if my manners aren't up to scratch, Alice, but I'm not some fop who'll tip-toe around you, minding my every word. You have to get used to it.'

'Aye,' she replied miserably, lying down again. Was it really that obvious? That no man had ever touched her? Why, the way he said it, it was if the words were painted on her face: virgin. She curled on to her side into a tight, little ball, away from him, spreading her cloak over her knees, her feet, to ward off the evening chill.

* * *

Something was digging into his right hip, Bastien thought, as he tried to find a good position to sleep in. He had slept fitfully, but now found himself wide awake, his limbs cramped and stiff. Or was the mound of hay too short? His legs dangled over the edge, squeezing his calf muscles. Or was it, he thought, as he drew himself into a sitting position, that he had become, in such short a time, used to home comforts again, to sleeping on a soft mattress after all these years of sleeping in makeshift beds?

On the other side of the barn, Alice's sleeping form snared his sweeping perusal. Her dark cloak was tucked around her, demurely, with a glint of her blonde hair shining above her face. And despite her best efforts, she had turned to face him in her sleep, her hands tucked under one cheek, as if in prayer. He recalled the deftness of those hands as she treated the woman, her whole manner practised, efficient, assured. Her skill seemed to surpass her years—why, she could not be above twenty winters. How different she was from the bumbling physicians who had accompanied them in France, the botched operations, the screams of pain. Somehow, you couldn't imagine such things happening with her; you would always feel safe in her hands, however dire the situation.

Her eyes shot open, dark lashes fanning her flushed cheeks. 'What's amiss?' She raised herself on one arm, staring at him, flustered.

'Rest easy, maid.' His velvet tones soothed her. 'You've only been asleep for a couple of hours.'

'Then why did you wake me up?' she glared at him,

grumpy, wrinkling her nose. Her face was soft with sleep.

He shook his head. 'You woke yourself up.' He sat, resting his elbows on his knees, relaxed.

'Can you not sleep?' she asked, pulling her cloak around her, tucking her hands in under the cloth. A chill draught blew in under the gap made by the ill-fitting door; her fingers were like ice.

Bastien picked up a long thread of dried grass, began winding it around one finger. 'I was thinking about what you did back there…for the woman.'

She smiled, imbuing her whole face with a sweet look. 'I shouldn't let that keep you awake…it was nothing.'

He raised his eyebrows, slashes of dark brown. 'You underestimate your own skills. I know of no other woman who would do what you did.'

She shrugged her shoulders. 'I'm not like other women. It drives my mother to distraction…but I am fortunate to have a father who is prepared to teach me all he knows.'

'What about brothers…or sisters?' He found he wanted to find out more about this puzzling maid, to discover what drove her.

Alice bit her lip, a raft of sorrow sweeping through her. 'I have an older brother,' she replied lightly. 'Thomas. He taught me to ride. At the moment…well, he's still in France.'

'Surely he would have returned by now,' Bastien replied without thinking, then saw the bruised look on her face and wished he'd kept his mouth shut.

Alice dropped her chin to her knees, crouching down.

'We…we're not quite sure where he is,' she informed him quietly.

Bastien said nothing. Any reply would have sounded trite, insincere. He knew, and he felt that she knew as well, that her older brother was dead. Too much time had passed since the end of the war in France; her brother would have been home by now, even if he had returned on foot.

'What about you?' Alice broke the silence, grateful to him for not voicing her own fears about her brother.

He tilted his golden head to one side, concentrating on unwinding the piece of straw from his forefinger, watching the red blood flow back into his fingertip. 'What about me?'

'Do you have any siblings?'

Her question hung in the fragile, hushed air of the barn.

'Not now.' His voice changed: a gruff burr.

'Not ever?' she asked, softly persistent.

He glared at her, teetering on the brink of trust. He never talked about Guillaume. Never. 'Are you normally this curious?'

'You don't have to tell me if you don't want to.' Her large, limpid eyes drank in the lean lines of his face.

'I had a brother,' Bastien found himself saying. His voice sounded overly brittle, bright. 'He was older than me by two years, a great knight. He was killed in a fight, a skirmish near our lands…' His voice trailed off, his eyes hollow and bleak.

'What happened to you?' she whispered into the shadowy twilight.

'I mislaid my breast-plate. Guillame, my older brother, the more experienced fighter, loaned me his.'

Bastien shook his head, as if in disbelief. 'It wasn't even a battle, just a stupid argument with some local ruffians. Guillame was stabbed in the chest; there was nothing I could do.' His voice shook, knotted with the memory: the blood on his hands, the unmoving form of his brother.

Horrified, Alice stared at his rigid features, the tight line of his mouth, trying to see what he had seen, trying to understand. 'God in Heaven, Bastien. I had no idea.'

His eyes narrowed on her, sharp, piercing. 'Why would you? You scarce know me.' The sympathy in her voice gouged at him, tearing back the thick layers of protection he had built around himself, peeling them back to expose the very rawness of his soul. He shrugged his shoulders, a note of dismissal in his voice. 'Forget it. It happened a long time ago.'

Yet it still haunted his every waking moment, she could see that now. In the chill hush of the barn, lit only by fragments of moonlight sneaking through the rough planking, she felt close to him, amazed that this man of war should reveal something so personal. It made him more human, somehow, more vulnerable, whereas up to now he had seemed invincible, immune to the vicissitudes of life. With the divulgence of this memory, he lost his hard edges, softened, and her heart longed to hold him, ached to comfort him. Kneeling on her bed of straw, she reached over, grasped his cold fingers in her small, now warm hand, prepared for rejection. Without speaking, his fingers squeezed hers, accepting her offer of comfort. Her heart soared.

'I don't deserve your sympathy, Alice,' he murmured gruffly. 'It was my fault he was killed.'

'Nay!' She hitched closer to him, took his other hand.

'Don't say that! You mustn't say that! It was not your fault—how could you have known what would happen that day?'

He drank in her vibrant features, her limpid eyes reassuring him, supporting him, and drew strength from those depths. How could one so small, so delicate, be such a source of strength, of energy?

'It wasn't your fault, Bastien,' she said again, her eyes imploring him to believe it. 'Nobody blames you.'

He sighed, gripping her fingers, hard. 'Nay, Alice, you're wrong. My mother blamed me for Guillaume's death. She has never forgiven me.'

Chapter Nine

The guard at the gatehouse of Abberley Castle planted himself firmly in front of the open portcullis, legs astride. In his right hand he held a lance, at least ten foot long; a narrow white flag fluttered from the top, just below the shining point, heavily embroidered with the colours of the King.

'What business have you here?' he asked roughly, jutting his chin up at Bastien.

'I have brought the Lady Alice home,' answered Bastien, nodding at the maid beside him. The guard scrutinised the girl riding at the big man's side.

'It's me, Albert,' Alice laughed as the expression on the guard's face changed to one of astonishment. 'It's really me.'

'Holy Mother of God, so it is!' The arrogant mask slipped from the guard's face as he blinked up at Alice. 'Where in God's name have you been?' He glanced curiously at Bastien. 'The whole place has been in an uproar looking for you!'

'Then I had better go in and find my mother,' Alice replied, her heart sinking slightly as she anticipated the tumult of questions.

'Oh, of course, of course!' The guard stepped back, nodding and smiling. Alice kicked her heels into the mare's flanks to set the animal walking once more. In the shadowed darkness of the gatehouse, she paused, knowing that once she passed through the gate, her charade of betrayal would begin.

'Lead on, my lady.' Bastien was at her side, his horse sidling so close to her that the toe of his boot brushed along the side of her hip. She flushed, grateful for the damp, cloying dimness of the gatehouse. 'And remember to play your part—' his voice held a warning '—because I'll be watching you.'

'No need to threaten me, Bastien,' she whispered back, conscious that the guard watched their backs, 'I value my father's life too much.' Last night, she had witnessed a softer side to this man, the briefest, fleeting glimpse of the sadness he had endured at the loss of his brother. Yet ever since that time he had been cold, aloof, behaving like a complete oaf.

'Then let's do this,' he said, impatiently. 'And remember, don't call me by my real name, make something up.' The slightest nudge from his heels sent his horse trotting out into the light of the inner bailey. The irritation that had plagued him all morning seemed exacerbated by the situation; he wanted to do the job quickly and leave, leave this maid who seemed to draw him in, closer and closer, with every moment he spent in her company. He had never spoken of his brother's death before; he had vowed never to speak of it. Christ, this maid was turning him into some maudlin' fop, ready to spill the beans about every little crisis! How had she managed to wring the words from him, undermining his normally rigid self-control? Many women had asked before, yet he had never told of the depths of guilt that laced through him. But he had been punished for it. His mother had made sure of it.

Grooms immediately ran to secure their horses, small boys scampering over the cobbles to grab the reins as Alice and Bastien pulled them in. Intending to dismount before Bastien could help her, Alice was dismayed to find him at her side before she had even slipped her foot from the stirrup.

'Let's start as we mean to go on.' He lifted her easily, swinging her down, his big, warm hands steady about her waist. But he didn't let her go at once, holding her so she was clamped against him, chest to chest, her toes dangling a good foot from the ground.

'Put me down,' she squeaked at him, outraged. Between the muscled cords of his neck, she could see his pulse beating strongly.

'Just remember,' he growled at her in a low voice, 'that you are eternally grateful to me for rescuing you from those barbarian Yorkists.'

Alice's toe made contact with his left shin.

He winced. 'Be agreeable…or else.'

Was it her imagination, or did she see the trace of a smile on his face? Was he actually enjoying this?

'I'll behave,' she answered quietly. 'But I can't say it's going to be easy.' At her words he allowed her to slide down so her feet touched the ground, holding her in such a way as to make the movement slow, deliberate. Her eyes met his, accusation in their blue depths. 'And you can stop that sort of behaviour,' she snapped. 'I'm betrothed.'

'So you said,' Bastien replied slowly, his eyes flicking over her bright head at the sight of an older woman emerging from a doorway, shrieking at the top of her voice. Spinning in his loose hold, Alice's heart sank. 'Prepare yourself to meet my mother,' she ground out, her teeth set.

'Alice, Alice, oh, my little Alice!' In a peculiar loping style, her mother half-walked, half-ran, across the cobbles, her palms upwards, outstretched towards her daughter. She was pursued by a gaggle of brightly dressed women, their satin slippers and fine silk skirts dancing across the inner bailey like bouncing butterflies: these were the ladies of the Queen's court, all anxious not to miss one moment of this emotional homecoming.

'Mother,' Alice greeted her mother tentatively as the older woman approached. She couldn't remember the last time her mother had been so concerned as to her personal well-being; this over-emotional greeting was completely at odds with her mother's normal manner towards her.

'Oh, my God, what has happened to you?' Beatrice's eyes were wild, searching, scouring her daughter's face for some kind of evidence that she had been through a terrible time. 'Where have you been?' Her hands fluttered over Alice, touching her face, her shoulders, in an agitated, nervous way.

'Mother, I'm well. Stop worrying.' Alice caught one of her mother's hands, bemused by her mother's effusive manner. 'I was captured by the Yorkists—'

'Captured! Oh, good Lord!' Beatrice moaned, sagging back into the arms of the other ladies. 'What happened to you…? What did those barbarians do to you?'

'Nothing happened…I told you…I'm fine.'

Beatrice drew herself upwards, her face pale, but angry. 'I knew this would happen. I told you, didn't I?' Her blue eyes, identical to Alice's, snapped over her daughter. 'By God, I warned you enough times, but would you listen…? Nay, you kept going off with your father…'

Alice knotted her fingers together over her stomach, resigned, allowing her mother's ranting to wash over her. This was more familiar; Beatrice's worried concern had lasted mere moments, only to be replaced by torrents of criticism. 'Mother, I am safe…' Alice managed to interject when Beatrice was forced to pause for breath. 'Lord…er…Lord Dunstan…' she frantically conjured up a name for the man at her side.

'And what did they do to you, eh?' her mother interrupted. 'Now, I'll have no hope of finding you a husband, damaged goods like you!'

Alice flushed painfully at her mother's crude remarks; usually Beatrice reserved the worst of her criticism for behind closed doors. Her mother seemed to have lost all sense of perspective, letting her true colours show in public. At her side, Bastien shifted imperceptibly— was it her imagination, or did he move closer to her? The bulk of his upper arm curved around the top of her shoulder; the warmth of him nurturing her in a surprising, unexpected way.

'Mother, please stop this. Nothing bad happened. Listen to me.' At her daughter's low, imploring tones, Beatrice's mouth clamped shut, abruptly. 'Lord Dunstan rescued me, brought me home,' Alice continued calmly, relieved that she had managed to stop her mother ranting on. The last thing she wanted was for Bastien to become embroiled in the grubby minutiae of family business.

'Yes, yes, of course. I was forgetting. Forgive me, my lord.' Beatrice raised her head jerkily towards Bastien, at last acknowledging his presence. 'I was so overcome to see Alice again…'

'No matter, my lady.' Bastien brushed her apology aside. 'Although you must rest assured that no harm came to your daughter.' Even as the words emerged from his lips, the image of himself, sprawled across Alice after she had stolen his horse, pushed vividly into his mind.

'It seems we are in your debt, my Lord Dunstan. I trust that you will take advantage of any hospitality we can offer you.' Having recovered her public persona, the formal words slid from Beatrice with ease; she had spent a lifetime dealing with guests and visitors, perfecting the art of receiving them to such an extent that little thought now entered the process.

'I thank you, my lady,' Bastien responded with a brisk nod of his head. How different the mother was from her daughter! Beatrice was all sharp angles, her fine court clothes hanging from her thin, bony frame, her eyebrows completely plucked away and redrawn, in his opinion, at a ludicrously high angle with soft charcoal. With her hair completely hidden by an elaborate padded head-dress, he couldn't even tell if it was the same colour as Alice's. Whereas warmth and light seemed to pour from Alice, this woman appeared cold, icy, despite her demonstrative behaviour.

Beatrice peered past Alice. 'And where is that hapless father of yours? Tending to the injured outside the castle gates as usual? Too busy even to greet his own wife? He could have brought you back on his own, surely, without having to trouble this good man here.'

'We were both captured by the Yorkists, Mother,' Alice explained gently. 'Only I was fortunate enough to escape.'

Beatrice's lips pursed together; two points of colour appeared high on her cheeks. 'Both of you…completely irresponsible. First Thomas, and now this.' She shook her head, a sharp movement that made every pearl in her head-dress shudder and jolt, before turning on her heel and marching inside, her back as straight as a poker inside the stiff folds of her court dress.

Alice stared after her mother for a moment, yearning, for a split second, for a different reaction from her. Then she shook her head as if to rid herself of that dreamlike thought, pulled her spine straight and angled her head up to Bastien, chin high and proud. 'I'll find someone to show you to your chamber.'

Bastien saw the hurt chase across Alice's gentle face, saw it quickly suppressed, hidden, unformed. The urge to comfort her, to wrap her in his arms and kiss away the forlorn look on her face, surged powerfully through him, an insistent desire. He clenched his fists by his sides, compelling himself to look away from her limpid features. Even though he was accustomed to the soldier's rough way of life, Alice's mother had been cruel, critical. Surprisingly, he understood.

Alice lowered her cold, naked body into the wooden tub of hot water, a small sound of delight emitting from her throat at the delicious sensation. The rising steam was fragrant, scented by the dried lavender sewn into the muslin bags that floated in the water. Leaning back, she rested the nape of her neck against the edge of the tub. She pressed the warm pads of her fingers against the shadowed wells of exhaustion beneath her eyes, and began to relax, relishing the sweetness of the water brushing against her tired limbs.

'Your mother's worked herself into a real state over you.' Joan, her mother's servant, appeared above her, slowly pouring another pail of hot water into the tub. The heated liquid trailed around her calves, her toes.

'She's always in a state about me, Joan.' Alice sighed, trying to blot out her mother's pinched, withering expression. Reaching for the cloth, floating languidly atop the water, she began to scrub herself with a fierce briskness. She didn't want to talk about her mother now, or even talk at all, preferring to empty her mind of all thoughts, to drift.

'She thinks something terrible has happened to you.' Joan's voice held a dramatic edge, no doubt fuelled by the gossiping women that surrounded her mother.

'So she sent you to try to wheedle the truth from me.' Alice grimaced at the shifting surface of the water.

Joan passed the empty pail to the boy who waited in the corridor to take it back to the kitchens, and closed the door. Turning, she wiped her wet hands down the front of her simple fustian gown. Her face was a little flushed; she had the grace to look ashamed. 'Any mother would be worried when their daughter disappears for days...especially in the company of...that man.'

'What? Lord Dunstan? He's completely harmless!' Alice buried her face in the cloth, knowing that nothing could be further from the truth. Even her protest sounded hollow, false; she hoped Joan wouldn't notice.

'Nobody in the castle knows him, so naturally people are asking questions, even the young Queen. She especially wants to know how he rescued you.' Joan began soaping Alice's wet hair, the pads of her work-roughened fingers digging into her scalp.

'How he…?' Mother of Mary! How had he actually 'rescued' her? Alice's mind scrabbled about for details, spluttering slightly as Joan poured a pail of water over her hair, rinsing it. She and Bastien hadn't even had the forethought to cobble a story together! Being quizzed by Joan was one thing, but Queen Margaret, with her incisive quick-wittedness, was certain to become suspicious if their stories didn't marry. And if Bastien's true identity were discovered, then her father was dead. Much as it galled her, it was her responsibility to ensure this didn't happen.

Alice stood up suddenly, water sluicing from her slender limbs, the wet strands of hair clinging to her skin, iridescent as a pearl in the glowing candles that lit the chamber. 'I will go and tell my mother the whole story, in detail, to stop all this speculation.'

'It's a good idea,' Joan agreed, handing Alice a large linen towel.

Drying herself quickly, Alice ran to the oak coffer and began to dress. A square-necked blue silk kirtle covered her linen undergarments, followed by a high-waisted gown in a heavier green silk. Joan secured the leather laces at the back, fastening Alice tightly into the dress.

'Let me sort your hair, Alice.' Joan frowned dubiously at Alice's tumbling mass of curls, already starting to dry in the heat of the room.

'There's no time.' Alice was already bundling the thick strands into a tight coil at the back of her head, driving in long, jewelled hairpins to secure the bulk of it.

'Here, cover your head with this.' Joan placed a small headdress on top of Alice's head, again, securing it with pins. A light, silk veil drifted down from the velvet padding that formed the U-shape. Joan stepped back, running an appraising eye over Alice. 'You'll do, as long as you're just visiting your mother. Now go, before she worries herself into an early grave.'

Alice didn't need telling twice.

Bastien would have been given a chamber in the west tower, she was sure of it. Closing her chamber door gently behind her, she leaned back for a moment, listening to the gentle puttering noises that Joan made as she tidied things away from Alice's bath. She didn't want Joan to see that she turned right down the corridor, instead of left, towards her mother's apartments. Swiftly, she moved along the dimly lit passage, her bare feet making no sound against the wooden floorboards. In her haste to reach Bastien, she had forgotten her shoes and stockings—too late! Instinctively, her hand trailed lightly over the hewn stone wall for guidance; darkness had fallen outside, and the corridor only had one burning torch to light its length, throwing its flickering light from the far end, next to the door to the stairwell. Her hand made contact with the iron rivets, sunk deep into the grainy wood of the door, and she pushed through, on to the spiral staircase. Tiredness had been chased from

her; revived by the bath, her mind ran with a cool determination. To create a plausible story with Bastien was
her main aim; it would enable him to dampen whatever
suspicions the Queen might hold of him, and facilitate
his audience with the King.

The stairs were unlit, so finding Bastien's chamber
was easy; light flooded out from beneath the door, and
she rapped sharply with her knuckles, three times. No
answer. Confident that no one else was about, she called
his name, softly at first, then louder. Again, no answer.
Her fingers curled into her palms, impatiently. Why did
he not hear her? The need to speak to him overrode her
hesitancy; calling his name once more, Alice turned the
handle on the door and stepped in.

Lit by several torches, the chamber blazed with light,
and she blinked rapidly after the dimness of the stairs.
A fire crackled strongly beneath a massive sandstone
mantel, filling the room with a sweet, soporific warmth.
The bed was made up, the horsehair-stuffed mattress
heaped with clean linens and woollen blankets. A tunic
and something white—it looked like a crumpled linen
shirt—had been flung across the fur coverlet, gleaming
in the firelight.

Too late she heard the sound of water splashing in
the side room to the chamber. She checked her hasty
stride, and halted, bare toes curling hesitantly against
the sleek elm boards. Indecision coursed through her,
then, in a moment, she spun around, intending to leave.

'Alice?'

She turned back at the familiar voice. Head almost
touching the stone lintel, Bastien emerged from the
ante-chamber, linen towel scrubbing at his hair, rivulets
of water running down the strong column of his throat

and over the smooth, solid muscles of his torso, before disappearing into the low waistband of his chausses. A leather lace darkened with water swung from his neck, a golden ring swinging against the bare, honed skin of his chest, sparkling in the ambient light.

'Oh...I'll...' Shocked, Alice stared, open-mouthed. A furious blush leapt uncontrollably to her cheeks; she put her palms up, trying to cover her face, to hide her reaction to him. A weakness surged over her and she staggered back, back, reaching her fingers behind her to grasp the door handle.

Bastien threw the towel on to the bed and stuck his hand in his hair, rumpling the glossy locks. 'To what do I owe this pleasure?' he asked, eyebrows raised in question.

Alice swallowed, her mouth dry, arid. 'I'll...er...I'll come back later.' Mother of Mary, she could hardly speak properly, her breath emerging in short little puffs. The door handle refused to yield under her useless fingers; it wouldn't turn!

Water droplets clung like diamonds to the muscled sleekness of Bastien's skin, the sculptured muscles of his chest glowing in the warm light. Her blood fired; her fingers itched to touch, while her brain told her to leave, to go, now.

'What is it?' he asked, curiously. The maid seemed rooted to the spot. 'What's the matter with you?' He took in the hectic skin of her face, her wild-eyed look. He walked over to her, and to his amazement, she shrank back, as if she was trying to disappear through the very wood of the door!

'Alice, what is it?' Concerned now, he reached for her hand.

'Put...your...shirt on,' Alice breathed out, both palms flat against the door for support. The honed steel of his chest was but inches away! Her eyes feasted on the beautiful sight before her, gulping in detail after beautiful detail. A fresh, invigorating smell lifted from him, the dampness from the water scenting his heated skin. His chest was covered with bronzed hairs, like burnished gold... Look away! her senses screamed. She ducked her eyes, only to be faced with the sight of his strong, flat stomach. In utter desperation, she closed her eyes.

'What's the matter....haven't you seen a man stripped to the waist before?'

Alice bridled at the taunt in his voice, eyes snapping open once more. 'What? Nay, don't be ridiculous, of course I haven't!' she blurted out.

His eyes moved over her flushed face. 'Of course, my apologies. I forgot.' Lord, but she was beautiful, standing before him, her delicate build framed by the rough-hewn oak of the door. The wide V-neck of her gown revealed an expanse of fragile skin below her neck, the dark fur edging the collar brushing against it. She had changed her gown, now wearing one that fitted her exactly; his eye traced the rounded curve of her bosom, the fine seaming that followed the indentation of her waist. Something knitted within him, deep within the kernel of his heart, igniting a delicious energy, a need. Inwardly, he groaned.

Alice frowned. Forgot? What was he talking about?

'I forgot you were an innocent,' Bastien answered her unspoken question. His voice was like silk, flowing over her, low, husky. He stepped a little closer, his knees brushing against the gathered folds of her gown, rustling. In the soft, white hollow of her neck, he could see her pulse, beating rapidly.

Her blush deepened. 'Stop teasing me. And go and put your shirt on!' Her palms sprang forwards, lay flat against his chest to push him away. Beneath her trembling fingers, his skin was hard, yet warm. He took a deep, unsteady breath, the green of his eyes threaded with gilded desire.

'You should have known better than to enter a man's chamber without knocking.' His voice was rough, husky. Unexpectedly, he leaned into her, over her, one hand above her head, palm flat against the door behind her. The warmth from his skin swept over her, tantalising, tormenting. Her heart squeezed, then accelerated, the blood hurtling around her body. Her innards dissolved in a flaming whirlpool of desire.

'Nay,' she breathed suddenly, quivering beneath him, sensing the change in him, her voice a whisper. 'Don't do this.' But even as the words left her lips, her treacherous body craved his caress.

His fingers grazed her cheek; a shiver of desire pulsed through her at that single contact, thrilling her. He bent his head, and she slanted her mouth up to him, knowing what she did was wrong, but desperate to quell the raging flames within her, eager to find out what before she could only have guessed at. Her senses scattered, logic deserting her to be replaced with a keen, ravening hunger.

His cool firm mouth descended, met her lips with a fierce longing. Wave upon wave of desire crashed through her at the unbelievable sensations bombarding her body. Her hands moved over his chest, clung to his shoulders for support as his lips moved over hers, slowly, languorously. Her mouth opened, like a flower in bloom, and he moaned, pressing his muscled length against her, wedging her up against the door, hard, as the kiss gained in intensity. In one savage, devastating movement, without his lips ever leaving hers, he lifted her up, pinned against the door, so her head was level with his, so her stomach pressed against his stomach, her soft thighs against his. He drank deep, and she gave, willingly.

'Lord Dunstan!' Someone banged on the door, loudly, insistently. Startled, Alice jerked against the door in fright, fear bolting through her, breathing fast. Bastien held her tight, her feet still dangling above the floor, lifting his mouth from hers reluctantly to put a finger to his lips.

'My Lord Dunstan, I have been sent to bring you down to the great hall!' the voice demanded from the other side of the door.

Alice wilted visibly. Edmund! It was Edmund who spoke through the door. Only the thickness of a plank of wood separated her from shameful discovery! She began to shake her head at Bastien, eyes wide with panic, drumming her fists against his chest, trying to tell him without speech that under no circumstances should he let the man in! Oh good Lord, what had she been thinking? Her body still hummed with the onslaught of Bastien's kiss, her lips felt bruised, her hands shook as she brought them to her face, ashamed.

'Who is it?' Bastien dropped his mouth to her ear, but she jerked her head away, unable to contend with his nearness, struggling to be free of his hold. She let out a deep, shaky breath as he let her slide to the floor. 'It's Edmund,' she hissed. Bastien looked blank. 'My betrothed!' she explained, moving to the safety of the centre of the room. 'For God's sake, don't let him in.'

To her utter chagrin, Bastien chuckled, the wide grin splitting his face with mirth, before he turned and opened the door a crack. 'I'm a little busy right now,' he explained to the person outside. 'I thank you...and I'll make my own way down.' Listening to directions, he nodded once or twice, then shut the door, turning the key with a satisfying clunk.

At the sound of Edmund's footsteps fading down the corridor, Alice crumpled back on to the bed with relief; her legs would no longer hold her. 'Oh, Lord, what have I done?' She dropped her face into her hands, humiliation churning in her insides.

Bastien approached her, studying her bowed head, the gossamer veil from her head-dress spilling forwards over her neat shoulders. 'Was it really so terrible?'

She wrenched her face from her hands, eyes wide, pools of translucent periwinkle blue. 'Nay...aye! It will be if Edmund finds out!'

'Why?'

'Why?' She frowned up at him. 'Because this marriage to Edmund has to work...for my parents' sake. They're desperate to see me settled, cared for, especially now, as...' Her voice trailed off as she smoothed her palm across the bed furs, thinking of her absent brother. 'It's possible that I'm all they have left.'

'And what about you?' Bastien asked calmly, the brilliant emerald of his eyes shining over her. 'What do you want?' His voice contained the husky edge of desire, nudging at her, reminding her.

She laughed, a hollow sound. 'What I want doesn't come into it, Bastien. I have to see that my parents are provided for in their old age. Marriage to Edmund will fulfil that.'

'Do you love him?'

She lifted her wide periwinkle-blue eyes up to his, her cheeks still burning fire from the impact of his kiss, her lips bruised. He knew the answer.

'Please don't make this more difficult for me.'

He shrugged his shoulders. 'It was a kiss, Alice,' he explained mildly, crossing his big arms across his chest. 'Nothing to get worked up about, nothing to worry about. But don't fool yourself it was all my doing. You were a willing participant.'

The vivid hue in her cheeks deepened as the memory of the kiss, vibrant, exciting, burst into her mind. She ducked her head, plucking at a loose thread on the embroidered skirt of her gown. He was right—she was just as much to blame as he was. Her flesh throbbed, pulsed from his touch; it was as if he had plundered the very core of her, turned it inside out and set it back differently. She had tasted the edge of danger in that compelling kiss, the promise of something more, and she ground her fingers into the soft fur of the coverlet to quell her heightened feelings. He had said it was nothing, and that was how she must think of it.

Alice flinched as Bastien reached past her, picking up his shirt. A golden ring, resting against his chest, spun forwards on a leather lace, snagging her gaze. Inadvertently, her fingers lifted towards it, touched the cool metal.

'A betrothal ring?' she stuttered out, anxious to deflect the attention away from what had just happened.

'You could say that.' Bastien yanked the shirt over his head.

'Who are you planning to marry?'

'No one. The girl I intended to marry is dead.' Bastien studied Alice's startled features, her forlorn, drooping figure. He would do well to remember Katherine now, the cool, linear beauty of his first, his only, love, and recall the agony of her loss. He would do well to remember the strict boundaries of his self-imposed restraint, locked into place at her death. Yet this kiss had surpassed those limits, sneaked through when his guard was lowered, carrying with it the promise of immeasurable desire, of love. This kiss had scared the hell out of him. He had told her it was nothing, a mere passing dalliance to assuage his physical attraction towards a beautiful woman. It should have meant nothing. In reality, the kiss had pillaged feelings he had thought long since laid to waste, and breathed new life into them. At the press of her rosebud mouth, the iron-bound shackles around his heart had begun to slip.

Chapter Ten

Edmund tripped carefully down the spiral staircase, smirking to himself. Lord Dunstan had a girl in his chamber, of that he was certain. Not in the castle above two moments and already he was dallying with one of the maids. Good luck to him! It was none of his business what Lord Dunstan did; only unfortunate that the Queen had spotted him doing very little in the great hall, and had asked him to escort the new visitor to the evening meal. He grimaced, his mouth curling down to a sharp little pout. Queen Margaret treated him like a servant, when she knew full that his father was a knight, albeit not a very rich one.

Once he received the money from his uncle, things would change—the Queen would have to treat him with more respect; why, he'd probably be richer than her! Poor Alice had no idea to what she had agreed; naturally, she trusted him, believed in him. He had all those years of friendship to thank for that; he hoped it would be enough to persuade her to elope with him. Only yesterday another message had arrived from his uncle; the man was growing impatient for his prize and would not wait for ever. Now Lady Beatrice was aware of the plan, it would make things easier; he had taken a chance by telling her, but she had agreed readily, believing her daughter, over time, would see the sense of it.

Edmund held his sleeve away from the gritty stone wall as he descended; a snagged thread on his tunic was the last thing he wanted. Soon, soon he would be able to buy all the fine new clothes he could possibly wish for, but for now, he liked to take care of the few garments in his possession. Rounding the bottom of the stairs, he scanned the corridor, ensuring it was empty. He smoothed back his floppy chestnut hair, a secret joy bubbling in his chest; with Lord Dunstan having no need of him, there was time to meet Beatrice. Now Alice had returned, they needed to discuss what they were going to do with her.

At the head of the stairs, Bastien waited for Alice to fetch her stockings and slippers before they went down for the evening meal. The tempting sight of her bare toes, her delicate pink toenails, as she sat amidst his bed furs, had sent a fresh surge of desire through his muscular frame. He wished he hadn't mentioned Katherine; surprisingly, he'd completely forgotten the ring that swung around his neck until Alice commented upon it. Yet his words had done nothing to diminish the power of that unnerving kiss with Alice. He had thought her naïve, innocent, which she was, but, Mother of God, the passion that burned under her diminutive exterior had almost made him lose his self-control. He had hoped it would be a disappointment, serving only to wipe out any further sensual thoughts towards her, but, in truth, it had left him wanting more. His brawny frame hummed, throbbed with the memory.

Through the dim haze of arrested passion, Bastien had been taken aback by the sight of Alice's betrothed, peering up at him through the crack in the door. Brown, obsequious eyes, weak chin, a slight lisping voice—God in Heaven, he chuckled to himself, Alice would walk all over him. Especially as her sense of loyalty, of duty towards her parents, had driven her to accept this man's offer of marriage. It was not an uncommon event—most noble marriages happened from convenience rather than love—it was only now that he baulked at the injustice of it all. Bastien's fingers curled into the stone ledge as he recalled the peculiar, lop-sided tilt of Edmund's lips, an acrid taste in his mouth. Something was not quite right about Alice's betrothed.

Through the open window, the setting sun warmed his back, highlighting the endless small stitches holding the pleats in place on the back of his tunic. The fading sounds of the day drifted up to him: a cartwheel squeaking on a distant path, the shouts of the grooms in the stables, a faint yapping of a dog. And, much closer, two voices. Two distinct, recognisable voices lifting towards him, hanging in the still air; the thin, reed-like tones of Alice's fiancé, and the higher-pitched wheedling tones of her mother. He heard Alice's name and the promise of coin; his heart grew cold.

The young Queen Margaret smoothed the white linen tablecloth beneath her palm, rubbing with her middle finger at the puckered crease set into the material. Frowning, she swept her eyes along the length of the high table, checking that everything else was properly set; she always insisted on the highest standards and it vexed her to see details out of place.

'I don't like it, Beatrice.' She turned to her lady-in-waiting, who sat beside her.

'It's the new laundress,' Beatrice explained, trying to interpret Margaret's stony expression. 'She hasn't quite—'

'Nay, not that!' Margaret stopped her speech, impatient. 'I mean your daughter. It sounds as if she landed herself in a proper tangle. Why did she not come and see me, the moment she came back? Surely she knew I would be anxious for details about our knights? I have heard nothing from the Duke of York, but I presumes he holds them.'

The young Queen leaned back in her high-backed chair, ornately carved with an intricate pattern of trailing ivy leaves, as a servant placed a steaming platter of roast chicken before the ladies. The hanging diamonds on her heart-shaped head-dress bobbed as she hitched forwards again, resting her elbows on the table.

'Alice was exhausted when she returned, in no fit state to see anybody.' Beatrice screwed her lips together. How many times had she had to excuse her daughter's behaviour? At least now, with Edmund's help, she had a solution for Alice.

Margaret lifted her silver goblet to her lips, drinking deep. She was exhausted as well, exhausted with dealing with the affairs of state whilst her husband languished in an upstairs chamber with only a single servant for company. A strange madness had overtaken him: he didn't speak, he hardly ate or drank, just stared blankly at the wall, unmoving. It had been months now, and Margaret knew her excuses for her husband's absence were wearing thin. The situation was tenuous, for if Henry were unable to rule, then the throne would be taken from him, and from the child she would bear very soon. Her hand rounded protectively over her stomach, her eyes narrowing. She knew just who would steal it from under their noses: her bitterest enemy—the Duke of York! She would do everything in her power to prevent that happening!

Beatrice nudged Margaret's shoulder. 'My lady, look, here's Alice now…and she looks much refreshed. She'll be able to tell you everything.'

'Who is that with her?' Margaret's eyes rested on the tall, commanding man behind Alice's diminutive figure in the doorway.

'Oh, er…' Beatrice searched her memory. Had the man told her his name? She had been so incensed by Alice's behaviour that she had failed to take anything else in. 'His name escapes me, my lady. But it was he who rescued Alice, and brought her back.'

'I see,' Margaret replied drily. Really, her lady-in-waiting could be remarkably dense at times. Names were important in these troubled times—why, you could scarce trust your own neighbour, let alone some complete stranger!

On the threshold of the great hall, Alice paused. Shame continued to rush through her, a deep red humiliation at her reckless, wanton behaviour. He had told her the kiss was nothing, yet her body told her otherwise: even now, as he stood behind her in the doorway, as the warmth of his breath fanned the vulnerable skin at the back of her neck, a flicker of excitement licked along her veins! She clenched her fists, willing herself to concentrate on the matter in hand.

The great hall was packed, thronging with the King's retainers; his knights and servants jostled for space on the trestle tables, while the nobles sat up on the high dais with the Queen. Servants brought out platter after platter of hot, steaming food; a delicious aroma filled the hall, mingled with the distinctive smell of wood smoke. Alice's heart failed as Margaret beckoned to her, unsmiling, indicating that she should join her on the dais. This was it; this was the moment she would hide the truth from her Queen about Bastien's identity. Against her stomach, her fingers knotted together, palms sweating.

'Keep going,' Bastien rapped in her ear, putting his hand to the small of her back to give her a gentle push.

Despite the raised noise levels, the chattering and clink of goblets, Alice felt every eye in the hall upon her, judging her. 'I can't do this,' she whispered. Her stomach twisted with nerves, panic radiating from every pore.

'Remember your father,' Bastien reminded her gruffly. To his surprise, he found himself hating this situation, forcing the girl to do something against her will, especially after the conversation he had unwittingly overheard.

'Come on,' he continued more gently. He wanted to comfort her, not push her on. 'Tarrying will not help.'

'But what if someone recognises you?' She turned to look up at him, eyes huge orbs of sapphire.

'It would be unlucky if anyone did; I've been out of the country for so long.' He put a hand on her shoulder, propelled her forwards. 'Remember what we agreed upon, and all should be well.' On the way down they had cobbled together a simple story of her rescue. Now, as Alice climbed the wooden steps to the dais, she rehearsed the scenario over and over in her head, the details churning in her mind.

'Come, sit with us, please,' Margaret swept out her arm, indicating that Beatrice should move down so that Bastien could sit on one side of her, and Alice in the empty seat to her left. Beatrice sucked her cheeks in with displeasure at the inconvenience of having to move her plate, her goblet, performing the task with an ostentatious clatter.

Bastien swept a low, formal bow. 'Your Majesty, Lord Dunstan, at your service. It is an honour to make your acquaintance.'

Margaret's liquid brown eyes travelled the length of the man before her. 'Have we not met before?' she asked, curiously. 'Please, sit down,' she added, indicating the seat at her side.

'I doubt it, your Majesty. I have been away for many years, fighting in France.'

'Ah, yes, of course. At least now all is resolved over there.' Margaret attempted to keep her tone neutral, a deliberate monotone. As the wife of the English King, she had to support all things English, but secretly she had celebrated when the English had returned in defeat. Her countrymen had won!

'And where are your lands, your family?' During the King's illness, Margaret had made some effort to try to learn all the names of the powerful families in England, all those dukes and earls who would support the King in battle. The list had been endless, full of unpronounceable English names that had made her head ache. Now, determined not to show her ignorance, she wished she had paid more attention.

'I have lands up in the north, my lady.'

Margaret shuddered; she had never, in her few years of marriage, ventured to the north, and neither had King Henry. It was a part of the country to be feared, full of desperate men living hand to mouth, proud and warlike, accustomed to a harsh life.

'How agreeable,' she commented lamely. No doubt he wanted money, some sort of reward for his pains in rescuing Alice—those sort of people always did. 'And what brought you to our part of the country?'

'I was travelling home from France, your Majesty, when I heard the Lady Alice's screams.' Bastien's tone was confident, measured. 'It was lucky that she lagged behind, guarded only by two soldiers. I was able to snatch her from the back, and ride away.'

Lagged behind! How dare he? Alice listened to his account with annoyance, nibbling on a bread roll. The crumbs stuck in her gullet, and she took a deep gulp of wine to wash it down. The fiery liquid spread down her throat, through her veins, steadying her slightly.

Beatrice leaned forwards, her face a white mask. 'And my husband was definitely taken prisoner?'

Bastien nodded. 'According to Lady Alice, he was captured as he went out into the battlefield to help the wounded.'

'Stupid, stupid numbskull!' Beatrice jabbed her knife into a slice of meat. 'Why must he persist in this foolish game…and involve *you?*' She bent forwards, staring past Bastien, past Margaret, to fix Alice with a baleful eye.

'If he hadn't been there, Mother, those soldiers would

have died where they fell. That's why he does it...and it's why I go; two of us are more helpful than just one.'

'Calm yourself, Beatrice,' Margaret said sternly. She checked that two guards still flanked the side door to the dais, to reassure herself, although she felt no threat from this man beside her. 'And now you are returned to England, I hope you support your King?' she ventured, wondering if he were aware of the grumblings amongst the nobles about the King's continual absence.

'I have six hundred paid soldiers at my command,' Bastien replied, his tone neutral.

Margaret laughed. 'Why, that is a small army in itself!' She managed to restrain herself from visibly rubbing her hands. So many powerful families had turned against the King in the past few weeks, and she had been too wary of this huge Northerner; by his admission of strength, he was obviously prepared to support the King.

Lean fingers curling around the stem of his goblet, Bastien fixed Margaret with his piercing gaze. 'I am naturally keen to meet the King, to discuss his future plans.'

Alice took another gulp of wine. The red liquid warmed her innards, relaxed her trembling hands. She chewed at the inside of her cheek, praying for the end of this conversation, praying for the end of the meal, when she could fly back to her chamber and hide her head in shame. How could such a man make her feel in such a way? He was a barbarian, the enemy, someone she should push away, yet every time he came near her, her limbs melted in treachery.

Margaret was shaking her head at Bastien. 'I'm sorry, my lord. He has been taken ill, suddenly, tonight, a bad headache, unfortunately,' she said smoothly, studying a speck of wine on the tablecloth that spread, blotting the white linen. 'But be assured that we will count on your support, and will call on you when you are needed. We pay those who support us well.' Her smile was wide, but foundered before it reached her eyes.

The wine trailed like liquid fire down Alice's throat as she stared out across the bobbing sea of heads below, not wanting to catch Bastien's eye, not wanting any part of this deception. Her neck felt rigid with the effort of keeping her head turned away. To her dismay, she spotted Edmund waving at her frantically from a trestle on the far side of the hall, his white hand flashing plumply in contrast with the richer tones of the tapestry draped down the wall behind him. He would want to talk to her, to be seen with her in his official capacity as her betrothed. Her heart thumped dully; she should go down to him.

At her elbow, the serving girl filled her silver goblet to the brim once more. Bastien's easy, affable manner had easily won over the young Queen, easing her suspicious mind, and now the pair of them chatted amicably, like old friends. The urge to yell out, to scream to all that he was a Yorkist, an enemy in their midst, surged strongly in her veins, only to be curbed by the image of her father as she said goodbye to him in Ludlow.

'So, what do you think?' Margaret turned her smiling face towards Alice. Her creamy skin glowed in the candlelight, sheened, like pale-coloured velvet.

'I beg your pardon, my lady.' Alice blushed. 'I didn't hear what you said.'

'Head in the clouds again?' Margaret teased. The strain slipped from her face as she smiled, making her appear much younger, her true age. This royal marriage was taking its toll on the young Queen's nerves. 'I was just saying that Lord Dunstan here should stay for the wedding celebrations of Lord Halston. The marriage is the day after tomorrow, with jousting in the afternoon.'

Alice's world began to unravel; the stone wall at the side of the high dais seemed to dip and lurch. 'Stay?' she managed to croak out. 'Here?' Her stomach flipped, then looped violently.

'Of course, *here!*' Margaret laughed. 'Where else would you have him stay?'

As far away as possible, thought Alice. 'I don't think it's a good idea.'

Margaret wrinkled her petite nose, puzzled. 'Why ever not? Surely Lord Dunstan must be rewarded for bringing you back to us, for rescuing you?'

Alice's eyes moved past Margaret's questioning features, trapping Bastien's bright eyes. He frowned, almost imperceptibly: a warning. 'Don't you need to be somewhere else?' she asked him directly, her fingers pulling nervously at a bread roll. The muscles tightened in her face, making her speech inflexible, forced.

'Not particularly.' His wide smile caused small, crinkled lines to fan out from the sides of his eyes. 'I can spare a few days.'

'Excellent,' Margaret chimed in, clapping her hands. Maybe when she told the King about this new ally, the impressive Lord Dunstan, it might rouse him out of his stupor. She could only hope, and pray.

Alice placed her hands flat on the table, then levered herself into a standing position. What was the matter with her? Everything seemed to moving around, dancing before her eyes. Bastien was changing the original plan; she had agreed to show him the location of King Henry's chambers, later that evening when the castle slept, when the King's valet would be asleep. After he had seen the King, he would then return to Ludlow, without delay, to release her father. Now, he was proposing to stay!

Bastien, half-listening to Margaret chatter on about some court matter, watched Alice sway upright. Her fingertips touched the table, enabling her to balance, and he smiled to himself. The stupid girl had drunk too much, or too much for her slight frame anyhow. Alice edged backwards, carefully avoiding bumping into the back of her chair, or Margaret's. She resolved to go and speak to Edmund, for, despite the unwanted betrothal, he was still her friend, she must not forget that. Talking through matters with him always helped.

'Oh, would you like to dance?' Bastien asked innocently, twisting around in his seat as she came level with the back of it. He tipped his head towards the main part of the hall, where some of the tables had been pushed back to create an area for dancing. Already a few couples had paired up while the musicians in the corner practised a few tentative notes on their instruments.

'Not with you!' Alice hissed nastily, low enough so that neither Margaret nor her mother heard it. As she walked unsteadily to the steps, she caught his light chuckle. Damn him! The cool, well-worn wood of the rail alongside the steps slid under her fingers, and she gripped it hard to stop herself falling.

All at once, the great hall seemed too hot, claustrophobic. With its high rafters and cavernous roof space, it was usually too cold for comfort. People bumped and jostled companionably against her as she made her way carefully through the throng, away from that man. Just wait until she told Edmund about him!

'Alice!' Edmund had managed to lever himself through the bouncing press of people towards her. His hair was pushed back from his wide, pale forehead; small pinpricks of sweat stood out on his clammy skin, and he wiped them away, smoothing his hair at the same time. 'We were so worried about you! What happened to you?'

It's still happening, she wanted to blurt out. But instead she shook her head dully, trying to ignore the ever-increasing swirling sensations in her head. 'I can't tell you here.' She raised her voice above the clamour of the music. 'Let's go somewhere quieter.' Alice clasped at his forearm, surprised at his resistance when he didn't move.

'We should dance together first.' Edmund looked down at her with warm brown eyes. 'Especially now that we're betrothed.'

You don't need to do this, Alice wanted to scream at him. You don't need to be loving, or overly attentive, or romantic in any way. Our marriage is to be a business contract, nothing more. Surely he knew that? For some inexplicable reason, nausea began to rise in her gullet.

'Edmund, I want to talk to you!' she whispered urgently. 'It's important!'

'One dance,' he cajoled. 'For appearances' sake, and then we'll go.'

Alice closed her eyes, then opened them quickly, finding the sensations in her head worse. 'One dance,' she agreed, finally, reluctantly.

He smiled lopsidedly, pulling at her affectionately to

join the throng of dancers holding hands in a long line, before they twisted in and out of each other. Then they split back into couples again, Edmund raising his arm to spin her around.

'Oh!' Alice staggered sideways, clutching desperately at her fiancé's sleeve.

Face set with concentration, Edmund twisted her the other way. The room wobbled crazily, spun in a whirling myriad of bright colours, of flickering candlelight; she began to fall, her head light and loose…

A pair of thick, brawny arms hooked around her waist, stopped her falling, wedged her firmly against a long, muscled body.

'Alice—are you all right, Alice?' Edmund's voice sounded from a long distance away, muffled, concerned.

'She's had too much wine,' another, familiar male voice growled. Oh God, not him! Not now!

Alice lifted her heavy head. 'I have not!' she protested loudly. A wave of sickness swept through her, and she touched her hand to her clammy forehead.

'She looks ill to me,' Edmund ventured. 'I thank you, my lord…for preventing her fall. I'll take her back to sit down.'

'I think I need to go to my chamber,' Alice mumbled. 'Edmund, can you take me?' Bastien's arm was firmly wrapped around her waist; if he removed it, she knew she would fall.

'Aye, of course,' Edmund agreed readily. Maybe this would give him the chance to talk to Alice about the wedding, persuade her to marry him sooner. In her present state, she might well agree to any of his suggestions. He nodded significantly at Lord Dunstan, trying to dismiss the high-ranking noble by expression alone, indicating that he should release Alice into his care.

'I'll take her,' Bastien announced firmly, locking his grip more tightly around Alice, now sagging alarmingly in his arms.

Edmund's mouth curled downwards. 'But I'm her fiancé,' he mumbled back, his face assuming the expression of a spoiled youth. 'I should take her.' Why did Alice not protest, instead of hanging in the man's arms like a limp and useless doll?

'I was thinking of retiring myself,' Bastien replied, trampling over his ineffectual protest. 'It's no trouble; she'll be safe with me.'

Puny wrists clamped to his side, Edmund glanced round with irritation as someone jogged into his shoulder. He was no match against the palpable strength of this man, and both of them knew it. Aware they were drawing curious glances, he coloured faintly, inadequacy washing through him. He knew when to back down. 'Then I thank you, my lord, for taking the trouble,' he agreed after a small hesitation.

'It's no trouble.' Bastien was already half-dragging, half-carrying Alice across the great hall, through the merry crowds, their laughing faces shining with sweat from the exertion of the dance. His muscled chest was warm against her back as he leaned around her to pull open the thick oak door that led out into the darkened passageway, pushing her through. She tottered unsteadily, before reeling against the cool stone wall, resting her head back, closing her eyes.

'I'll be all right now, thank you.' Her voice echoed faintly in the empty corridor. Away from the press of people, she found it easier to breathe.

'Did you tell him anything?'

'Nay, of course not!' she croaked, her mouth dry, a husk. 'Is that why you insisted on taking me to my chamber? Why would I do such a thing when my father's life is at stake?'

In the half-light of the corridor, her skin gleamed like polished marble; at her neck, her pulse throbbed, fast. Sweet Jesu, she was beautiful. Bastien rounded her shoulders with his hands, the quicksilver green of his eyes washing over her. 'I could see it in your face as you left the top table. Don't lie to me, Alice.'

'Then stop changing the plan,' she hissed back at him without admitting the truth. 'You agreed you would see the King tonight, and be gone on the morrow to release my father. I can't bear to think of him suffering at the Duke's castle...'

'He will be treated well.' His voice was low, liquid honey in the shadows. How could he tell her of the conversation he had overheard, of her mother and Edmund plotting together? She would never believe him. Alice was alone in this castle, with nobody, he suspected, on her side. He needed more time here, time to fathom what devilment young Edmund was about.

Another wave of nausea hit Alice; she lurched forwards, doubled over. The muscles in her legs turned to wet rope. 'I must go to my chamber,' she mumbled. At the precise moment she didn't care what Bastien did. 'I don't feel very well.'

'You've had too much wine,' Bastien replied, his tone matter of fact, studying her white, pallid face.

'I don't even like wine!' Walking forwards, Alice stretched her fingers out to hold the wall as she turned back to look at him, miserably. His shadowy bulk loomed behind her. 'Oh dear,' she giggled, as her toes became entangled in the hem of her gown, 'this really is difficult.'

'God's teeth,' Bastien muttered. He swept one arm around the back of her shoulders, and the other under the crook in her knees, hoisting her high against his chest in a swirl of skirts.

'Nay! I can walk.' Alice wiggled her slippered feet. Her cheek grazed the soft velvet of his tunic; the distinctive, heady scent of his skin rose to her nostrils, sumptuous, tantatalising. Her heart floundered.

'Aye, you can...' his voice was low, husky '...but it would take all night!' He strode off, bearing her light weight effortlessly. Her head lolled near his shoulder; and from her hair, confined in a pearl-studded gold mesh, sprung the glorious scent of lavender, reminding him of long, hot summers in France. Ducking beneath the oak lintel, he hoisted her more securely into his arms, in order to negotiate the narrow spiral staircase to the upper floors. He tried to ignore the tantalising firmness of her hip beneath his palm, the way the tips of his fingers brushed close to the rounded curve of her breast, as his arm supported her back.

Kicking open her chamber door with the toe of his leather boot, he manoeuvred her inside. Alice had gone to sleep; her breathing had deepened, her body lying softly against him. Her room was lit by a single torch, hanging in an iron bracket by the door, its flickering light casting huge, undulating shadows against the gleaming wood panelling of the walls. In one corner, a charcoal brazier smouldered, a delicious heat spreading around the chamber from its glowing coals.

Bastien lay Alice gently down on the bed furs, the

silk fabric of her skirts rustling delicately as the fabric settled around her limbs. Her eyelids fluttered open, lucid, searching, a hand reaching up to his cheek, a butterfly touch.

'What was she like?' Her voice, a muted whisper, lured him with its softness.

He knew of whom she spoke, but strangely, it mattered not. His mind sought the details, details long since buried but recalled with ease: Katherine, tall, willowy, her dark hair pinned to her head in elaborate braids, her composed, serious features.

'She was...nothing like you.'

A wide smile curved Alice's lips. 'That tells me nothing.'

His hand covered hers upon his cheek, her pulse beat, rapid, vital beneath his fingers. A lightness frothed around his heart, fetters loosening.

'You're still hurting.' Her eyelids fluttered with the effort of trying to hold them open.

He stared at her for a long while, watching her eyelids drift down, her hand falling from his face to rest by her side. Her breathing slackened.

'Not any more,' he whispered.

She smiled in her sleep, her dark lashes fanning down over her flushed cheeks as she nestled her head more securely into the linen pillow. Desire stabbed through him; hastily, he pulled off her embroidered slippers and dropped them to the floor, before stepping back, folding his arms tightly across his chest, to prevent himself from touching her again.

At what point had their relationship changed? A few days ago, she had been nothing but a minor irritation, a troublesome maid who he couldn't wait to be rid of. A wayward creature who flouted custom and convention at every turn, with an unerring ability to land herself in trouble. He should walk away, right now, yet oddly, every bone in his body yearned to taste those rosebud lips once more, yearned to protect her from danger. And after that conversation he had overheard from her so-called fiancé, he was in no doubt that danger was what she faced.

Chapter Eleven

Alice cracked open one eye, then closed it again, hastily. A heavy dryness clawed at her mouth, as if someone had stuffed a clump of straw against her tongue. Iron clamps bound her head, pressing tighter and tighter against her scalp. And that was before she moved. She opened her eyes again at the insistent thumping on her chamber door. 'Tell whoever that is to go away and come back later,' she croaked out to the maidservant. The girl placed the folded clothes on the oak coffer and went to the door. Alice lay back on the pillows, squinting against the bright sunlight shafting through the windows; she knew it was late, but, oh, how her head pounded! She must be ill!

'It's that man, my lady,' the maidservant whispered hurriedly to Alice, her eyes wide, 'and he says if you're not up in five minutes, he'll come in and drag you out himself!' Her face pinkened, bright with interest.

'Oh, he did, did he!' She threw back the coverlet

in a fit of annoyance, swung her feet to the floor. The lurching movement made her feel sick.

'Oh, my lady!' gasped the maid. 'Look at you!'

But in her fit of pique, Alice didn't hear her. She stomped to the door in her stockinged feet, and wrenched it wide, irritation rising in her chest.

The tall, formidable figure of Bastien, in radiant good health, filled the doorway. His green eyes sparkled, and the taut skin on his face held a ruddy glow, as if he had already been outside for hours. In contrast to his vibrant form, Alice felt pale, wan, and sick.

'Oh, good,' he said, cheerfully. 'You're dressed.'

'Wh-what?!' Stunned, Alice stared down at herself. She was, indeed, fully dressed. The delicately embroidered green silk panels of the gown she had worn the evening before shimmered back at her. How had that happened?

Bastien grinned down at her, the smile lifting the tanned contours of his face. Her heart flipped.

'Do you know why I'm still dressed?' Alice glared at him, suspiciously.

'I do,' he replied infuriatingly, withholding any explanation. He caught her limp hand, pulling her. 'It's time to fulfil your obligation.'

Alice resisted, holding fast to the door jamb, scrunching her eyes up at him. 'Can't you see I'm not well? I need to go back to bed, and you need to go away.'

He lowered his head near to hers, keeping his voice low. It reverberated in her ear, sparking a strange looping sensation in her stomach. 'I will go away, as soon as you take me to the King. Remember? The Queen's gone hunting, and taken half the castle with her. She thinks I'm with them, but I doubled back. We need to do this now! There may not be another chance.'

'The Queen…hunting?' Alice stared up at him, thinking of Margaret's condition. Should she be riding at this stage of her pregnancy?

Bastien caught her expression. 'She's gone in a litter,' he explained impatiently. 'She wouldn't do anything that would risk losing that baby; the child is too important. Now, come on!'

Vague, gut-wrenchingly awful details of the previous evening began to pop into her memory as she dipped back in the chamber to fetch her shoes. 'It was the wine, wasn't it?' she confirmed with Bastien, when she reappeared in the doorway.

He nodded. 'And I carried you up to bed.' His explanation seemed curt, abrupt.

'And…?' she hedged, almost holding her breath with the unpleasantness of it all.

His gaze was knife-sharp, glittering. 'And…nothing. You're still wearing all your clothes. Why, did you wish for something else?'

Her stomach plummeted. 'Nay, nay, of course not!' But a tiny kernel of desire twisted inside her; a forlorn hope, barely engendered, melted away.

'Follow me,' she said. 'It's not far.'

She led him along a wood-panelled passage that ran the full length of the north wall of the castle, then through a curtained doorway, and up one flight of stairs. 'It's along here…' she hesitated '…the door at the end. Walter, the King's valet, is an old friend of my father's; he'll be anxious for news of him. If I lead him towards the window, and keep him distracted, you'll be able to slip into the King's bedchamber, through the door on the left-hand side.'

Bastien laughed. 'And to think my plan was to overpower the valet, gag him and tie him up while I spoke to the King.'

'But then the valet would report your misdemeanour to the Queen,' she said, pushing a loose lock of hair back behind her ear and yanking her veil down to cover it, 'and you would have to leave.'

'I have to leave anyway,' he reminded her, 'in order to report to the Duke, and to release your father.' His fingers touched the pale skin of her cheek; for a moment there, she had looked so lost, so vulnerable.

'But…I thought you would stay for the wedding,' she blurted out. 'The Queen invited you.' Last night she had been so angry that he was planning to stay, but now, when he said he was leaving, her heart churned with the unexpected loss, the desertion.

'I didn't think we'd have this opportunity to see the King so soon,' he explained gently, 'and once I've met him I need to carry the information to the Duke.' His moss-green eyes shimmered, limpid with kindness.

'Aye—yes—of course,' Alice stumbled a little over the words, before turning and walking towards the door. 'Well, let's get this over with.'

Walter, the king's manservant, peered out through the crack of the open door, his wizened face brightening as soon as he recognised her. 'Alice, my God, you're safe!' He reached for her hands, tugging her gently through the doorway. A wave of betrayal rolled over her; she hunched her shoulders, feeling stained, soiled by her treachery. Her head thumped, punishing her.

Walter was one of her father's oldest friends; she had
known him for ever, and now she abused that trust by
allowing an enemy to walk into the King's room, right
under his nose. What if Bastien broke his promise, and
killed the King? Then the Duke of York would claim
the throne for his own. Her fingertips curled tightly into
her palms: she had to trust him, for her father's sake.

'Your father? What news?' Walter's bright hazel eyes
regarded her anxiously. Deep grooves filtered out from
the corners of his eyes, evidence of a past life toiling
in the fields. 'Has that Yorkist thug released him yet?'
Alice tucked her arm companionably under his elbow,
leading him over to the window. She hoped Walter's
curiosity about her father would distract him from bolting the door once more. Keeping her back firmly to the
doorway, and Walter by her side facing the window,
she began to recount the events of the previous days,
lengthening her explanation with every little detail, in
the hope of giving Bastien the maximum amount of
time with the King. She hesitated, when Walter touched
her arm, smiling.

'I would love to hear the rest, my sweet; it sounds
like you've been through an ordeal, but its time I helped
the King. Listen, can you hear the morning bell?'

Alice nodded. The small bell in the chapel had a
delicate ring, but would carry far around the estate,
summoning people to meal times, and to prayer, servant
and noble alike.

'I must prepare the King for the Queen's daily visit;
and she'll most certainly come when she's finished
hunting.'

'How is he?' Alice bent her head in the direction of
the King's chamber.

Walter shook his head, his expression immediately guarded. 'You shouldn't really be here, Alice. The Queen has given express orders that no one should see her husband.'

'But I didn't come to see the King.' Alice smiled, 'I came to see you!'

'And I thank you for it...' Walter placed his hand on her shoulder '...but now I think you should go.'

Reluctantly, Alice pivoted away from the window, praying that Bastien had had enough time to slip in and out, and that she wouldn't have to go through this whole charade again.

Emerging into the corridor, Alice looked left, then right. Where would Bastien have gone? She assumed he would be waiting for her somewhere, ready to tell her what he had found out, to say goodbye. Her steps quickened—but...would he say goodbye? Or would he slip away like a thief in the night, without a word? An unbidden sense of loss clutched at her heart—would he really leave without saying anything? She sprinted towards the west tower, to the chamber assigned to Bastien, knocking tentatively. No answer. She pushed open the door, eyes scanning the room. The bed had been stripped, ready to take fresh linens for the next guest. A pile of cold ashes lay in the grate.

She felt unsettled, cheated. Why did she expect anything more from the man? It had simply been a business arrangement: you do this for me, and I'll do this for you. Her mind told her to let him go, but her heart kept driving her on. The stables! That's where he would be! The hardness of the stone steps reverberated up her shins as she pounded down the spiral staircase, one hand running lightly over the central column of smooth stone in order to keep her balance, her skirts lifted high, bunched into her other hand. Rain misted her face as she dashed across the cobbled inner bailey of the castle, grey cloud lowering overhead. Checking her stride slightly, she plunged into the gloom of the stables.

He was there.

Breathless, Alice teetered on the threshold, trying to gather her scattered thoughts. 'You were going to leave without saying goodbye!' she gabbled, her voice shrill and accusing.

Bastien settled the heavy leather saddle on to his horse's back, the animal sidling a little at the unwelcome restriction. He thrust impatient fingers through the golden strands of his hair.

'Come here.' His voice was deep, velvety. Her heart strained, then squeezed, tight, at the husky danger in his words.

'I...er...' she hedged, unsure. Dear Lord, she had screeched at him like a petulant child. What in Heaven's name had made her say that? She pushed a palm against her forehead, feeling queasy. 'So, you're going then?' she continued, lightly. 'I only thought...' Her speech trailed off, dismally. What had she thought? That there was something more between them? Don't be ridiculous, she admonished herself strongly, it's perfectly obvious that he can't wait to return home.

'Come here...' Bastien repeated, a string of steel underlying his voice. 'I need to speak to you.' The thick layer of straw used for the animal's bedding rustled beneath his big leather boots as he drew back further into the stables, to an empty stall.

There was nothing he could do to her here, she surmised. And besides, she was anxious to know what he had found out, up there in the King's chamber.

'I was planning to find you before I left,' he explained as she approached, his voice curling over her, dark, rich and velvety. He leaned one bulky shoulder against the wooden planks forming the side of the stall, folding his arms across his chest.

Alice shrugged. 'I wanted to make sure that you were going.' The words sounded lame, a limp excuse for her earlier outburst. She smoothed one hand down the gathered folds of her gown self-consciously.

His expression was stern, serious. 'Alice, while I'm gone, I want you to take care.'

'What do you mean?' His words filtered through her, a shock. 'I'm in no danger.'

'I think you are. You need to watch out for Edmund.'

'Edmund?' she spluttered, astounded by his words. 'Are you mad? What would make you say such a thing?'

Bastien sighed. He was saying this all wrong; and now, it would only annoy her, set her against him. And even then he wasn't certain what Edmund and her mother were plotting. But if he said nothing at all... 'I overheard a conversation between Edmund and your mother... They were discussing you, Alice.'

She tilted her head up at him, hands planted firmly on her hips. 'There's nothing unusual in that, Bastien. My mother was no doubt discussing the details of our marriage.' Her speech wavered a little, cloudy with reservation.

'They *were* discussing marriage,' he agreed, 'but not between you and Edmund. Between you and someone else.' His hands rounded on her shoulders, secure, comforting.

Alice jerked her head back, confused. 'Why, why are you doing this? You're asking me to doubt one of my oldest and dearest friends. Someone whom I trust. Which is more than I can say for you…I don't even trust you to bring my own father back.' As if to emphasise her point she took a step back from Bastien, manoeuvring out deftly from his gentle hold on her shoulders. A loose thread from her gown snagged on a splinter of wood on the stall. She set her lips together in irritation, pulling roughly at her skirts, finally dislodging the stubborn material with a fraught, ripping sound. And all the time she felt his eyes upon her, burning into her.

'You trusted me with the King.' Further up the stables, his horse whinnied, jangling the bit between his teeth.

Alice glared at him, turquoise eyes wide and luminous. 'You were blackmailing me with my father's life!' she flared back. 'What was I supposed to do?'

'Fair point,' he agreed, equably. 'You had no choice. Alice, I'm just telling you to be careful.'

Alice tucked an errant strand of hair behind her ear. 'And I don't understand. You have the information you came for, so why tell me this? From this day on, you'll never see me again.' Even to her own ears, her voice sounded ravaged, forlorn.

'Is that why you came tearing into the stables like one possessed…' he chuckled gently '…because you're never going to see me again?' As he spoke the words, he knew it wouldn't be true. He would see her again. Even now, he had the strongest urge to bundle her up on to his horse, to take her with him, to protect her. He didn't want to leave her here, alone, vulnerable.

She stared up at him, realising it was the last time

she would see the beautiful, sculptured lines of his face, his easy smile, his devastating eyes. She had to accept that he was leaving, that her future was marriage to Edmund. 'I think you'd better go now, Bastien,' Alice said quietly, twisting away from him before he saw the sadness in her face, the threat of shining tears gathering in her eyes. 'And make sure my father comes back in one piece.' She turned on her heel in a flick of skirts and stalked out of the stables.

The Duke glared at his tall commander, followed his movements back and forth across the great hall. 'Oh, for goodness' sake, man, stop pacing around and sit down!' Bastien pitched his long body into a high-backed oak chair opposite the Duke, his sprawling attitude belying the fact that his every muscle quivered with a bristling energy.

Richard took a long sip from the pewter goblet, placed it back on a small table beside his chair. 'It sounds like the King is in a severe state of mental decline. No response at all, you say?'

Bastien leaned forwards, the coppery streaks in his blond head shining like darts of flame. The front edges of his cote-hardie fell open, revealing mud-spattered braies, boots. He had driven his horse hard on the way back. 'Nothing. I spoke to him, clicked my fingers in front of his face, even shook him a little. His eyes were open, but he merely stared straight ahead, blank.'

'And the girl helped you gain access to the King's quarters? She was amenable?'

Bastien's chest squeezed tight, catching him unawares. Amenable? Christ, she had been more than amenable when they had kissed! Even now, his lips tingled with the memory of the passion and desire he had seen in her eyes. He sprang up from his seat once more, moved to stand at the fireplace. 'Aye, she was amenable.' His words were clipped, sharp. He ran one finger around the inside edge of his fustian gypon; suddenly it seemed too tight around his neck.

The Duke threw him a crooked half-smile, saw the muscle twitch in his lean, ruddy cheek. 'Do I detect a certain attachment between yourself and the young lady?'

'You do not.' He had no inclination to discuss Alice; every word stuck needles of guilt into him, reminded him that he should not have left her alone in Abberley. Yet she was not his responsibility, not like Katherine, his betrothed, had been. And he hadn't been able to protect her, had he?

'I'll call a meeting of all those nobles that support me,' Richard was saying, 'and then arrange a meeting with the Queen; Henry is in no fit state to run the country. You'll come with me?'

Bastien pushed a fist against the high mantelpiece above the fire, levering himself away. 'I'll be at Abberley when you arrive there,' he said. 'I'm going to take the physician back, now he's free to go.'

The Duke looked up in surprise. 'I have several hundreds of soldiers who would do that job for me—why you?'

The image of Alice's sweet heart-shaped face swung into his mind. Lord, but the girl was making him soft in the head. He told himself he didn't have anything better to do, that he had no wish to return to his estates and lands. But the whispered conversation he had unwittingly overhead returned again and again to him; he smelled a plot with an instinct born of years dealing with unsavoury people, of tricksters and hoodwinkers. Men like Edmund needed to be dealt with. And he was the man to do it.

'It's just something that I need to do.'

The sun flared valiantly through the straggles of grey cloud, but there was no heat in the rays on this cold autumn day. In the walled garden to the south-west of Abberley Castle, smoke from the gardeners' fires rose listlessly into the still, damp air. The dead twigs and gnarled prunings crackled as they burned, filling the air with a sweet, woody scent. Under a heavy dew, the plants drooped, their leaves blackened and shrivelled from an overnight frost.

Walking along the stone-flagged path at Edmund's side, Alice stared glumly ahead, failing to notice the neat borders of dug-over earth, the line of clipped yews towards which they were headed. All she saw, in a wave of inexplicable misery, was Bastien's face as she had last seen him, deep in the shadow of the stables. Despair crushed her heart; she should have been rejoicing at his departure, yet all she wanted to do was lock herself in her chamber and weep. She would never see him again.

As the slick wetness from the flagstones seeped through the thin soles of her slippers, Edmund coughed in the damp air, muttering about his lungs, flicking a speck of lint from the voluminous gathered sleeve of his tunic. When she had come down for breakfast that morning, he had been desperate to talk with her, alone, and, heart sinking, she had suggested the gardens. She had to forget Bastien, had to concentrate on building a secure future for herself and her parents. Marriage to

Edmund was the only solution, however unappealing the prospect. At least he was young, and they were friends; but he would never make her heart sing, like… Nay, she must forget him!

Edmund tucked her hand companionably into his side; they squeezed together as the path narrowed and entered an avenue of pleached hawthorns, the shapes of the trees tied down, their growth contorted and controlled from an early age into an arch. Alice's skin glowed, fresh and rosy from the frosty air, her breath emerging in short misty puffs.

'I feel like I've hardly seen you since you returned from Ludlow,' Edmund grumbled lightly. He nibbled delicately at a nail, reliving the humiliation he had felt when Lord Dunstan had insisted on taking Alice to her chamber.

Alice ducked her head, flushed, knowing to whom he referred. 'I couldn't ignore the man,' she protested. 'He did rescue me, after all! I had to be polite.'

Edmund pulled her closer to his side, a reassuring gesture. 'Alice! I was only teasing!' She looked quite pretty in this dappled morning light, if a little untidy. Why didn't her mother force her to arrange her hair in the correct manner? Even so, he couldn't help thinking it was a shame he wasn't to have her after all. But the lure of the riches he would gain in his part of the plan was too great to ignore. With that sort of money, he could procure a much higher class of bride than this humble daughter of the Queen's lady-in-waiting.

The gravel beneath his feet crunched as he stopped in the centre of the four paths that divided the garden into equal quadrants. A stone urn, intricately carved, marked this centre, its pitted surface frothy with pale-blue lichen. Edmund disengaged his arm to hold both of Alice's hands in his, turning to face her.

'I think we should marry as soon as possible,' he announced solemnly.

Shock resonated through her slender frame; she clutched at the stone urn for support. She had the over-whelming urge to wrench her hands away, to run. It was all happening too fast; her toes curled inwards in her slippers, as if trying to slow the headlong rush of time. Her wide-blue eyes, set with incomprehension, roved over Edmund's placid features. 'But…but we were going to wait for a year, at least! You don't receive your inheritance for a year.' Desperation threaded her voice.

'Circumstances have changed,' Edmund replied slowly. 'My father is ill; he would see us wed before he…before he…' He choked on the final words, silently congratulating himself on his acting ability as he spotted the wave of sympathy in Alice's expression.

'Oh, Edmund, I'm so sorry. I had no idea he was ill.'

Neither has he, thought Edmund. He's probably tuck-ing into a large breakfast at this very moment, in the peak of health. But he would do anything, say any-thing, to lure Alice away from Abberley; the reward was simply too great.

'It came on very suddenly.' Edmund's expression was grave. 'I think we should leave on the morrow… travel to my father's castle.'

'My father might be able to help him.'

'Nay,' Edmund replied vociferously, 'he has the ser-vices of one of the best physicians in the country.'

Alice frowned. 'Who?'

Edmund shuffled uncomfortably, running one finger around the inside of his high embroidered collar. What was the matter with her? Why so many questions? He thought she would jump at the chance of marrying him earlier, yet her whole manner seemed to be one of reluctance, hesitation. 'Er...I'm not certain of his name,' he replied lamely. 'But rest assured he is receiving the best possible care.'

Alice nodded, appearing to accept his explanation. 'My parents may need more time to pack for the journey,' she continued.

Edmund placed a hand on her shoulder. 'I think it would be better if we kept it as a small ceremony,' he said carefully. 'Just us, with the priest and my father. He wouldn't care for a crowd of strangers standing around his bed. He is extremely ill, you know.'

'But...my parents would expect to be there!' A look of astonishment crossed Alice's face. 'They'll be so hurt.'

'I've talked to your mother already,' Edmund reassured her. 'I've explained the situation and promised her we would hold a larger ceremony back at Abberley on a later date. She is happy with that, and thinks your father will be in agreement.'

'If you're certain...?' Alice responded doubtfully.

Edmund nodded, a cunning glitter in his eyes. 'Your mother is in full agreement.' Little did the girl know that her mother was fully aware of his true plan, and stood to gain from it.

'I see.' But in truth she didn't understand at all. Since when had Edmund taken to going behind her back and speaking to her mother? Bastien's last words shot into her head, unbidden, warning against Edmund, his words corroding her thought processes. But she couldn't think of that now, or start to believe them; she had to think of the future.

Chapter Twelve

A wide expanse of rough, tussocky grass to the north of Abberley Castle formed the tournament field; a piece of land where knights triumphed or slunk away, heavy with the sense of defeat. Even at this early hour, stands had been erected for the spectators on either side of the lists, with a higher box for the nobility and the newly married couple. Fluttering pennants adorned stands, each flag embroidered with a white daisy, the emblem of Queen Margaret. As the sun rose, slipping its gentle light over the land, bringing colour into the washed-out hues of the pre-dawn, knights began to practise, lances flashing deftly as their laughter punched the cool air. A considerable number of men had accompanied William of Halston, the bridegroom, himself an eminent knight, and their brightly coloured, round tents were pitched in a far corner of the field. Several late risers were emerging from the tents, faces white and flabby with sleep, eyes bloodshot from their various excesses the previous night, as they cast weary, sideways glances at the men already dressed, already in the saddle.

Fabien Matravers saw all this as he trudged towards the castle. The soles of his feet ached; his stomach growled with hunger. Watching the flags snapping in the sharp breeze, he scoured his memory, trying to recall what the occasion might be. As he entered the castle gates, people scarcely noticed him, bustling about carrying piles of plates, and linen tablecloths hither and thither. Ah! He remembered: the marriage of Serena of Stow to young William of Halston. The lad possessed a mere five-and-twenty years, yet had already inherited the vast lands and estates of his father on his death a year ago. The Lady Serena was a close friend of the Queen, who had graciously allowed the marriage to take place at Abberley.

After some searching, he eventually found his wife in Alice's chamber, kneeling on the floor in front of a large oak coffer, rifling through their daughter's clothes.

'Fabien, it's you!' Eyes widening, wrinkles forming in her smooth forehead, she jerked round with a start of guilt, quickly suppressed, as he came through the door. The sun, streaming through the east window, shone full in her face, and she screwed her eyes up against the brightness. Her skin, heavy with white powder, gleamed like a mask, unnatural in the radiant light.

'Aye, returned to you, my love,' he quipped, 'and all in one piece!' He stepped over to her, bent down and took her limp hands in his.

'Why did they let you go?' Beatrice arched one non-existent eyebrow in query, a sulky twist to her mouth. Her abrupt question implied that she would have pre-

ferred him to remain a prisoner; indeed, she had hoped
Fabien wouldn't return until Alice was safely dispatched
with Edmund. 'I wasn't aware that the Queen paid a
ransom.'

'I fear she may have to pay a great deal more than
a ransom,' Fabien replied enigmatically, unwilling to
share the details of how Alice had been involved in his
release.

'No matter, you're back, safe and well,' his wife
replied. There was no warmth in her words. Already she
was turning back to the task in hand, shaking out the
gown spread over her lap, sighing with dismay. 'Really,
that girl does not possess a single decent thing to wear!'

'For the wedding?'

'For her wedding, Alice's wedding,' Beatrice corrected him. 'Edmund's father is ill, and he would like
to see his son and Alice married before he dies. It will
be a small affair.' She fed her husband the rest of the
explanation, all the while hoping that Fabien wouldn't
hear the distorted notes of fabrication in her speech.
He wouldn't approve of the real plan, not even with the
promise of wealth and comfort in their old age.

'It all seems so sudden,' Fabien mused. 'And she's
been through so much.'

'Of course it's sudden!' Beatrice rapped back at him.
'No one plans to be ill, do they?'

Fabien held up his big, capable hands, hoping to
appease her. He was used to such agitation in his wife;
rarely a day went past without some crisis or other
affecting Beatrice. 'How does Alice feel about it? I
know she and Edmund have been friends, but marriage…?'

'Alice has agreed to the marriage. It's the least she

can do after everything she's put us through.' Beatrice screwed her lips together, an expression of distaste. She lowered her head, unwilling to meet her husband's searching glance. Would he look into her eyes, pools of aquamarine, and read the lies in their blue depths? She had no intention of telling her husband exactly what she was doing; he would probably prevent it from even happening. He had always been far too sentimental over his daughter.

'Father!' Alice burst through the door. Beatrice winced, her shoulders lifting in tension as her daughter bounded into the chamber. Alice threw her arms around Fabien, laughing, hugging him close, burying her head in his shoulder to savour the warm, familiar smell of him. Stepping back at last, her hands still linked with his, she scoured his face for any signs of mistreatment.

'I am well, daughter.' His kind face twinkled down at her, immediately reaasuring. 'They treated me well.'

'Just look at your muddy boots! And your braies!' Concern brushed Alice's bright face.

'Since when has such a thing worried you?' Beatrice interjected. She adjusted her weight on her heels, trying to assuage the painful prickling sensation in her feet, before clasping the edge of the coffer to lever herself into a standing position. 'I'll leave you two now; I have other work to do.'

Fabien nodded briefly in his wife's direction by way of acknowledgement, but already the door was closing behind her.

'Did they make you walk the whole way?' Alice demanded.

'Nay, I rode most of it, and only walked for the last little bit.'

'On your own?' Her voice held the sting of accusation. Oh, but she wanted to blame these Yorkists for something!

'Not on my own, daughter,' her father answered in his measured, level tone. 'Bastien de la Roche came with me, most of the way, to be truthful.'

'Him!' The name sent unwelcome ripples of arousal piping through her slim frame. The memory of his skilful lips upon hers slashed into her brain; she caught her breath, shocked by the vivid image. How could a name affect her thus? Was she really so weak-willed that she couldn't drive him from her thoughts?

'Alice?' Her father touched her hand.

Disorientated, she smiled weakly at him. 'At least they had the decency to escort you.'

'As they escorted you,' her father reminded her, watching her closely. 'As he escorted you. Alice…did something happen on the journey?'

'Nay…nothing.' Her words rang hollow, the treacherous memory of Bastien's fingers sifting through her hair scorching her brain. Why did everything seem different since she had met him? It was if he had altered her internal perception, her way of looking at things.

'Did the Queen suspect anything while he was here?'

'She didn't. He was all charm. In fact, I think she was quite taken with him.'

'He's a clever fellow, and far better company on a journey than a lowly foot soldier. Despite his support for the Duke, I liked him as a man.'

Alice frowned. She didn't want her father to like Bastien, especially when she was doing everything in her power to not like him.

'And Bastien definitely returned to Ludlow?'

'Aye, I watched him gallop in that direction; I suppose that was his intention. The Duke of York means to have an audience with our young Queen. I think Bastien was going to meet up with them *en route.*'

'How much time have we before they arrive here?' Alice chewed at her bottom lip until it reddened.

Fabien shrugged his shoulders, rubbed a distracted hand through his shaggy blond hair. 'I'd say at the earliest, tomorrow.'

'Then Edmund and I must leave before they arrive.' Alice smiled wanly. 'I suppose Mother has told you?'

'Aye…but, are you sure this is what you want?'

Alice stuck her chin into the air, pulled her spine straight. 'Of course, Father. Edmund and I will suit each other very well.' But inside, her stomach crawled with doubt.

Bastien folded his arms across the broad expanse of his chest, and leaned back against the stone wall of a cottage, looking up towards the gatehouse of Abberley Castle. All around him, people streamed towards the castle, the dun-coloured rags of the peasants contrasting strongly with the brighter colours of the nobles and soldiers on horseback. The wedding would make it easier for him to slip back into the castle. No one gave him a second glance. For a few gold coins he had managed to secure some rough working clothes in a nearby village; he carried his own garments in a cloth bag slung over his shoulder. A low wide-brimmed hat shadowed his face, and a voluminous tunic with its frayed hems effectively hid his muscle-bound frame, though did nothing to disguise his height.

He needed to check Alice was safe; she wouldn't

even have to know he was there. As he had ridden further and further away from Abberley after bidding adieu to her father, an uneasy feeling began to grow, hard and unwieldy, in his gut. He had tried to tell himself it was better not to become involved, that he was a fool for interfering, but every time he did, his mind bounced back to Edmund's shifting brown eyes and Alice's bright open features. With a bolt of amazement he realised that he was involved already. Involved with *her.* Levering the bulk of one shoulder against the wall, he joined the busy throng of people trailing their way up to the castle.

Once in the stands, squashed between a large lady who smelled of fish, and an old man who shouted to his companion through a couple of rotten teeth, Bastien scoured the high benches on the other side of the lists where the nobility sat. An embroidered canopy covered the stands, shading the Queen and her entourage beneath from the strong sunlight. Bastien screwed up his eyes in an effort to discern the individual features of the spectators; his perusal moving steadily along the row of nobles, the gossamer veils of the ladies fluttering like pale colourful moths in the faint breeze. Alice sat at the end of the row, the polished skin of her face shining out with a healthy glow, compared with the heavily rouged and powdered faces of the court ladies at her side. At the sight of her, the muscles in his neck and shoulders slackened, his body slumping fractionally with relief. At least she was safe, for now. And that weasel Edmund was nowhere to be seen.

A bugle sounded to the left, signalling the beginning of the tournament, swiftly followed by a rousing cheer from the spectators. The two knights on horseback, who faced each other from opposite ends of the lists, lowered their visors and their lances, their horses pawing the ground in excitement. And then with a roar from the crowd they were off, hooves throwing up great clods of grassy mud, as they raced towards each other at breakneck speed, meeting each other with a clash of metal upon metal. No one was thrown, so the contestants carried on to the end, to turn, and have another go. In that moment, Bastien raised his head to look up towards Alice once more. The spot where she had sat was empty.

Alice had seen him. Her mind, busy with the details of her imminent departure with Edmund, refused to settle on anything, her eyes roving over the crowds, the contestants, anything, but never still. But then her gaze had hooked on to a tall peasant weaving his way through the crowded stands opposite, the big bulk gently shouldering people aside in an effort to gain a seat, and she knew, from the distinctive set of the broad shoulders, to the lean contours of the shadowed face beneath the hat—she wasn't certain which particular detail gave him away, but she knew. Her stomach flipped, then plummeted with the knowledge. If Bastien was here, then the Duke of York would not be far behind, and once he arrived, any thought of she and Edmund leaving would be out of the question. The castle would be seized, all movements in and out halted, whilst the Duke talked to the Queen. And as Edmund's father's life hung in the balance, they didn't have a moment to waste.

Her shoulders hunched forwards, as if anticipating the imaginary steel bars of a cage dropping over her. She and Edmund had to leave, and leave now! As soon as the two contestants set off, hurtling towards each other in an impressive blur of flashing steel and vibrant colours, she slipped away, unnoticed.

Edmund was sprawling in an ornately carved oak chair in front of the fire in the great hall, enjoying a late breakfast. Chewing slowly on a bread roll, he lifted a pewter mug of mead to his mouth to wash it down, following Alice's rapid strides across the hall towards him, her face stricken and pale.

'What's the matter?' He set down the tankard on the scrubbed wooden trestle table before him.

She stopped abruptly, skirts swishing over the flag-stones and leaned down to him. 'We need to leave, now!'

He sighed. Why did she always do this? Once a plan was set, why did she always try to change it, or alter it in some way? She was going to give him indigestion at this rate! 'But…the plan was to leave later on today.'

'It might be too late,' she whispered. 'My father tells me the Duke of York is on his way; we'll never be able to leave if he seizes the castle.'

'You're worrying too much.' Edmund placed a gentle hand on her shoulder. 'I've heard nothing about the Duke.'

Alice stepped back, chewing anxiously on a nail. Should she tell him about Bastien? 'Edmund, please, it's imperative that we leave today…or I don't think it will happen.' A pair of dragon-green eyes loomed before her.

Edmund spread his hands over his knees, studied his neat, tidy nails with admiration. Most of the plan was in place already—would it really make that much difference? Alice seemed jittery, out of sorts; it would be just like her to change her mind completely and refuse to go at all. And he wasn't about to let a chunk of money that would set him up for life slide through his fingers for the sake of a handful of hours.

'Very well—' he nodded '—we'll leave now.'

They rode in a northerly direction for most of the day, the wind behind them, helpfully nudging at their backs. No one had seen them ride out from the stables at Abberley, horses saddled and packed with leather satchels containing a few clothes.

'Don't take much,' Edmund had said, as he watched her stuffing a couple of gowns into the bag. 'Once we are married, I'll be able to buy you anything you need.'

She nodded jerkily, eyes downcast.

Edmund frowned; Alice looked tired, her face white and drawn. He'd need to make sure she had some colour in her cheeks when she met his uncle. 'Don't look so worried.' He smiled at her.

Alice tossed her head back, stretching her neck upwards towards the blue cerulean skies, the sunshine. Her cloak billowed out behind her, the material shifting and rippling over the horse's rump. Above her, a buzzard wheeled in the warm air, its haunting cry circling. Normally she would delight in galloping through the huge rolling green hills, the wind in her hair, but somehow, she couldn't help feeling she was riding towards her doom.

'Alice…. A…l…ice, stop, will you!' Edmund shouted at her back. Shifting around in the saddle, loose golden strands of hair fanning over her face, she was surprised to see how far behind he actually was. She slowed her horse to walking pace, and then to a halt.

'What is it?' The breeze threatened to whisk her question away.

'Don't go so fast,' Edmund whined, bumping irregularly against the saddle as his horse approached hers. 'We can't all be expert riders like you.'

'Sorry,' Alice replied, quietly. 'I thought we could make some good headway, across this open plain.'

'You must remember,' Edmund continued in a tight, fastidious tone, 'that this is something you do every day, whereas I—'

'Prefer the finer things in life. Aye, I know.' Alice grinned. Edmund made no secret of the fact that he positively detested any activity that took place outdoors. 'How much further is it?' Alice lifted herself up in the saddle, stretching out the muscles in her legs.

'We should be there by sunset, even going at my speed,' Edmund surmised. 'I wouldn't mind stopping for a while, to rest the horses, and have something to eat.'

Alice looked about her. 'We'd have to drop down into that valley to find water.' She pointed over to her left, where a line of stunted hawthorns indicated land sloping down.

Edmund nodded and kicked his horse onwards.

They descended into a narrow wooded valley. There was a faint sheep track that the horses were able to pick their way along, but before long it became impossibly steep, and they had to dismount, walking before the animals, leading them by the reins. As they descended, rags of white cloud above their heads seemed to bunch together and darken. Alice shivered as she led the way down, gnarled fingers of the trees snaring at her clothes like human hands. Access to the river was difficult, but eventually they found a place where the land levelled off to shallow water, allowing the horses to drink.

'I don't like this place.' Alice turned her wide blue eyes to Edmund. 'It has a sense of foreboding.' Her eyes flicked over the dense trees crowding the valley sides. 'Let's keep going.'

'Don't be silly,' Edmund said heartily. He had already spread his cloak over a dome-shaped rock and was proceeding to unwrap various packages of food. 'Come, sit beside me and eat. You'll feel better with a bit of food inside you.'

Alice wrapped her arms around her. 'Nay, I think I'll stretch my legs. I'll see if I can find another track leading out of this place in the right direction.'

Edmund frowned. 'Don't go too far,' he mumbled through a huge mouthful of bread. Crumbs spilled down over the front of his tunic; he brushed them away carefully.

'Nay, I won't.' Alice began to pick her way over the smooth rocks, towards the point where the trees formed a boundary with the river. In the muddy bank at the edge of the expanse of stones, tree roots had been exposed by the sporadic flooding of the river cutting into the earthen sides. She used their sinewy strength to haul herself up into the forest.

Out of nowhere, a large hand grabbed her questing fingers, pulling her bodily up the slope, wrenching her right shoulder. She was spun around, an arm clamped around her waist pulling her swiftly backwards, out of sight. Disorientated, shaken, she tried to open her mouth, to shout, to squeak, anything, but strong fingers over her face prevented all sound. Her eyes closed involuntarily as her attacker pushed her backwards against a tree, his other hand spread across her stomach, holding her there.

'Open your eyes.'

Fear turned to anger, hot blazing fury. Her eyes shot open.

Bastien stood before her—nay, towered over her, a wide-brimmed felt hat jammed at an angle on his head. Beneath the shadow of the brim, his eyes glittered, chips of green emerald. 'Are you going to scream?' His voice was low, a whisper on the breeze.

She shook her head violently, wanting to hit him. A thousand questions rippled through her mind. 'What are you doing here?' she hissed.

The warmth of his fingers dropped away from her cheek, her mouth. 'I'm saving you from yourself,' he replied enigmatically, lips twisting with a wry smile.

'You followed us?' she asked, astounded. 'Why on earth would you do that?

Why on earth, indeed? He had asked himself the same question countless times as he tracked the couple. 'Because there's something in me that can't seem to help pulling you out of tricky situations.'

'It's none of your business.' She jabbed him in the chest sharply. Her mind worked furiously. Had he returned to Abberley for *her?* Beneath the pad of her pointed forefinger his skin was hard, unyielding.

'You're a fool if you think that man is going to do any good by you.' He captured her hand against his tunic, lean powerful fingers around her delicate wrist.

'Why do you persist in trying to turn him against me? I've known him all my life; he'd never do anything to hurt me. He is going to marry me.' She lifted her chin up, challenging him. 'It's all planned out.'

But Bastien was already shaking his head. 'Nay, Alice, I can't be certain, but I think he has other plans for you, plans to marry a rich relative of his. I told you…I overheard a discussion between Edmund and your mother.'

Alice shook her head. 'And I told you why the two of them would be talking. Why would my mother ever agree to such a preposterous plan? A rich relative, indeed!' Her eyes glowed, lucent aquamarine. 'You're making all this up!'

'Why would I do that?' he replied mildly, shrugging his shoulders.

She didn't hear him, caught in her own fiery tirade. 'Why don't you leave me alone? I did what you wanted, didn't I? I got you in to see the King. What more do you want?'

I want you. The answer rushed into his head, stunning him. Her words hung in the air, shimmering between them. His eyes darkened, a brilliant jade, glowing over her with a simple promise.

A lone crow cackled above as he lowered his head down to hers, leaning his muscular frame into her. 'Nay,' she whispered, her voice shuddering under the closeness of his body against hers, her blood hurtling through her veins at the heightened sensations. She braced herself for the impact, the wide trunk at her back preventing any escape, but the moment his cool lips touched hers, her knees buckled.

'Aye,' he murmured, bracing her wilting frame with his big body, his hands cupping her neck, her jaw, as his lips roved over hers.

What in God's name was she doing? Even as her mind screamed at her to flee, to fight, her traitorous lips roamed against his, seeking more, much more. The feel of his lips sent shards of excitement, of desire, shattering through her flesh. Her hands crept upwards, curling around his wide shoulders, pulling him closer to her. Bastien groaned, his tongue flicking along the seam of her lips, seeking, questing. She opened her mouth beneath his like a flower in the sunshine, eager for his warmth, his passion, yearning for his touch.

Then, as quickly as it had begun, his head jerked backwards, his eyes closing as he fell against her, a dead weight.

'What...?' she cried out in alarm, as his big body slumped against her. She managed to support him for a moment, but he was too heavy for her, and he crashed to the forest floor. Behind him, Edmund, smiling triumphantly, held a bloodied rock.

'That should keep him quiet for a couple of hours.' He nodded at Bastien's prone form, spreadeagled amongst the brown, rotting beech nuts on the forest floor.

Alice was already crouching down, pulling off Bastien's hat to find the wound. He was very pale, but his breathing was steady.

Edmund pulled at her arm. 'Leave the bastard. Come on, before he wakes up!'

'Nay, I need to see he's alright. You could have killed him!'

Edmund frowned. 'What's it to you? He's just some local peasant taking advantage of a lone maiden. You're fortunate I found you in time.'

Beneath her fingers on his wrist, Bastien's pulse beat strongly. Thank God, she thought, still stunned by the violence of Edmund's blow—how unlike him! Tears pricked in her eyes at the unnecessary violence, a cold trail of unease crawling through her veins. Even now, Edmund stood over Bastien's prone form, holding the craggy rock aloft like a trophy, a smug, victorious smile upon his face.

Edmund didn't recognise him, of course. He had only met him that one evening at Abberley. She felt no inclination to reveal Bastien's identity and for the first time, a tiny seed of doubt began to grow in her mind. This was the second time Bastien had tried to warn her and she couldn't fathom out why he did it. Unconsciously, she smoothed one hand across the broad expanse of Bastien's chest, feeling his strong heart beat beneath her fingers.

Edmund yanked her upwards, pulling at her upper arm with a sharp tug. 'Leave him!' he ordered roughly. 'We must keep going!' He gave her a little push towards the horses. Alice hesitated, turning her head back in time to see Bastien's eyes begin to flicker as he surfaced back into consciousness. She had a powerful desire to tell Edmund to go, so that she could stay instead at Bastien's side.

Chapter Thirteen

Lord Walter of Felpersham, Edmund's uncle, was a portly, florid-faced man of about sixty winters. He slumped back in his chair, alone, at the top table, his fleshy lips slicked with grease. Stripping the chicken bone of its last piece of meat, he tossed it to one of the dogs trotting expectantly below the high dais.

'Welcome, welcome.' He lifted one arm in greeting, spotting Alice and Edmund entering the great hall through the main door. A long strand of grey hair fell across one eye; he pushed it away in irritation, peering with excitement at his new visitors.

'Well, well, well.' His small, sunken eyes feasted on Alice's slender figure as she mounted the steps to the dais. 'What a tasty morsel we have here.' He ran a thick tongue around greasy lips, nodding approvingly at his nephew. 'You have done well, Edmund. You promised me she would have beauty, and so she has.'

Alice's skin crawled at the thread of lust in Walter's words. Who was this man? Surely not Edmund's father!

'This is my uncle, Alice,' Edmund introduced her.

'And where is your father?' she shot back.

'I expect he is in his chambers.' Edmund raised his eyebrows in mock query at his uncle, who nodded back in conformation. 'How is he?'

Walter burped loudly, wiping his sleeve across his mouth. 'Not well, my boy, not well at all. Thank goodness you made it before…' His words faded as he stared at a point on Alice's chest.

'Then maybe we should go and see him,' Alice suggested, appealing to Edmund with a sense of desperation. Although it was not late into the evening, she wanted nothing more than to disappear up to bed. The uneasy feeling she had experienced on leaving Bastien sprawled in the forest had refused to diminish, but she continually damped it down, attributing it to pre-wedding jitters.

'Not yet, Alice,' Edmund countered. 'Let's eat something first. I'm starving.' He plonked himself down at the table, indicating that Alice should do the same. Sitting next to Edmund, she prayed that his lecherous uncle would retire, and leave them in peace, but to her dismay, he was already pouring himself a large goblet of wine, and for her, as well.

She shivered slightly, her limbs thawing in the heat of the room. Nothing about this journey northwards had been as expected; instead it was tainted with something unfamiliar, sinister. Guilt soaked through her, a rolling wave of shame, as her mind continually recalled the sprawling, unconscious figure of Bastien in the forest. She should not have left him, she realised that now— why couldn't she have been stronger, more forceful with Edmund? But somehow, she knew that if she had stayed, then the whole direction of her life would change for ever. And her future lay with Edmund. It was her duty.

A pewter plate was set before her, a servant placing a lump of barely cooked, gristly meat upon it, followed by bread, a few vegetables. She stared at it with no appetite, her mouth dry.

'Come on, eat up, my lady.' Walter jostled her from the left. 'You're going to need all the energy you can get.' His insinuation was unmistakable, and she blushed, a hot, livid colour flowing across her face. Her nose wrinkled; Edmund's uncle obviously hadn't taken a bath for a few days and now the smell of stale sweat mingling with meat fat made her stomach roil.

'You need to drink up, as well,' Walter continued, slopping yet more wine into her goblet, despite that fact that she hadn't drunk anything yet. The voluminous gathered sleeve of his tunic brushed across the table with the movement, gathering crumbs. Recalling her last brush with alcohol, she took a small tentative sip.

'Oh, come on, Alice, you can drink more than that,' Edmund accosted her jovially, leaning forwards so she could see his face past Walter's flabby jowls. 'Surely this marriage is a cause for celebration?'

'I don't see how we can celebrate when your father is lying upstairs,' she responded disapprovingly, surprised that Edmund hadn't even gone upstairs yet to visit him. She lifted the unwieldy goblet and took a few sips, just to appease him. Why did she feel so leaden?

Walter belched loudly, then pushed his chair back. 'Must go and see that everything is prepared. Especially that good-for-nothing priest of mine.' He winked sideways at Edmund, before prodding fleshy fingers into Alice's forearm. 'Not long to wait now, my lady,' he leered at her. 'Make sure this little lady drinks up,' he ordered Edmund before he rose, and lumbered off, his shuffling step accompanied by another powerful belch.

Relieved that he had gone, Alice leaned across to Edmund. 'Does that mean we'll be married tonight?'

Edmund grabbed her cold fingers. 'It's for the best, Alice. We have no idea when my father...' His voice trailed off, miserably.

Alice nodded, understanding.

'Have some more wine,' Edmund said helpfully. 'It'll make you feel better.'

Her head was swimming already; she was surprised at how soporific it made her feel. 'I'd better not drink too much. It makes me feel quite giddy.'

'Don't worry, I'll look after you.' Edmund's voice was gentle, reassuring. Was it her imagination or did Edmund appear to be a little blurred, as if he were in a dream? She shook her head, trying to clear her vision.

'I feel very strange.' Her tongue felt huge, unwieldy. Even speaking seemed to involve a great deal of effort. What was the matter with her? A trickle of panic gripped her stomach—what was happening to her? 'Edmund...I'm not well.' Her heart knocked against the wall of her chest, an irregular beat.

'Nay, you're exhausted from the journey.' Edmund's voice poured over her from a long way away. Now he was at her side, hoisting her bodily out of the chair. Her legs and arms refused to work in a co-ordinated fashion and she heard him summon a castle guard to take her other arm. 'I think he gave her too much,' Edmund chuckled above her head to the other man.

His words sent ricochets of fear slicing through her brain. Too much of *what?* Sweet Mother of Mary, what kind of nightmare had she landed herself in? As they half-lifted, half-dragged her towards the door, she forced herself not to panic, to slow her breathing and to think. 'Edmund, stop! Please stop!' she endeavoured to force the words out, but the two men either couldn't hear her or chose to ignore her. She sagged against their hold, thinking to slow them, but between the two of them they could carry her easily, even with her puny resistance.

Undefeated, she gathered every last vestige of strength to scream his name, to make him hear her. 'Edmund!'

At last! With one palm flat on the door panels, about to push it open, he paused in his determined stride, angling his head solicitously towards her. His features bobbled before her face. 'Aye, my sweet?' His tone held the faintest trace of mockery.

'What…is…going…on?' She forced the words out on a squeeze of breath, fighting the engulfing torpor that swirled in her brain. The soldier on her left adjusted his hold on her upper arm.

'Haven't you guessed yet?' His smiling mouth closed in on her face, a threatening twist to his lips. 'I would have thought your quick little mind would have worked it out hours ago. You're going to marry Felpersham.'

'Wh-what?' Every last thread of reality vanished into the shimmering light of nightmare at his words; her head jerked back in shock. Her fingers clung to the soft material of Edmund's tunic sleeve. 'But…I was going to marry you.'

'Felpersham's promised me a great deal of money in return for a maid like you.' His features, undulating close to her face, seemed to take on a weird sense of proportion, his mouth and nose huge, his eyes receding, tiny. Guttering candles lit his face from the side, giving him a monstrous aspect.

'Nay.' Her head drooped in sadness, shoulders hunching forwards, unable to look at him, shattered beyond belief at the huge betrayal. Sweet Mother of Mary, Bastien had been right all along, and she had thrown his advice right back in his face.

'How could you do this to me?' A single tear rolled over her cheek. 'How could you?' Nausea made her gorge rise; swaying, she wondered vaguely whether she might be sick.

'You never wanted to marry me anyway, Alice. Admit it. I have always been the friend, nothing more. Our marriage would have been dull beyond belief; this way I'll be rich.'

'So money means more to you than our friendship.'

'Aye, it does.'

Alice crumpled momentarily against the soldier, the flagstone floor looming close in her vision, blood pumping fast through her veins. Despite her outward appearance of weakness, of docility, inside her mind worked fast. Felpersham had obviously slipped something in her wine, hence the reason why they had constantly urged her to drink. But she had only taken a few sips, barely swallowed. Already her head was beginning to clear, and she could feel the strength returning to her limbs. If she could keep up the pretence of someone who was almost incapable of walking, then maybe she could seize an opportunity to escape. She tracked back to the moment they had arrived at Felpersham's castle, recalling details about the layout—had there been a moat, a high curtain wall? With those details steadily building in her mind, she might find a way out. She would not give up. She would fight, fight this man who she had believed to be her friend, and she would escape this fate he had engineered for her, even if she had to die trying.

Between them, the two men shouldered her through the thick oak door, its wide panels studded with iron rivets, and out into the cobbled expanse of the inner bailey. Above, stars twinkled in the vast bowl of dark blue velvet, the clear skies promising frost on the morrow. As the cool, sweet-smelling air rushed over her, Alice, her head still hanging with the supposed effects of the sedative, rapidly gained her bearings. The castle gatehouse sat to her left, heavily guarded; on her right, steps led up to the battlements. If they reached the chapel it would be too late; it was now or never.

She slumped heavily within their arms, stopping any forward movement, shivering dramatically. 'I don't feel too well,' she whimpered, raising one limp hand to her forehead. 'Edmund, fetch my mantle, would you? It's on the chair…back there.' She lolled her head in the direction of the great hall.

Edmund scowled, rolling his eyes at the soldier over her neat head. 'It's not much further, Alice, just over there.' He pointed out the arched doorway of the chapel, the stone fretwork of the windows from which a flickering light spilled, ominous. Inside, Felpersham waited for her, and if they tarried too long, he would no doubt come looking to see what held them up.

'Please, Edmund.' Her voice wavered; she was careful to keep the sense of urgency from her tone. 'It's only a couple of steps.' He must not guess, must not realise that she had regained her strength.

Edmund regarded her faltering, pathetic figure: she did look pale. 'Sweet Jesu!' He relented. 'This is going to take all night! Keep going with her,' he ordered the soldier. 'I'll be back in a moment.'

As soon as Edmund vanished through the oak doorway, the latch clicking solidly in place, Alice lunged at the guard, forcing him to stagger away. He released his grip, surprised by her sudden burst of strength. With the look of astonishment pinned to the soldier's face still in her mind, she ran. Ran as if her whole life depended on it. Blood pumped through her veins, her muscles, giving her the extra burst of energy she needed to fly from this awful place. Her nimble feet sprinkled over the cobbles, slippers barely touching the ground, bobbing and weaving through the milling servants, who, only after she had passed through them, heard the frantic shouts of the soldier, and of Edmund. 'Stop her! Hold her!' But she was already halfway up the steps to the battlements, her steps determined and sure, the green fabric of her dress shining against the grey stones of the wall. She climbed up, the muscles in her thighs tight with exertion, to the top of the grey wall, to the square-cut crenellations. Up here, the wind snagged at her hair, her veil, and she wrested the white fabric from her head, knowing it would flag up her position in the darkness. The battlement soldiers moved in towards her, one to her left, one to her right. They were grinning, believing she was trapped; there was nowhere else for her to go.

Panic laced around her heart, tightened its cold fingers. Stepping up into the gap between the crenellations, fingers rasping against the granular stone, Alice prayed that her judgement had been correct, that the wall, at this point, was not too high above the moat. She took a deep, steadying breath, and jumped. The rush of air ballooned out her skirts, searing her legs with icy breath. Seconds later, the waters closed over her head, and she plunged down and down, hoping her legs wouldn't suddenly judder and crumble against a solid bottom. But nay, the moat was deep, her saviour! She began to bob back up again, but before she reached the surface, she struck out to the right, underwater, hoping to confuse her trail. Thank the lord her brother had taught her to swim, to be strong in one's body! She pulled herself steadily under the water, until her lungs screamed out with the need for oxygen. Breaking the surface carefully, water streaming across her eyes and face, it took a moment for Alice to realise that the opposite bank was close by. She struck out towards it, knowing that it wouldn't take long for the castle guards to make their way around to this point. Her gown, saturated with water, clung around her legs, slowing her. She flung herself towards the bank, hands reaching out to slip futilely against the long strands of wet grass. Brambles, sprouting vigorously from the damp earth, tore at her skin, but in her anxiety to drag herself out, she grabbed at them again and again, making her palms bleed. Hot tears of frustration poured from her eyes—nay, not now! She couldn't fail now! Hopelessness clawed at her heart—was marriage to Felpersham to be her fate after all?

The winding creak of the drawbridge being lowered clanged dully in the breeze; her time was running out. Gouging desperately into the soft mud beneath the grass, her nails filled with sticky earth. Exhaustion began to sap her lively strength, the constant treading of water to keep upright in the deep water began to tire her; as the energy leaked out from her, all she wanted was to lay down her head and rest.

And then, out of the darkness, a hand, a warm rough hand, grasped her fingers.

Wild fear made her lunge backwards, trying to escape the grip, but she only succeeded in wrenching the muscles in her shoulder. The hand held her fast, began to lift her sodden weight out of the moat. Nay! Nay! She shook her head in dismay, despair. This could not be happening! The moment her feet touched the flat grass beyond the bank, she sprung at the dark shape, pushing, twisting to free herself. At her back, the sound of hooves, of raised voices.

'Nay!' she yelled at her captor, unable to push her matted wet hair from her eyes as both her hands were held by now. 'I'll not do it! You cannot make me do it!'

A hand came over her mouth, sealing her speech. 'Hush now, it's me. Come on!' The dark, looming shape took on more familiar lines, the broad shoulders, the high cheekbones…Bastien?

'What are you doing here?' Relief sapped at her knees; she stumbled alongside him over the rough ground, aware of his arm around her back, supporting her. His horse waited on the edge of a copse of trees, patiently cropping the grass.

'Up!' He hoisted her drenched form on to his horse, swinging his body into the saddle behind her. The hem of her skirts dripped sparkles of water over the animal's side, highlighted by the eerie light of a low three-quarters moon. Bastien kicked his heels inwards, urging his horse to move quietly into the shadow of the trees.

Her mind was rife with unanswered questions, cushioned against a background of pure, unadulterated relief.

'What are you doing here?' she murmured, pallid and wilting against him, grateful for the support of his wide, hard chest at her back.

Hot breath fanned against her damp ear. 'Talk later,' he whispered. 'The sound will carry easily in the night air. Hopefully they'll think you've drowned in the moat. Which, of course, is nothing less than you deserve.'

Alice's gown stuck uncomfortably to her in wet, cloying folds, making her restless, muscles tense. 'What is this place?' She clasped her arms tightly about her chest, trying to stop her teeth chattering.

Bastien shrugged his shoulders, glancing up at the crumbling stone walls, the shaggy green ferns sprouting from precarious heights. 'An old keep, by the looks of it. It should give us some shelter for the night.' The moon had risen high, its unearthly light slanting across the inner walls, illuminating Bastien's rugged outline as he looked across to her.

'Will they come after us? Will they find us?' Her fingers clenched nervously against her stomach.

He caught the fear in her trembling tone, and scowled, moving swiftly over the bumpy ground to pick up sticks for a fire. There would be time for questions later, after he had made sure she was warm and dry. 'Nay, it's unlikely. I think we've put enough distance between us.'

She sagged visibly at his terse reassurance, vaguely wondering if her legs would hold her. Their journey had been long and hard, conducted at full gallop, Bastien's heavy arm about her offering some security. Despite being used to riding, her whole body ached from the effort of trying to stay on the horse, the muscles in her cheeks stiff from the icy wind blowing into her face.

Alice hopped from one foot to another, aware of a frozen numbness creeping up her legs. Shame washed over her, as she watched Bastien hunch down over the small pile of sticks, shame at her own stupidity, for not believing him. 'Thank you,' she whispered. 'Thank you for being there, at the edge of the moat.' Her breath jagged on a rising sob, and she bit her lip to stop herself descending into a mass of quivering weeping. 'If you hadn't come…'

Crouched down on the earth, he paused in his efforts to light the fire, locked his head on one side, his eyes fierce. 'It was a foolish thing to do! You could have been killed!'

'Wh-what?' Shuttered by the cold, her fuddled mind refused to grasp his meaning.

He stood up, stepping towards her. Dry bracken crunched underfoot, the sound bouncing up the walls. 'Jumping off the battlements! What on earth possessed you?' He stopped, inches away, the silver thread of his cote-hardie gleaming in the moonlight. He had ditched the rough peasant clothes in the forest when he had come around from Edmund's attack.

'I…h-had no choice,' she responded jerkily. An uncontrollable shaking seemed to have taken hold of her, her hands unsteady as she lifted them self-consciously to her face. 'I…I had to get away before it was too late.'

Bastien shook his head, his mouth set in a grim line. Christ, when he had seen her there, perched up between the gap in the stone crenellations, her white veil float-ing in the air above, away from her, he had thought he

was too late. And then, when she had jumped, straight
as an arrow, her skirts flying about her slender limbs,
it was as if someone had driven a shard of glass direct
into the centre of his heart. In that single, heart-stopping
moment, he thought he had lost her, would never see
her bright sunny face again.

'I was coming for you.' The possessiveness of his
tone wrapped about her, warming her.

'Why?' Her voice wavered. 'You had no reason
to. Especially after we...I treated you so badly in the
forest.'

I had every reason to, he thought, yet somehow he
couldn't say the words out loud. Her quiet beauty drew
him at every turn; he couldn't let her go. 'I knew that
Edmund was up to something.' His answer was bland,
but she seemed to accept it.

'What a fool I was!' Alice stuttered the words out
through chattering lips, bowing her head. She had been
utterly and completely betrayed.

His fingers touched her chin, tipped her face so she
was compelled to look into those untamed eyes of green.
The weak light of the rising moon kissed her skin, turning it to pure alabaster.

'How could you have known?' he said gently. God,
but she was stunning! Coils of her hair fell down about
her face in loose wet tendrils.

Alice rubbed one ear, releasing a trickle of moat
water, a rueful expression playing across her features.
'I should have listened to you...' She lifted one shaking
hand, stretching it out towards his haphazard blond hair.
'How is it...your head, I mean?' Her question ended
in a violent quivering rippling through her body; she
seemed unable to control it.

'It was nothing.' He dismissed it easily. Yet when he had come round in that deserted forest, finding her gone, it had been everything. He had picked himself up, ignoring the trickle of blood at his collar, and scoured the area, his steps determined and resolute until he picked up their trail once more.

'I'd better look at it,' Alice ventured practically, trying to impart a brisk efficiency in her tone. What was the matter with her? Her movements were stiff, jerky as she came towards him, her stumbling feet like lumps of rock against the mossy floor.

He stopped her gently, wrapping loose fingers about her forearms to hold her away from him, smiling. How like her to concern herself with others when she herself was in trouble. 'Alice, I think you're more in need of my help at the moment.' His eye ran over her shivering, shaking frame, her skin pale and luminous in the rising moonlight, her lips violet-blue. 'You need to take off those wet clothes.'

'Oh…' Doubt creased her forehead. 'Nay, it's not necessary. I just need to sit down.' Her face blazed at the thought of undressing before him.

But already Bastien had moved behind her, his fingers at the knot that laced her gown together. 'I've seen great men felled by the cold,' he murmured, 'and I'm not about to let it happen to you, a girl barely half their size. Now is not the time for maidenly modesty.'

Alice closed her eyes, her body resisting, rigid against his vigorous tugging. Bastien was right about the cold, and she couldn't unlace the gown herself. She had no choice but to co-operate and retain as much of her dignity as possible.

His big knuckles scuffed the soft fur of her V-shaped

collar, as his fingers fumbled with the knotted end of the laces at the back of her gown. His heart lurched at the sensation, the delicate tickle of the fur sending his senses raging; inwardly he groaned. The water had swelled the fabric of the laces, tightening the knot fast. As his fingers worked, his eyes travelled up the delicate line of Alice's spine, to the nape of her neck where her hair drooped precariously, heavily, in its haphazard bun. His heart quickened; he took a deep shuddering breath, as his fingers dipped behind the bodice of her dress, brushing again and again against the soft, cool skin of her back.

'I suppose it's quite difficult,' Alice ventured. Her head lolled forwards; she was so tired. All that fear from before, the raw panic of having to think on her feet, knowing her whole future was in jeopardy, had been replaced by a sapping exhaustion.

'Aye, you could say that,' Bastien ground out. A sweet, fresh smell rose from her damp skin; he fought the churning desire in his body, his jaw rigid and set. He told himself what he was doing was entirely necessary; if the wet clothes remained next to her skin, then she would surely suffer. Concerned by the dullness in her voice, her wilting stance, he pulled out his knife, impatiently slicing through the length of criss-cross lacing. The two sides of her bodice fell sideways to reveal her damp, crumpled kirtle, and he seized the shoulders of the gown, dragging the fitted sleeves firmly down her arms, so that the skirts eventually pooled in a heap at her feet.

'You've broken it,' she chastised him miserably, raising her head in mild protest.

He didn't reply, merely repeating his actions with

the unfitted kirtle. Below, Alice wore a loose chemise, diaphanous in gauzy cotton.

'It was taking too long—' he rounded on her '—and you're just too cold.' He clenched his fists, trying to ignore the enticing shadowy curve of her hips beneath the thin fabric. 'Here,' he said gruffly, sliding out of his cote-hardie, settling the heavy fabric around Alice's shoulders. 'Come and sit over here, and I'll light a fire.' He strode away from her, leaving her to follow. She paused, savouring the weighted warmth of the pleated wool wrapped around her like a balm, stilling her shredded nerves. She tripped in his wake, holding the loose swinging sides of the cote-hardie together with frozen fingers.

Alice collapsed on to the blanket he had spread out for her, wriggling her hips to settle herself comfortably, watching Bastien as he squatted down to light the fire. Without his cote-hardie, the full dramatic length of his legs was revealed; the fine wool of his chausses strained against his big thigh muscles as he crouched over the sticks, striking a flint into a dry bundle of grass. A single strand caught the spark, flared. Shoving it into the middle of the sticks, Bastien breathed gently on it until flames licked greedily upwards. The sudden heat knocked against Alice's face, and she leaned into it, like a flower into the sun.

'What happened back there?' Bastien sat back on his heels, studying the fire. His voice was quiet.

Alice hunched forward over her bent legs, winding her arms around her shins. 'Edmund had arranged to marry me to Lord Felpersham.' Her voice hitched on the memory. 'Felpersham promised to pay him a great deal of coin for me.' She pressed her face into the warm fabric over her knees. 'It was horrible,' she mumbled into the cloth, her shoulders beginning to shudder. 'They put something in my drink, I couldn't walk…' Huge, great sobs stopped her speech, rolling up from the depths of her chest, racking her slim frame.

'Don't…' Bastien was beside her, arms coming around her back to hug her close. 'If only I'd reached the castle sooner.' Hot, blinding rage rose within him, the urge to kill, to kill Edmund and Felpersham for what they had done to Alice. His fingers curled in his palms, tight.

Tears streamed down her face as she turned to look at him. Her lashes fanned wetly against her cheeks. 'Why are you being so agreeable to me? You warned me, and I refused to listen. I brought the whole thing on myself. What a fool I am!'

'You were betrayed, Alice, by a man you had known since you were a child. How could you not trust him?'

'I should have seen it!' Her tears had stopped now; exhausted, her slim frame still racked with shudders, she rested her head into the wide crook of his shoulder, relishing the rumble of his low voice against the side of her face. 'We didn't love each other, but we both knew that. The marriage was one of convenience, but I thought it would work. For my parents' sake.' She hunched her shoulders into his big frame. 'It's difficult for you to understand.'

'Nay, I understand.'

'How?'

He tensed against her, silent. Alice crooked her head up towards him, trying to read his face in the shadows, sensing the tension in his body, the unspoken secrets behind his speech.

'Now is not the time,' he replied gruffly. 'You need to rest, sleep.' He adjusted his position against the crumbling stone wall, pulling her in more securely to his side. By his head, the limpid green fronds of a tiny fern clung precariously to the stone wall, sifting quietly in the warm draught from the fire.

'I've known Edmund since I was a child; he was my friend,' she said forlornly, 'I never thought he'd betray me. I'll never trust anyone again.' Her voice was constricted, rigid.

'Nay, Alice, that's not the way.' His low tones hugged her softly.

'Why not—surely it keeps you safe?'

Aye, but at what cost, he thought bitterly. After Katherine's death, he had shut himself off from the world, built a strong network of walls about himself, nurturing the memory of his fiancée in glorious isolation, but he had paid a high price. He had become cold-hearted, a ruthless brute with a fearsome reputation. Aye, he had friends, men he could have a laugh and a joke with, but he never trusted any of them completely.

'Safe, but removed from life, from living,' he replied. 'You could never be like that.' In the short time he had known her, he had come to cherish her bright ways, her ability to put everyone's needs, however lowly, before her own, her inner courage. He couldn't bear to think of her shutting herself off, damaged by Edmund's betrayal, curbing her passionate liveliness, her vitality.

Sparks crackled upwards from the fire into the gloom, illuminating the stone walls around them, coating them in a rosy glow.

'Why not?' she responded. 'You don't trust anyone. You seem to cope.'

She heard his sharp intake of breath, a tension rippling through his body against her.

'It's no way to be, Alice,' he said finally, his voice hollow. 'It's something I'm only just starting to realise.'

Chapter Fourteen

Alice's eyes snapped open, pure fright arcing through her body. For a moment she had believed herself to be back there, at Felpersham's castle, trapped at the side of the moat, scrabbling in the mud, helpless. But nay, she was safe. Her parcelled breath expelled slowly; relief flooded her veins. A delicious warmth penetrated the flimsy covering of her chemise; she lay on her back, Bastien's heavy arm slung over her midriff. The sides of the cote-hardie that Bastien had wrapped her in for warmth had fallen open in her sleep, but she did not feel cold now. The heat emanating from his forearm pulsed through her, setting off small, dangerous flickers of desire. The tension in her limbs softened, her initial fear on waking revolving swiftly into dangerous anticipation.

Slowly, slowly, she twisted her head on Bastien's tunic, her makeshift pillow, unwilling to wake him, hearing his deep, steady breathing. He lay just a fraction away from her, the heady, intoxicating vibrancy of him heating the length of her body. Her stomach somersaulted, peculiar sensations flipping through her veins. So close! In the moonlight, his tousled hair shone a pale gold colour, his bold features appearing as if carved from stone. She studied his profile: the proud, straight nose that flared around the nostrils, giving his lean face a gentler look; the full dramatic sensuality of his mouth.

She wondered at this man, this man who had burst into her life, so violently, so vividly, that all else seemed to fade dully in comparison. Why had he come after her, when she had refused to believe him about Edmund? He hadn't criticised her, or chastised her, merely understood. He'd been kind. Aye, he had been kind, a behaviour of which she hadn't thought him capable, this brusque, athletic man of war.

His eyes sprang open, watchful, attentive, saw her eyes glimmering wide in the darkness. 'What is it?' he whispered, his half-awake voice low, slumberous.

I love you. The thought, stark and intense, burst into her brain, a shocking truth. Alice gasped, stunned by the raw, naked simplicity of her feelings.

'Are you ill?' Bastien propped himself up on one arm, concerned by her silence. Strands of golden hair fell over his forehead, shimmering in the light of the fire. Over their heads, the wind chased gently through the ruined battlements, a drawn-out, keening sigh.

'Nay,' she breathed, 'it's nothing, go back to sleep.' The cote-hardie slipping from her shoulders, she sat up abruptly, unable to think straight, pinioned by his incisive glance. 'Actually, I think I need something to drink.' She licked her lips, knowing full well that her dry mouth had little to do with thirst. Rolling sideways, she made as if to stand up, but he held her back, a hand on her shoulder.

'Let me. I'll fetch my flagon.'

Bastien returned a few moments later, carrying the leather bottle that had been strapped to the saddle, pulling the stopper out as he handed it down to her. 'Here.'

She stretched out her arm, accepting the bottle gratefully. The wide, loose sleeve of her chemise fell back along her arm, revealing its white, lustrous length, the delicate wrist, the fragile crook of her elbow. Bastien stared at it, transfixed, his heart beginning to pound. Her skin looked like silk; he ached to touch, to test its fineness beneath his fingers. Sleep chased from him; every nerve-ending came alert, shivering with awareness, with arousal.

Alice tipped the wide-necked bottle up to her lips, drank greedily. She had been thirsty after all. In her haste to drink, trickles of water spilled out from the sides of her mouth, running down over her neck. Bastien followed the sparkling path of the droplets, down, down over the hollowed curve of her throat, down to the low, gaping neckline of the chemise, and took a deep, shuddering breath.

'Oh dear!' Alice laughed self-consciously, springing to her feet to hand the bottle back to Bastien, wiping the sides of her wet mouth with the back of her arm.

'I didn't expect that!' She crooked her head to one side, attempting to smile, conscious of a curious tension between them. The air was thick with expectancy. 'Bastien?' she ventured, willing him to break the silence.

He didn't answer. The moon, emerging briefly from behind a wreath of cloud, shone behind Alice's diminutive figure, highlighting every single, delicious curve of her body through the gossamer fabric of her chemise. The soft indentation of her waist, the tempting push of her rounded breast against the flimsy fabric, the rounded flare of her hips, all were revealed to him with striking, vibrant clarity. The heart-stopping sight of her punched him, hard, in the gut.

Self-control ruptured, blunt need clawing at him, driving out all logic, all sense of right or wrong. The water bottle dropped from his fingers, landing on the mossy earth with a soft thud. Big arms reached forwards, snaring her waist, pulling her towards him, hard, close. Alice didn't ask, didn't question; she knew what was about to happen and welcomed it. One rough thumb smoothed away the single pearl of water at the corner of her mouth, before his lips descended, brutal, rough, demanding.

Just one kiss. That was all. Just one touch of her lips to bury that burning need that consumed him, ripped through him like a forest fire. He ducked his head, dark gold strands falling over his eyes, mouth slewing over hers, insistent, demanding. At the cool press of her lips, his blood hurtled faster, his need to claim her threatening to overwhelm him. He was out of control, desire ripping through him like a wild animal, and he knew it.

Alice sank into him, cleaving her body into his, her toes grazing the ground as he hauled her against him, feeling his hardened muscles against her softness. As his mouth roamed over hers, her breath came in short, rapid pants; huge waves of desire crashed over her, relentless. She teetered on the edge of an unknown place, a place of no boundaries, of endless promise. She would go there with him, with this man she loved. The past, the future, nothing mattered any more, only this driving need, this craving that he had triggered within her, for something more than she had ever known.

With supreme effort, he wrenched his lips away, green eyes glittering, slicing over her. 'Stop me.' Blunt desire jagged at his voice. His hands cupped her shoulders, steadying her, steadying himself. A ruddy flush grazed his high cheekbones.

Alice tasted the sweetness of his breath. 'I don't want to.'

'You know what will happen.'

She nodded.

With a groan he claimed her mouth once more, bearing her down to the rumpled blanket in one easy movement. He ached to possess her, but schooled himself to go slowly, to take his time and savour this beautiful maid. There might not be another time, or place. Dragging his lips away, his hands snagged urgently in her hair, pulling out the securing pins, scattering them as the long cascades of rippling gold rope spilled around her face, down her back.

Sweet Jesu! He buried his face in that sweet-smelling mass, imbued with the fresh, clean scent of lavender. Alice laughed, sheer joy bubbling up in her heart, her tentative fingers reaching up to trace the jutting contour of his jaw, curling around to smooth the silken fronds of hair at the back of his neck, urging his head down.

'Don't stop,' she whispered.

He heard the shaky need in her hesitant plea and his heart flowered with pleasure. Such passion tucked into that slender frame, a brimming energy that matched his own vigorous desire. He had never known a woman so warm, so eager. Katherine...nay, not now. His hand slid beneath the hem of her chemise, travelling slowly, sensuously up the satiny length of her calf, her thigh.

'Bastien…?' Her stomach muscles flexed, then squeezed forcibly with gathering awareness, excitement melting within her.

'Hush now…trust me,' he whispered, his breath rasping hot against her ear. Against the velvet green of the mossy ground, her skin appeared as if covered in a sparkling net of dew. He stretched his sinewy length beside her; ripples of surprise jolted through her as she realised he was naked.

So soft, she was so soft.

He moved over her, enfolding her within the burly embrace of his body, clasping her tight, shielding her from the bright, knowing light of the moon. She gasped out loud as the scorching need of him nudged her thigh, before sliding into her tender folds, the very nub of her womanhood. Her limbs liquefied, lucid thought chased from her mind, intoxicated by the very feel of him. Her hands clung to his neck as she succumbed to the wild, tumultuous frenzy that drove through her heart, her blood.

Unable to rein himself back, he sank into her in a blaze of unstoppable passion. His blood ran fast, unchecked and wild, his heart thumping out of control as he drove into her, barely checked by the momentary resistance of her virginity, filling her completely, utterly.

Her arms fluttered outwards, the slightest whimper on her breath as he surged into her, her eyes closing under the all-consuming, forceful impact of him. Yet within a moment, the stinging ache was replaced by a mounting, churning fullness as Bastien began to move within her, sure and steady at first before gaining pace, faster and faster. Her body responded, matching his rhythm, rising in his arms to meet each increasingly powerful thrust, clinging to his shoulders as they rocked together. Moving with him, animal instinct guiding her, she let him lead her, take her. Her breath emerged in short, brisk pants, her mind dissolving into a gamut of strange flickering sensations building within the very core of her, rounding and swelling.

A tingling spasm shot down her legs, weakening them, curling her toes, and as his lips sealed to hers once more, the boiling, swelling knot within her pushed beyond its fragile limits, bursting into a thousand scattering stars. She clung to him, desperately, shimmering lights streaking through her mind, as wave upon wave of shattering desire convulsed through her.

'Mother of God!' Reaching his own climax, Bastien collapsed over her, his breathing snatched and tattered against her ear, his heavy frame quenched, replete.

The creak of branches and the rising, sifting breeze woke him; the swift reverberations of birds' wings against the cacophony of twitterings and chatterings signalling the imminent sunrise. Above him, through the tumbled stone opening of a former arched window, the three-quarter moon shone, alongside a star, sparkling like newly minted silver. And in his arms, Alice, sleeping soundly.

In the aftermath of their love-making, his body still hummed, satiated and replete. He was astonished at how he felt, astounded at the place they had reached, together, two souls locked in singing harmony. After Katherine's death, he had thought himself incapable of ever making love to a woman again; yes, he'd entertained the rough couplings with the battleground whores, suitable purely for physical release, but this? This had been something entirely different. For the first time in as long as he could remember, the lump of metal that caged his heart seemed smaller, lighter somehow, the memories of Katherine, of his brother, receding into the shadows. He touched the ring at his neck, waiting for the familiar knock of painful memory. Nothing. Only the briefest hint of something that had been lost.

Alice had done this, made him feel whole again, this small, courageous maid at his side: brave enough to stand up against convention for what she believed in, yet gentle and kind, always putting others before herself. It was her *naïveté,* her belief that people were essentially good, that had landed her in trouble, yet he admired her for it.

Alice shifted against him, nuzzling her face into his shoulder, but she did not wake. In the luminous morning light, her skin was like the inside of an oyster shell, pellucid and pure, imbued with a delicate rosy blush. Her dark gold hair, mussed and tumbled, fell around her face, over his bare arm at her back. She had barrelled into his life, unexpected, chaotic, and had set him at odds with who he thought he was. He told himself he had gone after her because that's what anyone would have done for a woman known to be in danger, but he knew it was a lie. He had gone after her because he wanted to be with her. Because he craved everything about her, her odd little mannerisms, her generous, spirited, courageous company, her quiet, powerful beauty. But he'd gone too far.

'Bastien?' Alice uttered tentatively.

Guilt caved his chest—how could he have done such a thing? He'd taken advantage of her when she was at her most vulnerable, his base, physical instincts surging through him, consuming him, consuming her. He was no better than Edmund, the way he had behaved. Shame washed over him, corroding his soul.

Unable to look at her, Bastien extricated his arm, rose to his feet. 'You'd better get dressed,' he ordered her tonelessly. 'And then we'll leave.' He strode over to his horse, bending over to pick up the saddle and fling it into place.

'What's the matter?' Alice propped herself up, the morning air chilling her body, the flimsy chemise billowing about her. She hugged her arms about her chest.

His eyes bore into her questioning features. It was better this way, he told himself. He would poison her sweetness, sully that bright smile, her gentle, kind ways. She was better off without him.

'Nothing,' he said abruptly. 'We need to move on, that's all. Felpersham and his men might still be out searching. I'd feel happier if we were behind stone walls.'

A huge lump balled in her chest, a horrible sense of wrongdoing, of wilting disappointment. What had felt so right the night before now felt terribly, terribly wrong. Scrabbling to her feet, she reached for her kirtle, her gown. The severed laces on the back bodice of her dress mocked her, filling her with shame. Her movements were jerky, tense as she stepped into the kirtle, then pulled the gown up around her shoulders.

Reaching down to scoop up his cote-hardie from the ground, she turned towards him, bundling his garment haphazardly in her arms. 'Aren't you going to say any-thing?' Her tongue moved woodenly in her dry mouth.

'About what?' His harsh tone scoured her.

'About…us?' she replied timidly, a hectic flush rising on her throat. She clutched desperately on to Bastien's cote-hardie, a woollen boat in a storm-tossed sea.

'What's there to say?' His face was devoid of expres-sion, closed. 'What I did…it was unforgivable.'

She smiled crookedly. 'I forgive you.'

He jerked roughly on a thick leather strap, securing the saddle. 'You need to forget it. I took advantage of you. For that I am sorry.'

Her wide, candid blue eyes followed his succinct, practised movements, his strong fingers fastening the buckle beneath the horse's belly. 'I was fully aware of what was about to happen. You gave me a chance to stop it.'

His fingers stilled, his bleak, glittering scrutiny shredding her flimsy confidence. 'Then why didn't you?' he ground out. 'Christ, woman, why didn't you stop me?'

Beneath the heavy folds of the tunic bunched before her, her fingers curled against his anger. Everything was wrong; she had done something wrong. How could she tell him how she felt towards him, that every time she looked his way, or heard his voice, or felt the brush of his hand, her heart filled with such a sense of joy, of belonging, that she felt it would burst with happiness? Edmund's utter betrayal only intensified her feelings. How could she tell him, when his rejection of her was all too obvious in his behaviour?

'I'm not sure.' She threw him a feeble smile, picking furiously at an errant thread, trying to hide her shame.

'Well, let's hope you don't regret it,' he threw back roughly.

Alice paled. 'Don't be like this,' she whispered. Her plea wavered, fragile in the shimmering air.

'I suppose you've already conjured up some rosy image of us growing old together, with four or five snotty-nosed children running around us, a comfortable castle, table groaning with food—'

'Stop it!' Alice paced over to him, fury lacing her voice. 'How can you be like this? How dare you defile something that was so…?' Her voice trailed to nothing. Something so beautiful, she had been about to say.

'Because this is what I'm really like, Alice. A black-hearted soul who will never change.'

'Nay!' She thumped the cote-hardie into his chest. 'Nay, you're not like that! You would never have come back for me if you were! People can change. You can change.'

'Alice, you see the best in everybody,' Bastien said wearily, his voice softening a little. 'You probably thought Felpersham was a kind-hearted elderly man, until he revealed his true character.'

'Nay, I…' But Bastien held his hand up, stopping her speech, setting his leonine head at an angle. In the distance, a faint sound: the baying of dogs. His eyes narrowed, dragon-green gimlets.

'They're on to us.' Bastien scowled. 'Come on, we need to move.'

She shrugged her shoulders. 'Maybe you should just leave me here. It would certainly save you from all the effort of being nasty to me.'

He grimaced at her. 'Don't be silly. I went through all that trouble of rescuing you, I'm not about to give you up now.' Her heart surged with hope at his words, although she was fully aware of his intended meaning.

Bastien sprung into the saddle, kicked his foot free of the stirrup. 'Mount up before me,' he ordered her briskly. The horse, sensing his master's tension, pawed the ground, eager to move.

Alice stuck her toe into the high metal stirrup, as Bastien leaned down to bring her up before him. The two sides of the back of her gown gaped open, the tattered laces dangling forlornly.

'Oh!' she muttered in surprise, clutching at the sagging front of her bodice, as she swung neatly in front of Bastien. 'My dress…!'

Bastien glowered. The ruined garment tormented him; he remembered the softness of her skin against his fingers, the swift rasp of his knife as he had impatiently sliced through the laces. He dug his heels into his horse's flank, spurring the animal into a fast trot.

'We'll sort it out later,' he ground out.

Through the open, dipping sides of her gown, Bastien's iron-hard chest bounced against her rigid spine, tantalising, warm. Alice jerked forwards abruptly with each jolting contact. Even as her body still thrummed with the after-effects of their love-making, still yearned for his touch, she endeavoured to hold her slim frame away from him. Her muscles, her nerves, strained with the effort, making them sore, frayed. They had galloped steadily over several miles, splashing through fast-flowing streams to confuse the dogs, but now, as the track narrowed through the trees, Bastien adjusted his grip on the reins, slowing the horse to a walk.

Alice studied his tanned, sinewy fingers looped

around the worn leather of the reins, fingers that had played over her body, thrilling her, igniting her with their touch. Her mind was in turmoil. Last night, she had wanted to be with him so much, all reason, all conscious thought deserting her. Had she turned to him merely out of comfort, her mind and body shattered and hurt by Edmund's betrayal? Nay, she doubted that. This feeling, this desire had been building between them for a long time, but she had refused to acknowledge it. What had happened between them was inevitable; Edmund's treachery had merely been the catalyst.

Even if this was it, she was still glad she had taken the chance to be with him, glad of those few precious, exquisite hours she had spent with this amazing man. Even if her life was nothing from this moment onwards, at least she could hold that memory tight against her heart.

'I suppose you'd better take me back to Abberley,' she pronounced finally, her voice sad, closed. Without him, she could try and rebuild her life, gather together what little scraps of dignity she could find, and start again.

The saddle creaked under Bastien's weight as he dipped forwards to avoid a tree. His face brushed against the bundle of Alice's hair, loose and tumbling around her. Guilt clawed in his gut; he heard the tint of wretchedness in her voice and knew he was responsible.

'Will you take me there?' Alice repeated.

Huge oaks towered around them, rooks' nests studding the bare upper branches, spiky balls of twig in a wooden mesh. As they passed beneath, the rooks rose up in one mass of black, flashing blades, protesting at the human presence, cawing and cackling.

'Nay, it's not safe.'

The warm slenderness of her back nudged constantly against him with the gentle rocking of the horse, despite her best efforts. Holding her thus was sheer, utter torture, constantly reminding him of her naked body in his arms.

'Not safe?' Alice turned around awkwardly, trying to see his face, but only succeeded in nearly tipping off. She clutched at the mane as Bastien's arms tightened around her. 'But Edmund wouldn't show his face there again. Not after what he's done.'

'It's not Edmund I'm worried about,' Bastien replied tersely. 'I told you before, I'm sure your mother is involved with Edmund. What's to stop her doing the same thing again?'

Her spine tensed against his chest. The light dappling through the trees brushed the top of her hair, sending flame-coloured sparks through her golden tresses. 'I can't believe my mother was involved. Are you sure it was her voice that you heard?' When she finally spoke, the faintest trace of hope threaded her voice.

'Nay,' Bastien found himself replying. 'Nay, I'm not certain.' He could protect her from the truth, at least for the moment.

'Abberley is safe, I'm sure. Remember, my father is there.'

'There's nothing to stop Edmund coming back for you.'

'He wouldn't dare! Do you think I'd go with him, after what he's done?'

Bastien laughed, the sound rumbling deep in his chest. This was more like the Alice he had come to know, spirited and courageous.

'My manor is not far from here. You'll be safe there.'
But even as the words flew from his lips, he wondered at
the truth in them, wondered at his own self-control. She
had probably believed herself to be safe in the forest,
yet he had abused that trust. But even now, even after
all that had happened between them, he couldn't let her
go. 'That is, of course, if you wish to go with me,' he
added, hesitation hitching his voice.

Alice nodded shakily, a tiny smile lifting her lips.
Hope flowered in her veins: he had asked her to go
with him! She had believed he would take her back to
Abberley, leave her, but no! He had asked if she wished
to go back with him to his home; little did he know that
she would go with him to the ends of the earth. She
simply needed time to convince him.

Lady Cecile de la Roche sighed, hunching forwards
to plant her gnarled, arthritic hands on the stone windowsill, her bright green eyes scanning the ground
below. Always the same view, the same unending pattern of rippling, gently sloped hills, the forests beyond,
vanishing into the blue distance. Lands that her husband, Guy de la Roche, God rest his soul, had set out
all those years ago, lands that should have belonged to
her beloved son, Guillaume. Her knuckles tightened,
nails rasping against the cool stone.

'My lady?' Lady Cecile's maidservant shouldered
her way through the door, arms piled high with folded
clothes. 'Are you ready to dress?'

Lady Cecile turned slowly from the window, her ash-
blonde hair swinging in two long braids either side of
her head. Countless years of scraping it back into the
fashionable styles had made it dry, straggly; thank the

Lord she could cover it up every day, hide the evidence of her ageing. She raised one non-existent eyebrow. 'I suppose I should,' she responded listlessly to the maid's enquiry, holding her arms up so the girl could remove her nightgown. She let Mary choose what she wore now; clothes held little interest for her, as long as she looked presentable.

'There's some news, my lady,' Mary blurted out excitedly, tugging at the nightgown's sleeves.

'Oh?' Lady Cecile replied in a bored tone. Nothing ever happened at Foxhayne, only the same dull, repetitious daily routine: the meals, the occasional travelling noble in search of board and lodging, the interminable cycle of the seasons.

'Lord Bastien is coming.'

Lady Cecile's half-shuttered eyes snapped open. Her mouth pursed, fine lines radiating out from her thin lips. 'Who?' she enquired tonelessly.

'Lord Bastien,' Mary repeated, suddenly feeling as if she had stepped onto treacherous quicksand. 'Your son, Lord Bastien. One of our guards met him on the road; it will not be long before he arrives.' Maybe her lady was going mad after all; there was talk of it in the kitchens, but Mary had always vehemently denied it, staunchly supporting her mistress.

'What does he want?'

Mary slipped the silk kirtle over her lady's head. 'This is his home, my lady. He has come home.'

'Aye, but he never comes home if he can help it. Why now?'

Mary frowned. She was finding it difficult to read her lady's moods these days.

'He has a girl with him. Beautiful, she is.'

'A girl? Curious. I thought he didn't bother with woman after…well, after poor Katherine.'

'Aye, my lady,' Mary responded in hushed tones. 'That was a terrible business.'

'It was, wasn't it? Lady Cecile smiled, then clapped her hands briskly. 'What are you waiting for? Lace me up quickly, my girl. This could prove to be very interesting indeed.'

Mary suddenly wished she had said nothing at all.

Chapter Fifteen

The manor at Foxhayne sat in a wide, sparsely wooded valley surrounded by fertile pastureland, still verdant green despite the lateness of the year. Cattle grazed the lowland fields, tails swishing back and forth to dispense the flies, while sheep worked their way across the rough, upper pasture. A river cut through the flat bottom of the valley, crowded trees on the banks marking its snaking, glittering path. The manor itself was built of the local sandstone, a pleasing jumble of circular turrets and crenellated walls, bowing out with age. No soldiers strutting along the battlements, no moat or drawbridge. No sign of any defences whatsoever.

Bastien reined in the destrier at the brow of the last hill, scanning the wide bowl of land that contained his home. The last time he had seen it had been above two winters ago, when he had left for France. He had believed then that he would never return to those walls, this land. So many memories! He remembered his mother's ravaged face, her screams of revenge when she'd learned of Guillaume's death, her triumphant look that he'd caught on her face at Katherine's funeral. The sweet smell of Alice's hair drifted upwards as she relaxed against him, and he closed his eyes, savouring the intensity of the moment. Maybe now was the time to stop running away, immersing himself in one battle after another; maybe it was time to confront those memories, and his mother.

He noted Alice's silence. 'Not quite what you're used to, I suppose,' he murmured. 'No royal guard, or succession of noble guests. No pomp or ceremony.'

'You know I have no call for such things,' she replied, her voice like a bell in the clear air. Aye, he did. He had never known a woman so unaffected by all the trappings that riches could bring. He knew her.

Alice shifted in the saddle, the curve of her hip nudging against Bastien's upper thigh. 'What a beautiful place,' she said. Dark green ivy clambered up the walls in places, softening the stone. Briar roses scrambled round the door, the last pink flowers clinging on until the autumn frosts would blacken them. A garden had been laid out to the left of the manor: paved walkways hedged with dark yew trees. 'Not at all what I expected.'

'What did you expect?' He gritted his teeth against the tantalising touch of her hip.

'Oh, I don't know,' she replied teasingly. 'Some sort of grim fortress teeming with soldiers, a deep moat, a portcullis.'

'Something more suited to me, you mean.' A muscle jumped in his jaw. 'These soft touches have nothing to do with me. My mother's had the run of the place for several years now, since I've been fighting in France. I only come here on brief occasions, to check up on things.'

'Then why come back now, if you feel nothing for the place?'

'Because it was the closest.' He tried to fob her off with the easy answer, not willing to share his thoughts about confronting issues he had long since buried. In truth, he was questioning his own sanity in returning. The breeze washed over him, lifting the short strands of his hair, cool air against his scalp. He wanted to stay there for ever, his arms cradling Alice, feeling the gentle press of her body against his. Sheer, utter torture.

'Will your mother be there?' Alice's voice shook him from his reverie.

'Aye, she never goes anywhere now. She lost all contact with the outside world when Guillaume died. All she has now is a handful of servants, and Buchan, my bailiff, who manages the land for me.'

'How sad.'

'She brought it on herself, Alice.' His tone was brittle, uncompromising.

'It can't have been easy for her, with no husband, losing a son like that, and another son away in battle.'

He caught the sympathy in Alice's tone. 'I think you need to meet her, before you make any judgements,' he replied carefully.

'And if I'm to meet her, then I can't go in looking like this!' Alice exclaimed. 'Look at my hair!' She pushed one desperate hand into the tumbling mass, 'And my dress!'

He loved her the way she was, the glorious silken threads of hair spilling over her shoulders, clinging to the front, the sleeves of his velvet tunic, the flimsy silk of her kirtle shining between the ruined sides of her gown.

'She'll not notice, Alice.'

'Even if she doesn't, the servants will,' she replied, throwing one leg frontways over the horse's neck and slipping to the ground. 'Haven't you got anything to secure the back of this?' She clutched the slipping front of her gown to her breast.

Bastien sighed, dismounted, and began to rummage in one of the satchels tied to the rump of his horse. 'I thought you gave no care to how you looked,' he remarked, withdrawing a long coil of leather lace from the bag. 'You never follow the fashion like the other ladies at court.'

'Bastien...' she grinned at him, her small teeth white against her fine, blushed skin '...there's following fashion, and there's being presentable. I'm not even close to being presentable! What's your mother going to think if I meet her looking like this?'

Like I've made wild, passionate love to you, he thought. The fact that Alice had spent most of the night in his arms was patently obvious. Her hair was mussed, her eyes danced with brilliant light, her lips were red, tender from his kisses.

'You have a point,' he replied crisply, his heart thudding with the memory of the night before. 'Although I doubt she'd even care.' He turned her about, concentrating on threading the fiddly lace through the rows of holes punched down each side of the gown.

'Have you threaded every hole?' Alice asked suspiciously, when, after a very short time, Bastien announced that he was finished.

'I have,' Bastien lied, eyeing the huge gaps in the lacing. Impatient to finish, unwilling to torture himself further with the warm feel of her flesh against his fingers, he had skipped a few holes. He wrenched at the tailing ends of the laces, so forcefully that he made her stagger backwards, and tied them in a double knot.

Alice raked her fingers through her hair, endeavouring to comb it, and began to bundle it into a long, fat braid. Her arms ached; normally her maid would do this for her. 'I've got no pins to secure it.' Small white teeth chewed at her bottom lip in frustration. 'Life would be so much easier with short hair.' She glared enviously at Bastien's short, ruffled strands.

'But so much less beautiful to look at,' he murmured. Briskly, he secured the curling end of the plait with another length of lace.

'How do I look?' Alice stood before him, elbows akimbo, the breeze billowing out her skirts behind her, a sweet smile on her face. Sweet Jesu! His body tensed treacherously in response to the bewitching sight of her. How in Heaven's name was he going to get through this?

Bastien swallowed hard. 'You'll do,' he muttered.

Cecile stood at the top of the stone steps leading to the wide, arched entrance door of Foxhayne, carefully positioned so she was shadowed from the glare of the noon sun, surprisingly hot for the time of year. She lifted one dainty hand to check her head-dress was positioned properly; the gold mesh rasped against her knuckles. She had dressed carefully: a silk velvet gown, lavishly embroidered, with a pleated bodice and a high neck framing her thin, peevish features. The padded heart-shaped head-dress, the sides fashioned of stiff gold netting, successfully hid every scrap of hair. The sleeves of her gown fell in vast, voluminous gathers, deliberately designed to fall back and show off the tight, colourful sleeves of her kirtle. Cecile raised her chin, her narrowed cat-green eyes watching the approach of her younger son, the unknown girl. She was ready.

Bastien walked slowly up the track from the gate-house to the manor, leading his horse, the girl at his side. She was at least a head shorter than him, slender, her blonde, uncovered, hair shining in the sun like spun gold. Cecile watched closely, noticing Bastien deliber-ately curbed his long stride to match the shorter pace of the maid.

Dispassionately, almost with no interest, she studied her younger son as he approached; big, brawny, the breeze shuffling his blond hair, so like her husband, both in looks and temperament. His brother, Guillaume, God rest his soul, had been more like her, delicate, sen-sitive. Grief ripped through her belly. Bastien had been a difficult baby, full of energy, desperate to talk, to walk, and once he could, there was no stopping him. He had been exhausting, such a shock after the calm, passive Guillaume, who would gurgle quietly from his cradle, his eyes wide, adoring. And now Bastien was home.

Bastien halted at the base of the steps, lifting his chin up to the woman who had rejected him all those years before. He saw the same brittle, rigid features set in the bleached, parchment skin, the pursed-up mouth, the high forehead. 'My Lady Cecile,' he greeted her formally, nodding his head briefly.

'Bastien,' Cecile breathed. Her mouth sat in a grim line. 'To what do I owe this pleasure?'

A groom ran up from around the side of the manor, and led Bastien's horse away, its hooves slipping on the cobbles as the boy led it to the stables.

'This is the Lady Alice,' Bastien explained. 'She is in need of a place to stay.'

'So you chose Foxhayne.' Cecile's voice was a clipped whine.

'It was the closest.'

'No maidservant?' Cecile looked down at Alice with a disapproving stare.

Alice stepped forwards, smiling, and curtsied. 'Please forgive the way I look, my lady. Your son rescued me from a…a…situation.' Her voice wobbled. 'At this moment I have nothing more than the clothes I stand up in.'

The girl was pretty, Cecile had to admit. And no doubt from noble stock, despite her uncovered hair, her unplucked eyebrows. She spoke like a noble. Her dishevelled clothes were fashioned from expensive cloth, obviously fitted by a proper seamstress. Whatever her son's faults, he had good taste in women. Katherine had been a beauty, too.

'Then we must see what we can do to accommodate you…my lady,' Cecile responded with a hint of a smile towards Alice. She had to make some sort of effort if the maid were to trust her. The thick powder on her skin cracked into tiny wrinkles with the unaccustomed movement of her face.

'Call me Alice, please.'

Bastien frowned. This wasn't how he'd expected the initial meeting with his mother to go. He'd anticipated tears, accusations and outright abuse from Cecile, but this? He couldn't remember the last time his mother had smiled.

'Well…Alice,' Cecile continued, 'I'm sure you must be hungry. Bastien, why don't you take her to the great hall, and I'll instruct the kitchens to bring you some food. You must excuse me, though.' She noted the swift glance that passed between the two of them, the way the maid seemed tucked into Bastien's side. Nothing was really obvious, but Cecile knew. Oh, there was something momentous going on between these two, something bigger than Bastien's relationship with Katherine, she felt it in her bones, she saw it with her beady eyes. She needed time to think, to plan.

Bastien led Alice through the doorway, and into a long passage, its floor set with large, uneven flagstones. After the warm sunshine on her back, the corridor was dark and cool. Alice blinked, trying to adjust her eyes to the half-light. A wonderful smell of beeswax and lavender rose to her nostrils, filling the air with the scents of summer; no doubt the mixture was used to polish the wooden furniture in the manor. Tapestries and paintings crowded the walls, full of vibrant colour and intricate stitches.

'What a lovely home,' Alice exclaimed in delight. After all the horrors of the previous two days, it was a delight to be in a place so warm and welcoming. Especially when the man she loved was at her side.

'Is it?' he replied tonelessly. He was still trying to decipher his mother's uncharacteristic behaviour; he didn't trust her one bit. Pushing aside a thick curtain hung over a doorway, he entered the great hall, Alice following. At this time of day, the double-height space was deserted, apart from a single servant stacking the used plates together, clearing up from an earlier meal. Sunlight shafted down from the high windows, gilding spinning circles of dust.

'It's certainly very different from all the draughty castles that I've spent time in,' Alice continued. 'It's warm and cosy.'

'I suppose it is,' Bastien said, sprawling into one of the chairs at the top table, watching Alice's graceful movement as she tucked herself neatly into the chair beside him. 'I've been away for so long.'

'What a shame you couldn't spend more time here.'

His green eyes pierced her face. 'Our country was at war with France, Alice. You don't have much time to be idle.'

'But when you did have time, did you come back here?'

She rested her arms across the table, then leaned forwards; his eye traced the blue veins on the top of her small hand, hands that had held him, caressed him. He should have resented her questioning, but curiously he welcomed it. He wanted to tell her, to share the details of his life with her.

'Nay.' He broke off a hunk of bread. 'I stayed with the Duke. I wasn't welcome here.'

'But your mother seems kind.'

'Nay!' He thumped one fist against the table, making the used crockery, the goblets and platters, jump. The servant, heading for the kitchens with a stack of empty plates, swivelled his head round, startled. Bastien leaned forwards, his face inches away from Alice's. She smelled the sweet, heady scent of his breath. 'Nay, Alice,' he breathed, 'she is not. Do not do what you always do, trying to see the good in everyone. Believe me when I tell you that you will not find it in her. You will never find it.'

* * *

Trying to shake off the deep layers of slumber, Alice moved her head first one way, then the other on the pillow; the fine linen rustled beneath her hair. She felt as if she had slept for days. Stretching her arms and legs, she relished the cool, crisp material of the sheets against her limbs, the delicious, relaxed feel in her muscles. She opened her eyes carefully against the bright sunlight flooding in through the iron casement windows. Under the window, a carved oak coffer was pushed up against the wall, a large bowl and jug set upon it for washing. Colourful garments were slung across an elm chair on the other side of the room; the clothes were not her own, but no doubt intended for her. Sitting up abruptly, pushing her wayward hair from her face, her mind felt alert, energised by restorative sleep. She bounced out of bed, eager to see Bastien, a fleeting, tantalising hope burning along her veins. Was it possible that they could be together?

The door clicked open, and a maidservant, about the same age as herself, bustled in, smiling widely at Alice who stood in the diaphanous nightgown beside the bed. 'Oh, my lady, you're awake! The mistress sent me to see if you needed any help. My name's Mary.'

Alice beamed at her. 'Aye, Mary, I need to dress.'

'I picked these clothes out for you, my lady.' Mary turned to the pile of garments on the chair. A troubled frown wrinkled her brow. 'I'm afraid your other gown has to be repaired.'

'Thank you.' Alice flushed, not wishing to share the details of how her gown came to be in such a state.

'You look so much better than when you arrived, my

lady. You were exhausted.' Mary lifted up the chemise in readiness as Alice pulled the nightgown over her head.

'Why, I didn't see you,' Alice said in surprise.

'I hope you don't mind, my lady, but I took the liberty of peeking out of the window. We don't receive many visitors at Foxhayne. It was a right treat to see a pretty maid like you standing on the doorstep, and the master too. We...' Mary glanced behind her, as if she were expecting someone at the door '...haven't seen him for a long time either.'

'His relationship with his mother is not easy, I understand.'

'Oh, nay, mistress, that's the reason he never comes home; it sends her into such a state, for days at a time, so I think—'

The door opened.

Mary's words froze on her lips, a violent flush flooding her broad features. Cecile came in, her smile pulling taut over her teeth. 'Good morning, Alice.' She nodded in her direction. The veil, hanging in perfect, starched pleats from the back of her headdress, hardly moved as her head bobbed forwards. 'Mary, I can hear you chattering away down the corridor. Look at this poor girl, freezing, half-dressed, while you babble on.' Her critical gaze alighted on Alice's toes, curled up against the bare floorboards.

'I'm...' Alice was about to say she was all right, that she was as much to blame for encouraging Mary's friendly talk, but Cecile's continuing words ploughed through any further speech.

'When you are dressed, you can visit me in the solar. I normally spend my days there, and it would be a pleasure to spend some time with you.' Cecile placed one bony hand on Alice's shoulder, the gemstones in her rings sparking coloured fire in the light.

'Oh, but I…' The urge to find Bastien, to talk to him, danced in her breast.

'Is that a problem?' The cold fingers clutched around her shoulder, digging in.

'Nay, I look forward to it.' Alice slumped into agreement. Lady Cecile was only trying to be kind, to make her feel welcome. It was the least she could do.

The stone turret, into which the solar had been built, was positioned so that it gained the maximum amount of sunlight during daylight hours. The chamber was warm, flooded with light from the large, south-facing window constructed in a curve to follow the circular line of the wall. As Mary led Alice in, Cecile was sitting in a high-backed chair, facing away from the window with her hands flat on her lap, staring blankly into space.

'Ah, here you are.' For such a delicate-looking woman, her speech seemed rapid, forceful. Cecile indicated that Alice should sit on the low upholstered footstool beside her, waving the hesitant Mary away. 'Go, girl, I have no need of you now.'

She smiled faintly at Alice. 'You seem much rested, my child.' The kindness in her voice seemed strained. 'Are you happy with the gown that Mary picked out for you?'

'What? Oh, aye, thank you.' Alice glanced down hurriedly. As usual she hadn't paid much attention to the clothes she had been laced into. Blue silk velvet flowed over her lap, the skirts embroidered with silver thread, a shimmering trellis design. 'It's lovely,' she added, after a pause, shifting uncomfortably on the seat. She felt all wrong, awkward, being here with Bastien's mother, with the woman he'd warned her against. It was as if she was betraying him. The sooner she could escape from this hot, stuffy room, the better.

'I thought we were about the same size.' Cecile's gnarled hands twisted in her lap. 'And the head-dress becomes you.'

Alice forced herself not to grimace. She had backed away when Mary had produced the padded, U-shaped roll, protesting that she never wore such encumbrances, but Mary had insisted. 'Do it for the mistress, my lady,' she had advised, pulling Alice's hair into a tight, confining bun at the back of her head, stabbing it with long pins to hold it in place. 'She likes to see ladies properly dressed.' Mary had driven another set of pins against her scalp to hold the thing in place; even now she felt them gouge her scalp, wrench cruelly at her hair.

'So…how do you know…Bastien?' Cecile's tongue stumbled over her son's name.

'It's a long story, my lady,' Alice hesitated. She had no wish to confide in this woman who she hardly knew, especially as Bastien had warned her, told her not to trust her.

'I have time.' Cecile threw her a half-smile of encouragement.

'He rescued me from a betrothal, a betrothal that went wrong.' Alice squirmed in her seat, uncomfortable with the confession.

In a waft of rose-scented perfume, Cecile leaned forwards, the huge pearl necklace dangling from her white throat, swinging into space. Her strong, vein-ridged fingers grasped at Alice's clasped hands. 'I'm sorry, my dear…about the betrothal. It must have been difficult for you.'

Alice hung her head, still feeling ashamed of her gross misjudgement of Edmund. 'I was betrayed by someone who I thought was my best friend,' she mumbled out, hoping that Cecile would prod no further.

Cecile nodded, collapsing back into her chair, removing her fingers. In the brilliant sunlight, her skin adopted the quality of parchment. 'Then it was fortunate for you that Bastien was able to help?'

Alice grimaced. 'If it hadn't been for him, then…' She paused.

'Then what…?' Cecile's voice snapped out, unexpected because it was so different from her earlier modulated tones. Her face took on a predatory air, anxious for details, sniffing them out like a bloodhound.

Alice remained silent, staring at her fingers.

Cecile patted her hands. 'Too painful to talk about? Tell me another time, my dear. I have a feeling that we are going to be the best of friends.'

Alice nodded, clearing her throat. The awkward silence ticked away in her head. 'I understand Bastien has not been home for some time.' The words stuttered out of their own accord, born of Alice's anxiety to deflect the subject away from herself.

Cecile's thin mouth twisted downwards. 'I'm surprised he hasn't told you why.' She cocked her head to one side, tapping her fingers against the wooden arm of the chair. 'He and I had a falling-out, a silly argument really. He's never forgiven me, even after all these years. He never visits me, barely speaks to me. You saw what he was like when he arrived. Is that a normal way for a son to greet his mother?'

Alice recalled the spontaneous way she would throw her arms around her father. 'Nay,' she agreed, wondering whether Cecile would tell her the true details of what had driven them apart.

'You can change him.' Alice frowned at the woman's unexpected words. 'Already I see a change in him. He would never have come here if it hadn't been for you.'

'He didn't have much choice, my lady,' Alice replied. What was Cecile thinking? That she had any influence on Bastien?

'Nonsense. He had the pick of all the best homes in England. He is a renowned knight, with friends everywhere, all eager to throw their doors open to him.'

'I had no idea.'

'Talk to him, my dear. He respects you, listens to you. I could see that from the moment you arrived, how close you were. Try to persuade him to forgive me.'

'I'll try,' Alice replied, nodding gamely, covering up the vague, cold sense of doubt in her heart.

Cecile seemed to slump down in her seat, her diminutive body becoming even smaller with the hunching movement. A white hand moved up to her forehead, resting there. 'I'm tired, my child. Off you go now, find him, talk to him.'

Alice sprang upwards, eager to leave. The footstool skittered back on the polished wooden floor. Cecile winced at the harsh, grating sound it made, her narrowed eyes fixed on the door. As it closed behind Alice, the simpering mask fell from her features, and she laughed: a harsh, corrosive sound. 'That's right, you run to him, little girl. How sweetly protective.' Cecile sipped from the goblet of wine at her elbow. 'He doesn't deserve it. He doesn't deserve *you.*'

Chapter Sixteen

Alice emerged from the solar, her mind a whirl of confusion. Bastien's description of his mother did not seem to fit the woman she had just encountered. Indeed, Cecile seemed at pains to make amends to Bastien. Maybe, just maybe, some chance at reconciliation between the two of them was possible.

'My lady?' Snared in her thoughts, Alice jumped as Mary appeared at her side. 'I thought I had better wait for you…to show you the way.'

'Thank you, Mary. I would be hopelessly lost without you.' She followed the maidservant down the stairs, trailing her hand over the curving stone wall to keep her balance on the uneven steps, allowing her breathing to steady after meeting Bastien's mother. For some reason, Cecile's friendliness had set Alice's nerves on edge; now, she took a deep breath, trying to shake off the feeling.

'How did you find my Lady Cecile?' Mary paused on the stairs, the hem of her simple fustian gown bunching on the higher step behind her. She nodded up at the door of the solar, indicating the source of her question.

'She seemed very friendly.'

'God's truth?' Mary's eyes widened with surprise. She clapped a hand over her mouth, then lowered her eyes, crestfallen. 'My apologies. I wasn't sure how she would be, you know, after seeing Lord Bastien again. It might have opened old wounds.' Mary's voice dropped to a hush.

Alice smiled. 'I think she wants to repair the relationship with Bastien.'

A look of relief passed over the maidservant's face, and she turned to continue down the steps. 'Come and break your fast, my lady,' Mary said when they reached the dim corridor at the bottom of the steps. 'The great hall is this way.'

The wooden floorboards creaked under Alice's slight weight as she paused. 'Have you seen Lord Bastien today?'

'When he heard you were still sleeping, he went out.' Mary searched Alice's features with a lively interest. 'Not far, I suspect, because he didn't ask the groom for a horse. He'll be about the gardens somewhere.'

'I'll find him.'

Alice stepped through the door, and out into the blustery air. Immense, rounded lumps of cloud had begun to form to the west, moving over the blue sky, obscuring it. A few random drops of rain, carried in on the wind, touched her face as she descended the steps to walk around the wide, cobbled pathway circling the perimeter of the manor. The strengthening breeze clamped the blue velvet of her gown against the slender contours of her figure, the silver embroidery sparkling in the darkening light, but Alice was oblivious to the covert, admiring glances of the few people who were at work around the place. Her head-dress tugged at its anchoring pins, and Alice, raising one hand to steady it, fervently wished it would rip from her head, fly off, and never be seen again.

The stables were situated at the back of the manor, the low, undulating slates that formed its roof as grey and dark as the lowering sky above them. Behind the stables, a narrow path led to the chapel. Huge, fat drops of rain started falling, spattering the cobbles, the slick wetness revealing a myriad of colour in each individual stone. Maids ran out from the kitchen door, on the north wall, laughing and shivering as the rain flew into the faces, bundling up the laundry that had been spread over the bushes to dry. Their girlish chattering rose into the wind, the end of the sentences ripped away, lost in the breeze.

Alice had no intention of dashing back inside. After the sour fugginess of Cecile's chambers, the cool rain acted like a blessing on her skin, strumming at her senses, enlivening her. Through the lines of rain sweeping across the cobbles, her eyes lit on the chapel, surrounded by its own neat stone wall, two massive yews either side of the arched doorway. The wooden gate at the top of the cobbled path sat open and she walked through, the long, bending heads of grass on either side of the path brushing wetly against her skirts.

Her fingers grazed the wrought-iron latch; the solid oak door swung in silently, on oiled hinges. The musty air breathed out from the dim interior, a salvation; here, she could seek refuge from the rain, from Cecile and gather her senses before searching for Bastien once more.

The hushed air of the church clung to Alice's skin as she stepped inside. A trickle of rain slid from her temple, an icy trail down the side of her face. She wiped it away, her eyes adjusting to the light. The church was empty, gloomy with the lowering light outside. Alice moved towards the rows of wooden pews, intending to sit for a while. She reached out to touch the ornately carved end of the back pew; under her fingers, the polished wood was smooth, silky. A small movement flickered in the corner of her eye; she stopped, suddenly, caught.

He was there.

Her breath looped, surged. Her heart thudded, noisy in the billowing silence. Every muscle, every nerve in her body stilled, tensed. She had no wish to intrude. Up at the front of the church, to the right of the altar, Bastien crouched, his big body kneeling down on the flagstones, his elbows resting on the edge of a tomb, palms pushed against his face. His dark green tunic curved around the broad frame of his shoulders, bunched on the flagstones in crumpled folds around his knees. And between his fingers, something dangled, spinning in the damp, silent air. A ring. Katherine's ring.

Her heart plummeted, a vast sense of loss flooding her limbs; her chest gripped, squeezed suddenly in a vice of desolation. His hunched position spoke to her of a widening expanse between them, a gulf, a chasm that she couldn't cross. She was unable to fight this, for how could she fight the dead? He was caught in a world that she could never enter. What had she been thinking—that he would forget his first, his only love, because of her? Even after they had spent that wonderful night together, he had warned her, told her of his black-hearted soul that would never change. And here was the reason: Katherine, his fiancée, his love, the girl he could obviously never forget. The clues had been there all along if she had thought about it; but she had chosen not to, ignoring the obvious. Such arrogance on her part! Slowly, tentatively, her heart swollen with grief, she began to back away discreetly, hoping, praying that he wouldn't notice her.

Immersed in his own thoughts, Bastien failed to hear the door slide shut behind him. Exhaustion dragged at his eyes; he had been at Katherine's tomb since daybreak. The stone pressed into his forehead as he leaned his head against the carved edge, closing his eyes, trying to relieve the scratching feeling within them. He had spent the time remembering, remembering those brief happy moments with her, the horror of her death. It was time to say goodbye. He had done the right thing in returning to Foxhayne; the dark memories that he had believed would overwhelm him if he returned to the family home had failed to materialise, and he knew why.

A newborn lightness danced around his heart, a surge of hope; the promise of a future he could never have dreamed of only a few weeks ago. And all because of one bright maid, all because of Alice. She had challenged him, back in the forest, told him he could change, but he hadn't believed her, dismissed her words. Christ, she had even forgiven him for making love to her, and he had thrown it back in her face! But now, returning to Foxhayne, with Alice's words ringing loud in his ears, he realised that it was possible. Between his fingers, the ring swung, the golden circle that had rested on Katherine's slim, white finger, the leather lace that had lain all these years against his chest. It was time to say goodbye. Leaning forwards, he hung the lace with its ring around the small stone cross at the head of Katherine's tomb.

Alice stumbled from the church, blindly, the heavy rain sluicing down her fine features. Great, gulping tears surged from her chest, from the very core of her, splinters of anguish driving deep into her heart. Where could she run, where could she hide, now, to curl up and lick her wounds in private? Maybe the stables, they were often a quiet place to go. She rounded the corner of the house, sprinting fast, and cannoned straight into a wall of solid muscle. Her hands reached out instinctively to brace herself, and she squinted up through the raindrops, her breath emerging in swift short gasps.

'Careful now,' a brisk, stern voice advised. A short stocky man stood before her, steel helmet tucked under his arm. His split-sided white tunic bore the distinctive arms of the Duke of York, the falcon and the fetterlock embroidered into the heavy wool. His steadying hands fell from her shoulders, and she made as if to walk past him. 'Hold a moment, my lady.' The soldier peered at her with interest. 'Have you by any chance seen Lord Bastien? I have to find him—it's a matter of some urgency.'

'Wh-what?' she stuttered out, her mind refusing to work.

'Lord Bastien,' the soldier repeated patiently. 'Do you know where he is?'

She wanted to weep at the mention of his name, but

she gritted her teeth, forcing herself to hold the tears in, to push the words out. 'In the chapel, over there.' As she turned to point the direction through the slanting rain, Bastien's tall frame emerged from the low door, his blond head bright, distinctive against the stone lintel. 'There he is,' she whispered, wanting to run, to flee. Nay, nay! She couldn't be with him at the moment: her whole body quaked with vulnerability, with the very rawness of the situation, as if her skin had been scoured with brambles. She had to go.

'Excuse me.' She stepped around the man, still intent on gaining the solitude of the stables. She couldn't face Bastien now.

'Alice, wait!' Bastien called after her, his strong velvet tones punishing her with their beauty. She carried on walking, pretending not to hear. 'Alice, stop!'

He covered the ground in great bounding steps, too quick for her to escape, ignoring the soldier trying desperately to gain his attention, catching at her fingers, pulling her back to him. 'Stay with me,' he murmured, the fronds of his wet hair brushing her forehead. 'I need to talk to you.' His lips moved close to the sensitive lobe of her ear; she quivered at the familiar thrill arching through her slender frame. Why didn't he ignore her? Why did he have to make it so difficult for her to leave? Surely he didn't really want her here, after the touching scene she had so recently witnessed?

'Lord Bastien?'

Bastien regarded the squat figure of the soldier, wrinkling his straight nose with mild irritation. 'What is it?' Droplets of rain clung to the ends of his hair, sparkling diamonds on gold.

'The Duke needs you, my lord. He's at Abberley. He

sent this.' The soldier handed Bastien a roll of parchment. Releasing Alice's fingers, Bastine unrolled the thick paper, scanned the scrawl of writing, and groaned. The lustrous green of his eyes roved Alice's face. 'I have to go, Alice, the Duke does need me.' He shook his head. 'Believe me when I tell you it's the last thing I want to do at this moment. There is so much I want to say to you, to share with you.'

Alice frowned at the softness in his voice, the tenderness she saw lurking behind his eyes. Her heart reached out to him, even as she tried to close herself down against his devastating nearness. 'Let me come with you, to Abberley,' she whispered. Suddenly she longed for the predictable stability of home, the security and warmth of her father's hug.

'Nay, it's too dangerous; the Duke has surrounded the castle.'

'But…my parents?'

'I'm sure they are safe. I'll bring back news of them.' The rain had eased up momentarily and he touched one lean finger to the yielding dampness of her cheek. 'Promise me that you'll stay here until I return. You'll be safe.' His lips curved into a smile, dazzling her, scraping cruelly at the open wound of her loneliness.

'But…your mother? Will she mind?' Alice inspected his angled face with wide blue eyes.

'My mother will be all right. It's me she hates, not you.'

Alice plunged her hands into the powdery flour, kneading her fingers into the softening clots of butter, amalgamating the two by rubbing them together. Pouring in a few drops of water from an earthenware jug, she brought the mixture together to form a dough.

'Here, use this for a pie dish.' Mary placed a clay platter on the table at her side. Hand on her hips, she regarded Alice with a smile, her small blue eyes twinkling in a rounded face. 'You know, for a noblewoman you're quite adept in the kitchen.'

Alice scooped up a lump of spare butter with her fingertips, began to grease the dish. 'I enjoy it; I like to be busy.' And it keeps my mind from dwelling on Bastien, on what he might say to me on his return, about whether I've done the right thing by staying, she thought. Several days had passed since his departure; the loss of his steady, vibrant presence sliced through her like a cold blade. Her misery at seeing him in the church had refused to slacken, instead heaping in great folds inside her, tormenting her, crumbling her hopes, her dreams, to dust.

'There.' Spreading a thin layer of loose flour across the well-scrubbed kitchen table, Alice thumped down the lump of dough, proceeding to roll it out. She laid the wide, flat disc over the dish, pressing at the smooth surface, trimming the top edge with a small knife.

'He'll be back soon, you know.' Casting a sideways glance at Alice's downcast face, Mary began to lay the chunks of apple into the pastry lining.

'I'm not so sure,' Alice replied doubtfully. 'There's nothing for him here.'

Mary blinked, her busy hands stalling on the peeled apple chunks. She laughed out loud. 'You're here, Alice.'

Alice wiped her hands down the front of her borrowed apron. 'Nay, Mary, you have that wrong. His heart is elsewhere.'

The maidservant frowned. 'But…who?'

Alice lifted trembling, flour-clogged palms to her face, trying to stop the tears from spilling. All the unhappiness that had built up since the day she had seen Bastien at Katherine's tomb seemed to gather now in one big fist around her heart. 'It's no use, Mary, I saw him, I saw him at Katherine's grave; he's never going to forget her.'

She collapsed into vast, shuddering sobs, her small frame shrinking inwards, bundling her arms about herself in an effort for control.

'Oh, my dear, I had no idea you were feeling like this!' Mary pulled her into a big hug, as Alice wept uncontrollably on her shoulder. 'You have got yourself in an awful state, haven't you? Now, come on, calm down, I'm sure you have it wrong.'

Alice shook her head miserably in response.

'Nay, you definitely have it wrong. Why, even the Lady Cecile noticed that he had eyes only for you. Come on, dry your eyes.' Mary plucked a large, clean handkerchief from one of the voluminous pockets in her skirts, and Alice lifted her damp face, accepting it gratefully.

Stepping back out of Mary's comforting arms, Alice wiped her face and blew her nose decisively. A drifting rootlessness had possessed her since Bastien's departure, a gaping uncertainty about the future. He had asked her to stay, and stay she would, if only to be told by Bastien the words she dreaded to hear: that no future existed for the two of them together.

'I'm sorry, Mary.' Alice handed back the creased linen square.

'Ah, there you are!' Both women turned in unison at the familiar shrill voice in the doorway. Lady Cecile moved gracefully into the kitchens, her pinched smile overlaid with a trace of irritation. Her shrewd green eyes clamped onto Alice. 'Why must you persist in these menial tasks, girl? I have enough servants to perform such duties.' She folded her pale hands across the countless pleats that fell from the high, tightly fitted waistband of her gown.

A wan smile tugged at Alice's features. 'I was keeping Mary company.' She hadn't seen very much of Bastien's mother in the past few days, and had assumed that the older woman preferred to be alone.

'Well, come and keep me company. I'm sitting all on my own in the solar. If you're intending to marry that son of mine, then I think I need to know you a little better.'

Untying her apron, Alice's hands stilled on the linen strings. 'I beg your pardon?'

Cecile raised non-existent eyebrows, the thin skin of her forehead wrinkling upwards like old parchment. 'You heard me well enough, girl.'

Mary nudged her in the elbow. 'You see, Alice. I'm not the only one to have noticed. Everyone has seen it except you.'

Except that you didn't see him in the chapel, Alice thought limply. You didn't see him. Even I thought there was a chance before then, a chance that we could be together. But it was obvious both Mary and Lady Cecile had made up their minds and she was too exhausted and confused to argue with them.

'Come, Lady Alice, let's leave this place.' Cecile whisked a disparaging glance around the cluttered kitchens, the rank of copper pans shining from the wall next to the cooking fire, a servant scrubbing energetically at some pots in the deep stone sink. Her critical gaze moved back to Mary. 'Tell that cook, wherever she might be, that I want to speak to her. This place needs some sorting out.'

Placing her apron on the table, Alice threw an apologetic glance towards Mary.

'Go on,' Mary whispered in response. 'You're doing her good; I haven't seen her this happy for ages.'

Alice followed Cecile's nimble figure down the corridor, blinking in the dim light after the brightness of the kitchens. The older woman carried herself ramrod straight, her head held high. Every detail of her elaborate attire was perfect: the tiny pearls sewn in lines across the fashionable turban headdress, the stiff, pressed edges of the high, linen collar that she wore, the knife-sharp pleats of her bodice. Alice drew level with her as they emerged into the hallway, and instinctively turned to the right, thinking they would mount the stairs to the solar. Cecile laid one bony hand on Alice's forearm, stalling her.

'There's something I wanted to show you, before we go up. I think you might find it interesting.'

'What is it?' Alice hesitated.

Cecile tapped her nose, adopting a teasing girlish tone that sat at odds with her starched, formal demeanour. 'Oh, Alice, I didn't really want to spoil the surprise.'

Alice hung back, unsure. There had been too many surprises recently.

Cecile laughed, a brittle, tinkling sound echoing up to the high vaulted ceiling. 'Don't be silly.' She clutched at Alice's sleeve, her claw-like fingers digging in to the fine silk velvet. 'You trust me. You know more than anyone how much I want to make it up to Bastien, after all these years of estrangement.'

Alice curled her toes up in her thin-soled shoes, embarrassed by her hesitation. She could hold her own against Cecile, surely? They were equally matched in height and weight. And Bastien's mother seemed to be making a great effort to change, despite her autocratic ways.

'I wanted to show you a place where Bastien and his brother Guillaume used to play; a special place that I thought you might like to see. I go there myself, sometimes.'

The wistful air of Cecile's words pulled at Alice's heart. This woman meant no harm; she was merely trying to help Alice connect with the family, with Bastien's past. Cecile's shoulders wilted slightly, her fingers fiddling nervously with her rings. And in that single gesture of self-consciousness, Alice's guarded heart succumbed, went out to this poor woman, who had lost one son, and was desperately trying to win back the affection of the other.

'I would love to see it.'

A wide, undulating river flowed steadily at the northern end of the manor, its shallow banks on the opposite side frilled with drooping willows, their leafless fronds tickling the surface of the water. The feeble warmth of the autumn day was dropping fast now, the sun low on the horizon. Cecile led Alice to the back of the manor, where the river slapped up against the steep, sheer sides of an old perimeter wall.

'I had no idea the water came this close!' Alice exclaimed.

'The original castle was built on a bend in the river; it provided an excellent defence in times of attack,' Cecile explained. 'My two boys used to love it when they were young; they came down here all the time.' A gentleness embraced her voice. 'They had a little boat, which they would tie up here.' She pointed down to the right, to an uneven flight of steps disappearing into the slopping waves of the river, to an iron ring set in the stone wall.

'They used to argue about who would hold the oars,' she continued, her tone adopting a sing-song musing quality. Alice shivered; despite the rays of the setting sun shining on the two women, there was no warmth in the air.

'It's a beautiful place,' she agreed with Cecile, 'but don't you think we should go back now? It's getting late.'

'They used to hide from me, you know.' Snared in her own memories, Cecile seemed not to hear Alice's words. Her eyes acquired a distant far-away expression. 'Look, down here.' She began to descend the stairs, her hand moving along the stone wall to keep her balance, not noticing how the long sleeves of her gown trailed through the slippery green slime that coated each step.

The undulating movement of the black, murky water against the stone wall made a jerky, smacking sound. Apprehension washed over Alice; she wanted to support Cecile, but maybe dragging up old memories was not helping the older woman. Cecile reached out for the iron ring in the wall, pulled it, and to Alice's surprise, a small door opened in the stone. 'See?' Cecile glanced up at Alice triumphantly, her face white, strained. 'I haven't forgotten after all these years! Oh, the times I spent calling those two scamps! And they would be hiding in here, playing their games, dreaming their dreams!' She leaned inside the dark interior, the stiff pleats of her veil scraping against the top of the doorway.

'It's exactly the same, the same as when they played in there.' Cecile withdrew from the small chamber, her expression clouded with memories.

'I think we should go back now, my lady,' Alice announced practically from the top of the steps. Fear grew like a hard lump in her chest. 'Why not come back and look at it in daylight?'

Two deep creases appeared between Cecile's high-drawn eyebrows. She frowned at her hands, studying them closely. 'My ring!' she gasped in horror. 'My wedding ring. I've dropped it!' She ducked her head and shoulders back through the wooden door. 'It's so dark, I can't see anything.' Encased in the stone chamber, her voice emerged as a muffled moan. 'It's the ring that Guy gave to me, I can't lose it! I just can't!'

Galvanised by Cecile's distraught tones, Alice sprang down the steps. 'Let me look, my lady. You're too upset. Look, careful now, I'll swap places with you.'

Cecile backed out carefully from the chamber, pale, distracted, visibly shaking. Tears squeezed from her eyes, already red-rimmed. 'You're a good girl, Alice, such a kind nature.' She moved up one step, allowing Alice to bend her head, to look inside the dark, dank space. Her voice changed swiftly, thick and dark, guttural with hate. 'My son doesn't deserve you.' With one almighty heave, Cecile pushed at Alice's unsuspecting back, tilting her off balance, bundling her into the chamber. Before Alice had time to blink, or breathe, or wonder what in Heaven's name had happened, Cecile had slammed the door shut, and bolted it from the outside. 'And he's never going to have you.'

'Cecile!' Alice shouted. 'Let me out, let me out of here!' In the rancid blackness, she twisted her body around, pummelling the thick, intractable wood with her fists.

'Not a chance, my child.' Cecile slumped against the outside of the door, the jewels on her head-dress fiery sparks in the dimming light. She wiped away the faint sheen of perspiration peppering her forehead. 'I promised myself I would have my revenge on Bastien if it were the last thing that I do. And with you, I have my revenge.' Cecile's voice moved over her like poison, seeping into her pores, leaving a sharp, sour taste in her mouth.

'Nay! You don't! You have it all wrong! I mean nothing to him! He still loves Katherine!' Incensed, Alice threw her shoulder against the door, bruising the soft flesh.

'He loves you, Alice. I could see it. I could see it in his every word towards you, in his every gesture—he loves you. I loved Guillaume and he took him away from me. That gives me the right to take you away from him.'

'It does not give you the right! You're wrong about him and me!' Fury brought Alice's voice to a high-pitched volatile squeak. 'You couldn't be more wrong!' Sobbing with frustration, Alice sank down on to the stone floor, her head in her hands.

'Goodbye, my child,' Cecile chanted, smiling woodenly at the bolted door. Checking that all her rings were in place, she made her way quickly up the steps, her step light. Revenge was certainly sweet.

Chapter Seventeen

In the corridor outside King Henry's chambers, Bastien waited. He sat on the low stone window ledge opposite the door, arms crossed high over the pleated folds of his tunic, his long legs stretched out across the polished wooden floor. He hoped today would be the last day of negotiation, that the lengthy discussions between the Duke of York and the Queen about who would rule the country whilst King Henry was ill would finally come to fruition. Impatience made him restless; for the first time in his life he found himself not wanting to be at the Duke's side, despite their friendship. He wanted to be with her, with Alice, and he wanted it with all his heart. These machinations of power meant nothing to him; all he wished for was to be set free from his duty to Richard so he could return to Foxhayne, to her.

He stuck a hand through his hair, pushing the blond locks away from his forehead, ruffling them. These last few days away had been torture; he constantly wondered what Alice was doing, what she was thinking. The sweet memory of her soft touch, her captivating expression, the light fragrance of her hair as it brushed against his chin—all taunted him, pulling his mind constantly away from the task in hand. Only weeks ago such distractions would have irritated him, but now, now he cherished them.

The door clicked open, and the young Queen Margaret emerged with a group of ladies-in-waiting. Dark circles ringed her eyes, and her slender frame bowed with fatigue. Her pregnancy protruding out from the pleated front of her gown only served to make her look more fragile. Bastien felt some sympathy for her; she had a lot to bear for one so young. The last few days had taken their toll, but she had fought for her side competently, arguing strongly for the rights of her husband, and for any child that she might bear. Her chin jutted in the air at the sight of Bastien; she had not forgiven him for his earlier deception, and no doubt regretted entertaining him on that previous occasion when Alice had brought him under false pretences into the castle.

Beatrice Matravers was among the ladies accompanying Margaret, bringing up the rear of the group, carefully shutting the door behind her. Her eyes skimmed over Bastien's hulking frame leaning against the windowsill, failing to connect him with the man who had ostensibly rescued her daughter. She merely saw him as another of the Duke of York's thuggish henchmen. Did she have any idea where Alice was now? Surely Edmund must have told her that the plan to marry Alice to old Felpersham had failed?

Beatrice's mouth dropped open in shock as Bastien stood up, gripping her sleeve with strong fingers, hindering any forward step.

'I need to talk to you,' he ground out, one fist curling at his side. He had promised himself he wouldn't throttle her, for Alice's sake.

Eyelashes fluttering with panic, Beatrice stared wildly at the rest of her party disappearing down the corridor, gowns like colourful butterflies against the dark wood panelling. She opened her mouth to scream, the red wax she had applied to her lips bleeding into the thick white powder on her skin.

'I need to talk to you, about Alice.'

Beatrice snatched her lips shut at his gruff words. Two bright spots of colour appeared on her cheeks, rash-like, frenzied. She sucked in a fitful, jerky breath. 'What do you know about Alice?'

'I know what you did.' His voice carved into her.

'Wh-what?' she replied, her tone faltering. Her blue eyes raked his face, trying to place him, to remember.

'And I know where she is.'

Beatrice swayed, clutched at his arm. 'Oh, my darling girl. Is she…is she…?'

'She's as well as can be expected.' His voice emerged, clipped, condemning.

'Tell me where she is.' Beneath her thick powder, Beatrice's skin had turned ash-grey.

'Later,' Bastien said, disengaging her clutching fingers from his sleeve. 'We'll talk later.' Putting one hand in the small of her back, he propelled her along the corridor. 'I'll find you.'

He was watching Alice's mother vanish through the door at the end of the corridor, when the Duke burst out from the King's chamber's, his square-shaped face wreathed in smiles.

''Tis done.' He approached Bastien. 'The Queen and

the Bishop have agreed to my rule, for the moment. The King is still quite insensible.' Richard clapped Bastien heartily on the back. 'I would never have achieved this without you, Bastien, I thank you for all your support, especially...' The Duke paused, cocking his head sideways, brown eyes twinkling.

'Especially?' Bastien supplied.

'Especially as you obviously have other things on your mind.'

Bastien grinned; it would be pointless to deny it. 'Is there much more to be done here?'

'Nothing that I cannot do myself, or with the help of my aides. You have done more than enough. Now go and saddle up your horse and claim that maid of yours.' Bastien was already striding off down the corridor. 'And don't forget to invite me to the wedding!' Richard called after him.

Alice's mother was easy to find, her bird-like figure perched on a bench in the gardens, twisting her fingers first one way, then the other. She sprung up at Bastien's approach, then sat down again abruptly, as if all her strength had suddenly failed her.

'I only did what I thought was best for her.' In the flimsy morning air, her voice echoed shrilly. 'What was best for all of us.' Her breath surfaced, misty wraiths on the cool air, and she shivered, clutching her slim arms about her. 'With Thomas gone, we had no one to support us, no money of our own. Alice was prepared to marry Edmund, but when he confided in me that he had no money of his own, and that his uncle had offered—' she ducked her head in shame '—I thought...I thought...'

Bastien threw his satchel on to the ground by the

bench; it landed with a scuffling sound, scraping on the gravel pathway. His large frame loomed over Beatrice, shadowing her. 'How could you have let her go with that man? And all for money.'

'Nay! Not just for the money. I couldn't curb her ways, she wouldn't be told; I had to do something, she was running wild! Edmund told me that his uncle was a decent, law-abiding man; he assured me that he was!'

'He lied. That snivelling, two-faced boy lied to you. Have you seen him?' Bastien paced up and down the path in front of her.

Beatrice raised one tentative hand to her head, checking her veil, patting the delicate fabric in place. 'Nay, he never returned. I assumed he'd decided to keep all the money for himself.'

Bastien stopped, spun around lightly. His calf-length leather boots strained with the rapid movement. 'Didn't you once think about what you'd done, about how she might be feeling?' His piercing tone slashed into her.

She hunched away, wincing, cowering from his furious expression. 'Oh, my lord, I think about her every day.' Big fat tears began to run down her face, creating runnels through the layer of white powder on her skin. 'I love her, I love my Alice. I pray she can find a space in her heart to forgive me for what I have done.'

Bastien's eyes travelled over her forlorn, drooping figure. 'Oddly enough, you seem to have bred a daughter with an amazing capacity for forgiveness,' he replied grimly.

'I'm so sorry. I'm so sorry,' Beatrice kept saying, over and over again. 'I've already told Fabien; he's angry with me, frantic with worry. Now that all the business with the King is over...' she waved one feeble hand in the direction of the castle '…he intends to ride to Felpersham's castle tonight.'

'She's not there.'

Beatrice lifted one trembling hand to shield her eyes as she looked up at him. 'Where is she?'

Bastien sighed. He lifted his head, watched the puffy clouds scudding across the sky. Beatrice Matravers seemed truly sorry for what she had done. He hoped he was making the right decision.

'I'll take you to her.'

Bastien slowed his horse to a walk beneath the trees, tall stately oaks that formed a deciduous forest to the east of Foxhayne. Leaning forwards, he patted the horse's neck, feeling the animal's sweating coat beneath his fingers. He had set a relentless pace from Northampton, leaving the lurching cart carrying Alice's parents far behind. They were happy to follow at a more sedate pace, grateful to him for saving their daughter, looking forward to seeing her once again. As he left them, they had been talking quietly together, Beatrice weeping a little in her husband's arms. Bastien knew that, despite what Beatrice had done, their relationship would soon be mended. Fabien Matravers's kind, generous spirit would make sure of that.

Foxhayne lay quietly under the hazy cloud of noon; he suspected most of the workers would be eating their lunch at this hour. How different his feelings were from the last time he had approached, in a mixture of trepidation and curiosity, with Alice's soft frame folded against him. As he trotted into the courtyard, a stable lad ran out to meet him, nodding furtively at Bastien before taking the reins of his horse. Bastien began to remove the leather satchels from the back of the saddle.

The main door of the house was wrenched open on its hinges.

Bastien turned, a smile on his lips, expecting to see Alice. His heart perched on the edge of happiness, of joyous expectation at seeing her once more.

He saw Mary.

Mary, his mother's servant, her mottled pasty skin ravaged by tears and fatigue, her fingers bunching continually into the folds of her apron.

'Oh, my lord, my lord!' She stared at him, hollow-eyed, quaking.

Dropping the bag, he sprinted towards her, leaping up the steps in two strong strides, grabbing her upper arms, supporting her. 'Mary! What in God's name is the matter?'

Mary's head lolled; he gave her a little shake. 'Tell me,' he said more calmly, ignoring the lick of fear in his veins, 'tell me what's happened.'

'It's your mother,' Mary stuttered out. 'She's locked herself in her chambers; she refuses to come out.'

Bastien laughed, a slashing hollow sound. 'So what's new? She often does that.'

Mary withered visibly. 'I think she's done something dreadful.'

'What? What is it?'

'We can't find Alice.'

Fear snipping at his heels, his mind tottering on the brink of crazed disbelief, Bastien fought for logic, for the cool control for which he was renowned. It could not be true; Mary must have it wrong! Striding across the hallway, he bellowed orders left and right to the

milling servants, to look, to search for, to find Lady
Alice. Like a soul possessed he tore up the stairs to his
mother's chamber, pounding on the door with his great
fists, shouting, yelling at her to open up. Blood hurtled
through his veins at a frenzied pace. Alice! Alice! his
mind screamed at him, what has she done to you? His
guts roiled—he should never have left her!

The door would be secured with a length of wood
fitted horizontally into two iron brackets either side
of the frame. On his orders, two burly servants raced
upstairs with a sturdy length of tree trunk: an effective
battering ram. The three men worked together, their
combined strength pounding at the door until the top
planks splintered; Bastien reached in, down, to toss the
wooden barricade away.

He stepped into his mother's chamber.

Closed, locked shutters made the room dismal,
gloomy, stifled with acrid air. His eyes searched the
shadows, heart thumping heavily in his chest. Cecile
lay on the bed, sprawled, a frail, shrunken figure, still
wearing her gown, her head-dress, her shoes. Her eyes
were closed, her white skin stretched taut over the bones
of her face; with a jolt he thought she was dead until
he caught the faint rattle of breath emerging from her
partially open lips.

As Bastien approached, her eyes snapped open,
intent, glittering evil.

'You're too late.' The words rasped out from dry,
cracked lips; a bitter uneven gasp.

Reaching down, the blood pummelling the inside
of his ears, he seized her shoulders, crushing her thin
bones beneath his fingers, and shook her, hard. Her
head bounced back on the pillow. 'What have you done

with Alice? What have you done?' A guttural rawness soaked his voice.

A wavering cackle escaped Cecile's mouth. She seemed to be having trouble breathing, her chest caving deeply with every shaky intake of air. 'Oh, this does me good, Bastien,' she wheezed. 'This is what I wanted, to see you suffer like this.' Her eyes narrowed, gimlets of hatred. 'Just as I suffered when you took Guillaume away from me.'

'You've punished me enough for that,' Bastien replied grimly, his face a mask of anguish.

Cecile's lips grimaced, a semblance of a smile. 'Nay, not enough, my dear boy,' she mocked, 'not enough.'

His hands leapt to her throat, tanned, sinewy hands against her scrawny neck, wanting to throttle her, to squeeze every last breath from her body. But his hands fell away as she laughed in his face, the uncontrolled, maniacal laugh of the truly mad. 'I've saved you the job, dear son. I've drunk enough poison to kill several men. I'll be gone soon, to join your brother.'

'Where...is...Alice?' he bawled at her, heart cleaving with desperation, springing back from the bed. 'Tell me, please, before it's too late!'

Cecile raised a finger to her lips, coquettishly. 'Now, that would be telling! Without her, you will suffer, just as I have suffered.'

Futility slashed at his face. 'Nay, she's not dead!' he bellowed at her. If he spoke the words often enough, then maybe it wouldn't be true.

'Aye, she is. Or at least, she soon will be.' A fit of choking drowned out her last words.

Bastien paced the room, frantic, ripping open the shutters to stare out. The normality of the bright blue sky, the small figures of people working in the fields below mocked him, laughed in his face. How could he make Cecile tell him? His mother had nothing left to live for. His mind scurried through the nooks and crannies of his home, through dusty stairwells, into disused rooms. Where? Where was Alice? Cecile would not have gone far with her—where could she have taken her?

At his back, Cecile's breathing laboured. It would not be long now. His heart splintered, vitality draining from his legs, his arms, the thought of losing Alice almost too great to bear. Whirling around, his gaze travelled the length of his mother's body. Even in the throes of dying, she was perfectly turned out: jewelled head-dress, expensive gown, shoes threaded with silver, the pale leather soles turned towards him.

Her shoes.

Bastien blinked, then lunged for the door. The soles of his mother's shoes were dirty, smeared with green slime. He knew where Alice was.

He flew down the stairs, feet barely grazing the polished wood, every muscle in his body charged with new-found energy. Alice could only be in one place, the place where he and his brother had played when they were young. He even recalled his mother's voice from all those years ago, chastising them both as they returned, tired, hungry and happy with playing, their clothes and shoes covered in the green slime from the river steps. Bounding down into the courtyard, he cannoned toward the river, oblivious to the astonished stares around him.

'Alice! Alice!' Almost falling down into the river in his haste to reach the hidden chamber, Bastien fumbled with the iron bolt, skinning his knuckles as he wrenched the door open.

Nothing.

Black, foul-smelling darkness, but no Alice. His heart howled.

Desolation scoured him, grinding into his bones. He buckled, his big body crouching down on the steps, face sunk in his hands. His mind was blank, frozen. He had been wrong, and now it was too late.

'Bastien.' A hand caressed his shoulder, warm, tentative.

Joy kindled in his veins, flowing around his heart, gathering momentum as he twisted on the step and saw Alice standing there, whole, *alive*. Her gown was torn and dirty, her veil streamed in tatters from her curling blonde hair, smudges adorned her face but he didn't think he could remember a time when she had looked more beautiful.

'Christ in Heaven! It is you!' He sprung upwards, crushing her body to his, tears of pure relief springing from his eyes. Enfolding her into his arms, he relished the tender, sweet feel of her. 'Sweet Jesu, woman, I thought I'd lost you!' He wrenched her veil from her head, sending jewelled hairpins flying, stroking the fine strands of her hair, tipping her face up towards his. 'I thought I'd lost you,' he murmured once again. Beneath his taut, tanned features, his skin held a grey tinge, shocked.

Her blue eyes sparkled up at him, blazing sapphire, her pale skin tracked with old tears. 'She wanted to be rid of me,' Alice stuttered out. 'She shut me in there.' She pointed at the chamber, finger trembling. 'She left me to die.' Her voice faded to a tremulous whisper.

Anguish hollowed the shadows beneath Bastien's eyes. 'I should have never left you here; I should have taken you with me, kept you at my side.' He paused, frowning. 'But, how did you…?'

'She forgot about the passageway,' Alice supplied, heart flaring at his possessive words. She would stay by his side for ever, if he would have her.

Bastien's face cleared, the ruddy colour of health returning to his cheeks. 'Of course, it leads to the other side of the wall. Very narrow, as I recall, even when I was a boy.' He glanced over her ripped gown, his green eyes grim.

Alice grinned. 'It was a bit of a squeeze.'

'Thank the Lord you found it.'

Her hand moved gently over his velvet sleeve, the thick muscles of his forearm solid beneath her fingers. 'You would have found me anyway.'

'Aye, I would have,' he concurred, hands falling from her face, gripping her shoulders. His square chin jutted forward with determination. 'I would have taken this manor apart, stone by stone, until I found you.' Raw emotion thickened his voice, the sinews in his throat constricting.

Alice's eyes sparkled up at him, blazing sapphire. 'Cecile believed…' she took a quavering breath, attempting to find the words '…she thought that it would destroy you, if I wasn't here any more.'

His big, capable hands moved back to her face, one thumb moving across her lips, petal soft, a dewy rosebud. 'It would have killed me.' His eyes glittered, haunted with the prospect of what might have happened. A shudder rippled through his lean, broad body.

'But…but…when I saw you at Katherine's tomb…?'

'You were there?'

'Aye, for a moment.' She had to be sure, be certain.

'I was saying goodbye, Alice. I had spent a lifetime grieving, and a lifetime fighting against it, until the day I met a maiden who gave me hope once more, who showed me how to love again.'

Her breath caught, suspended on a gossamer thread of flimsy hope. A sudden breeze from the river whipped at her skirts, the embroidered hem flailing around his sturdy leather boots. 'You mean…?'

'I mean you, Alice. From the moment I saw you, surrounded by soldiers in the forest, threatening them like a cornered terrier, you began to change me.' He stroked her hair as she leaned into him. His heart thumped solidly against her ear. 'I will never let you go again, do you know that?'

'I do now.' Delight shivered through her, her heart bursting with utter rapture. She wrapped her arms around him, hugging his big frame to her. 'Oh, Bastien, I almost dare not to believe it!'

'Believe it, Alice. Believe that I love you, that I cherish you, and want to spend the rest of my days with you.' He smoothed away a wayward strand of hair from her forehead; she shivered under his light touch, a moth's wing of sensation.

'As I love you, Bastien. With all my heart.'

With a groan, he lowered his head, gathering her slight body into his big frame, sealing his lips to hers in a kiss to claim her for a lifetime.

* * * * *